THE
WICKED
OATH

THE WICKED OATH

Book Two of 'The Oath' Trilogy

Michael L. Lewis

The Book Guild Ltd

First published in Great Britain in 2020 by
The Book Guild Ltd
9 Priory Business Park
Wistow Road, Kibworth
Leicestershire, LE8 0RX
Freephone: 0800 999 2982
www.bookguild.co.uk
Email: info@bookguild.co.uk
Twitter: @bookguild

Typeset in AldineBT 401

Printed and bound in Great Britain by CPI Group (UK) Ltd, Croydon, CR0 4YY

ISBN 978 1913208 844

British Library Cataloguing in Publication Data.
A catalogue record for this book is available from the British Library.

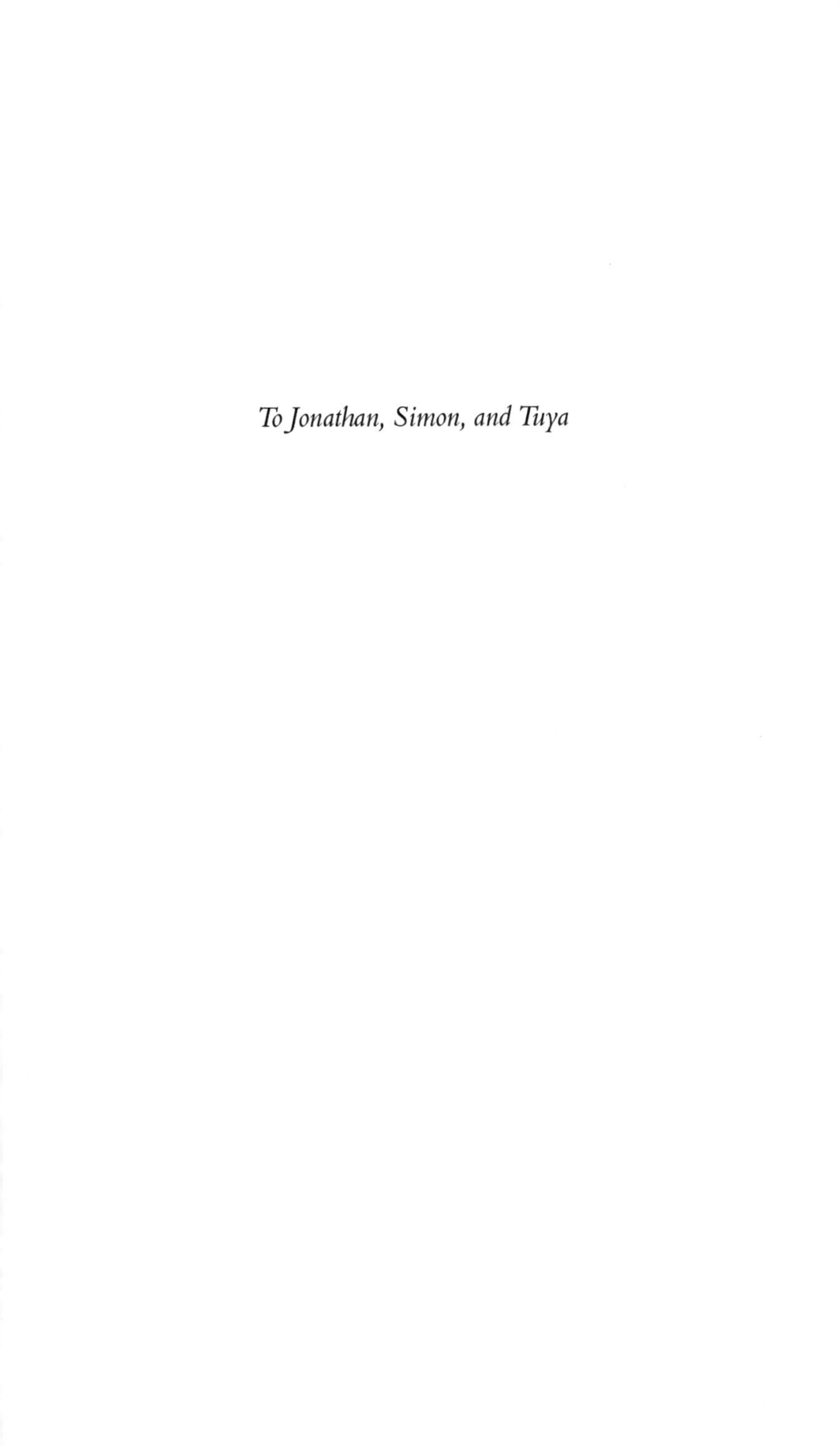

To Jonathan, Simon, and Tuya

*"By the pricking of my thumbs,
something wicked this way comes."*

– Act 4, Scene 1, *Macbeth*

PROLOGUE

August 31, 1956 9PM

Heavy rain pounded the high road south of Bedford. Nevertheless, the driver couldn't resist putting his new machine to the test. With a burst of power, the black and tan Bentley streaked like a bolt of lightning towards London and his flat in Knightsbridge. Edward Flicker was heading home a day early from a business trip. His wife and son would be surprised to see him.

He turned on the windscreen wipers to full speed. With exhilaration, the driver watched the speedometer effortlessly climb to eighty then ninety mph.

The man relished the power of the flawless engine. *Life*, he mused, *belongs to the strong*. This was the lesson he'd conveyed to his eighteen-year-old son, now a senior at Blackleigh School. Edward had read James's school reports and knew that other boys feared his son, who was a natural leader, domineering, with a quick temper.

James was revered at Blackleigh by most of the other prefects, who, with the support of the Housemaster, had elected him to the coveted position of Head Prefect in his House.

Edward and his wife Chloe planned to take James to Paddington Station on the following afternoon for the train journey to Enderby in Yorkshire and James's last term.

With a deep roar from the engine, Edward increased his speed to beat the orange traffic light up ahead. Only then did he glimpse the oncoming lorry, laden with gas cylinders, also speeding perpendicular to him, across the intersection. He jumped hard on the brake with both feet.

★★★

James went to bed early. He faced a big day ahead preparing for the afternoon train to Blackleigh. Around midnight, James awoke with a start. Did he hear voices in the family's Knightsbridge flat? *Probably a dream*, he decided. Since he was awake, James went into the adjoining bathroom and used the toilet.

While washing his hands, he glimpsed his reflection in the mirror. Although James needed a shave, his lithe figure struck a handsome pose: tanned with swept back black hair and piercing dark brown eyes. The fencing scar on his left cheek added to his charismatic aura.

"No!" He heard his mother's voice cry out from a distant room.

James threw on his dressing gown and rushed down the corridor to discover his mother in the living room, on her knees, sobbing.

Two uniformed policemen stood in front of her, holding their helmets. James went over to his mother, knelt, and enveloped her in his arms.

"What's wrong?" He looked back and forth between his mother and the policemen. "Mum?" he beseeched, but she was unable to speak. In a blink, James sprang to his feet, grabbed the closest of the two policemen by his dark-blue lapels, and yelled, "Tell me what's happened!"

The other policeman, the bigger of the two, wrapped his arms around James from behind, pulled him back and said, "Easy, lad, easy. I'm sorry to tell you, but your father had a car accident."

James went limp. "Is he...?"

"He didn't survive," the shorter policeman said solemnly.

James returned to his mother and helped her up onto the couch. He sat in a daze beside his mother, comforting her.

The short policeman cleared his throat, then said, "There was a terrible collision... near Bedford. Your father's car came to an intersection at the same time as a lorry carrying gas cylinders. There was a huge explosion. The Bentley went up in flames. If it's any consolation, he would have died instantly."

James shook his head in bewilderment. This was all too much to take in. He needed to be alone with his mother. "We appreciate you coming to tell us, but I must ask you both to leave now."

"Are you two going to be al..."

"Please go." James cut him off. "Thank you, but go."

They nodded and left.

James helped his mother to bed, assuring her that he'd take care of everything. He gave her a sleeping pill and waited until she was asleep, then returned to the living room and dropped down on the couch. His head was spinning.

His father had been a hard, unforgiving man. He'd wrongly blamed James for his favourite son Nick's death in a hotel fire, a few years before, and never forgave him. How ironic, James thought, that both his father and Nick died in a fire.

James was faced with a dilemma. On the one hand, he didn't know how well he could trust his father's business partners to run the family business.

On the other hand, his new responsibilities as Head Prefect at Trafalgar also weighed heavily upon him. The task he'd been entrusted with was difficult, most believed impossible. How to change a hundred years of tradition at Blackleigh, a school with an underbelly of fear and brutality, now metastasising in the rising power of seniors Sleeth, Tunk, Miller and the minions who supported them? The younger boys, called "juniors", were relentlessly targeted for abuse – both physical and mental.

The school year would start tomorrow. A further uncertain element was the appointment of a new and unknown Headmaster. James shook his head and lamented, "Everything's changed. What should I do?"

1

JONATHAN'S RETURN

September 1, 1956 9:30PM

The coach full of boys pulled up in front of Trafalgar House, at Blackleigh School. Jonathan Simon felt a combination of excitement and nerves at the start of his second year at Blackleigh. Nervous because he'd expected James Flicker to be on the train but saw no sign of him. *Something isn't right*, Jonathan worried.

Trafalgar was one of eight Houses, where the boys lived, slept, did their homework and participated in sports. They ate at assigned tables in the dining hall in the Administration Building with those in their House and joined with the rest of the school in attending classes and activities.

Jonathan wore his duffel coat and school scarf, black with yellow stripes. He stepped down from the coach onto the forecourt and joined several others, some walking, but most running to Trafalgar in chill darkness. Jonathan shivered in the gusty wind. He'd forgotten how bitter cold this place in northern Yorkshire could be at night.

The fourteen-year-old hauled his carrier bag into the lobby, jostled his way forward to the front of the crowd, and scanned the House noticeboard. Boys were pushing from all sides, but he held fast. Jonathan put on his glasses, aware that boys were talking, with surprise, about two meetings scheduled for the following day. Their concern prevailed over the usual cacophony of greeting friends and raucous conversation about the previous summer holiday.

The first notice on the board was a hastily handwritten note by Mr Alec Morton, the Housemaster, announcing that attendance was mandatory in the Houseroom at nine on the following morning. Jonathan hadn't known Morton call for a compulsory meeting this early in a new term and wondered what was up.

A second typed notice was on the new Headmaster's letterhead. At 1:00PM, on the same day, Dr Robert Macleod would be introduced to the full school in an assembly at Blackleigh Hall in the Administration Building.

Jonathan surveyed the Houseroom for his two friends, Peter Wynn and Jim Bhasin, hoping they knew what was happening. Like Flicker, they were nowhere to be seen. He reluctantly heaved his carrier bag up the stairs to the dormitories on the second floor.

To his dismay, from another list on the noticeboard, for some unfathomable reason, Jonathan saw he'd been assigned to the Middle dorm, predominantly for older boys.

After his first year at Blackleigh, he'd looked forward to renewing friendships among his peers with the juniors. He never anticipated that he'd be one of the youngest boys sleeping in a friendless place, for a lengthy period.

Jonathan only knew the handsome, athletic Keith Rayner in this dorm, who waved to him from across the cavernous room. They'd both started at Blackleigh the previous year. The two very different boys had bonded when Jonathan saved Keith from an attempted rape by Sleeth. And later, they'd escaped together from the Bell Tower, in the old cemetery near the school, where Sleeth had tried to exact revenge, before Flicker stepped in and shut him down.

Jonathan found his assigned spot among the twenty-five beds, spaced evenly apart. His bed adjoined a wall, the headboard next to a window. On the other side, Sean Gabriel, a standoffish boy, a year older, sat on his bed. Gabriel had barely acknowledged him in his first year. In fact, it now occurred to Jonathan that Gabriel made a point to avoid him.

Gabriel's appearance was stark: white, short hair, pinkish eyes and chalky skin, a condition that Jonathan knew was called albinism.

Jonathan offered his hand. "Hello, I'm Simon, know anything about the meetings tomorrow?"

"There are two notices in the lobby," Gabriel replied without looking at Jonathan and ignoring the offered hand. "Can't you read?"

The curt response caught Jonathan by surprise and the rejection stirred up his insecurities about both the birthmark on his cheek and being the only Jewish boy in the House. Jonathan decided to overlook the rebuff and began unpacking his carrier bag. He made up his bed with the pile of sheets, blankets and pillows provided, changed into his pyjamas, then tried a second attempt at conversation.

"I've seen you around. You're Gabriel."

"Yeah, I know you too, Simon," he sneered. "You and your pal, Bhasin, that little bugger from India, reported my friend Tunk to the authorities last term. You two snitches better watch your asses."

Jonathan knew at once he was in enemy territory and said no more. He climbed into bed, acknowledging, *A friend of Tunk is no friend of mine.*

After a difficult first year, Flicker had turned out alright in the end and the two formed a respectful relationship. *When Flicker shows up*, Jonathan figured, *I'll ask him for permission to move back into the junior dorm.*

Jonathan closed his eyes and reflected on the life-changing event of the previous term. Sleeth and Tunk had publicly humiliated Jonathan and his two closest friends, Ian Gracey and Arthur Crown, forcing the three of them to smear themselves with feces as part of their "House initiation". Afterwards, the three boys swore a Blood Oath that if any one of them was bullied again, the other two would retaliate, no matter how difficult – no matter the cost.

A short time later, Ian Gracey slipped and fell to his death from the Bell Tower. Arthur, lost without Ian, stole items from the Houseroom lockers to get himself expelled.

This left Jonathan, who remained determined to honour their oath and not to take abuse from anyone in his second year – starting with Gabriel.

The dorm door opened and slammed with a bang, and in strutted a tall, barrel-chested lad. He wore an expensive dark blue duffle coat with wood toggles, and a trendy peaked cap. The young man flung his cap on a bed, exposing a scruffy mop of greasy hair. His rotund face, marked with angry acne, appeared to be fixed in a sneer. The new arrival sported an ostentatious thick gold bracelet on his right wrist.

"Welcome back, Roooodge!" a ferret-faced youth shouted.

"Fuck you, Jasper!" Rodge snapped back.

Several others laughed along with Rodge.

Jonathan's half-mast eyes jerked wide open when Gabriel reached over, tapped him hard, and said, "Do you know who *he* is?"

"No, should I?"

"Hell! You don't know shit, Simon." Gabriel snorted. "That's Rodge Miller. He'll oversee your initiation to our dorm."

"I had my initiation last year." Jonathan shuddered at the memory. "I'm not having another."

"We'll see about that," Gabriel snickered. "Just look at him! Ever seen anyone that huge, and so-o strong? Wait till you see the size of his fuckin' hands. He's captain of the boxing team. Never lost a match. Miller's the boss here. He decides what happens…" Gabriel gave Jonathan another tap, "and to *whom*!"

"Thanks for the warning. I'll make sure not to pick a fight with… Roooodge," Jonathan said, imitating Jasper. "But I won't have another initiation," he added boldly.

"You don't have a say. One day, maybe soon, some of the seniors and others will be waiting for you. It's a House tradition. We all go through it."

"I'm sure you'd want to be there," Jonathan said, attempting nonchalance.

"Wouldn't miss it for the world," Gabriel chuckled.

Jonathan rolled over in bed and watched as the windows were flung wide open and cold air blasted in. The naked bulbs hanging on a wire were turned off and Holt, one of two seniors in charge, called out, "No talking!"

Jonathan reflected, *Things already look bleak. I'll need Flicker for backup this term more than I thought.*

2

THE HOUSEMASTER

The next morning, after breakfast, Jonathan was relieved that Jim Bhasin saved him a seat in the crowded Houseroom. Last term the two of them had broken the school's "no snitching" code by reporting Tunk to the police after he'd lied, and two young men from the nearby town of Enderby were wrongly arrested and imprisoned.

After their release, one of the men, a semi-pro boxer, hunted Tunk down and used him as a punching bag. Since then, Tunk had been on medical leave. The fear constantly plagued Jim's mind that Tunk also had it in for him on account of his dark skin, and would sooner or later return to school and seek revenge.

The seventy boys present stirred restlessly, knowing it was unlike the Housemaster to call a full House meeting on the first day of term – usually just the new boys were required to attend.

"I miss the junior dorm," Jonathan confided in Jim. "At breakfast, I'm stuck sitting at the end of a hostile table. Everyone's on edge as if looking for a fight. Have you seen Flicker?"

"No," Jim replied. "Perhaps he's with the Housemaster? All I know is that something weird is going on."

Those in the Houseroom became respectfully silent when Mr Morton came out of his study, followed by RG Ring, the diminutive Assistant Housemaster, who shuffled in. Mr Ring, who was French, rarely spoke in English. The French master had been a fixture at the school for so long that few recalled when he first joined the teaching staff.

"My God," Jim whispered, "the holy shit's hit the fan. Look who's come in with the masters!"

Jonathan stared in shocked dismay. Accompanying the two members of the faculty were his two worst enemies: Sleeth and Tunk.

Hugh Sleeth, with shaven head, reddish pock-marked complexion and thick, veiny neck, stood proud. His physique and broad chest filled out his impeccable grey suit. And to the surprise of everyone in the room, Sleeth was wearing a black silk tie with three small gold crowns. Only James Flicker should be allowed to wear the distinctive Head Prefect tie.

At Sleeth's side, stood a lanky, stooping figure, with black strands of hair combed forward. Tunk had dark, strange features. When he opened his mouth, in lieu of one centre tooth, there was a prominent gap. For some reason, known only to him, Tunk refused to have the space filled. Tunk was dressed in a funerial black school blazer, with yellow bands at the end of each sleeve, a yellow "B" on the chest pocket, a white shirt, and a standard black school tie with two thick yellow stripes. Tunk looked around, with his usual smug expression, and appeared to be relishing some secret triumph, only known to himself.

Jonathan thought, *Please, someone, wake me from this nightmare!*

The Housemaster looked serious. In his usual dark grey suit, sweater and black tie, the tall, balding man stood at the main table and spoke in his avuncular manner. "First, I welcome you back to Trafalgar, and I extend warm greetings to our newcomers. I'll be seeing new boys in my study this evening for an orientation. I called this meeting to make an important announcement. I regret that we face a sad and serious situation."

Jonathan instinctively knew that whatever Morton had to say would be especially bad news for him.

Morton went on, "A family tragedy has befallen James Flicker, our newly appointed Head of House. His father was killed two days ago in a car accident."

A gasp rose from the crowded room.

"James has been forced to leave us to be with his family at this difficult time and help with his father's affairs. He will not be returning to Blackleigh. James Flicker will be sorely missed."

Jonathan saw Sleeth discreetly nudge Tunk, who cracked his knuckles in response.

This announcement meant someone would have to fill Flicker's place. Even though Sleeth was already wearing the Head of House tie, many hoped, and even prayed, that it was some sort of mistake. Sleeth's idea of discipline would be to run the House like a penal colony.

Mr Morton continued, "In light of this news, an esteemed senior has stepped to the forefront and volunteered to assume the role of Head Prefect. I must say I'm surprised, given that he took himself out of the running last term. Nevertheless, we are indeed fortunate to have an able and responsible replacement for James Flicker in Hugh Bradley Sleeth."

Stoic silence. Sleeth looked to his left and right around the Houseroom to take note of anyone who dared disapprove of his promotion. He saw a tight grimace on Harry Bates' round face. Bates was an unfortunate boy with glasses from Leicester, in his second year. He was known for being incredibly dumb and lacked the guile to hide his feelings. Sleeth shot him a look as if to say, *You're on my radar.*

The Housemaster gestured at Sleeth and said, "Hugh has recommended someone he feels is amply qualified to take his vacated spot among our five prefects. I appreciate his advice and have appointed VH Tunk, who has fully recovered after his medical leave last term."

The Housemaster paused to give the Houseroom an opportunity to acknowledge his choices. There was scattered applause. But most remained in stony silence and disbelief.

Jim whispered to Jonathan, "I can't believe this. Excuse me for saying, but with Tunk a prefect, I may be finished here."

Mr Morton went on, "James Flicker asked me, as a parting wish, to appoint his study mate from last term, William Croat, as an extra prefect. I'm glad to honour his request."

The overweight senior, with receding hair, stood up and gave a brief self-conscious wave to the gathering. Behind Croat's back, some juniors referred to him as "The Bloated Frog", or "Frog" for short. Croat was relieved that Flicker had kept his promise and stood up for him; yet he wondered how he'd get along this term with the power-hungry Sleeth, and the volatile and slithery Tunk, now both dead set against him.

Croat knew that Sleeth despised him for having supported and plotted with James Flicker against Sleeth in their rivalry last term to become the next Trafalgar Head. Tunk was Sleeth's trusted friend, strongest supporter, and henchman.

The Housemaster went on, "I remind you all that at Blackleigh, we place a high value on our one hundred years of tradition. Unlike other schools, here the prefects, not the faculty, have sole authority to reprimand students for any lapses in good behaviour. I confidently place my faith in our new leadership and know that our House is in good hands.

"As we start another year, I remind you that our House is part of Blackleigh, a great school, founded over a hundred years ago. Here, you receive an elite education, leading to opportunities at universities and in the top professions.

"Some of you, in the distant future, may even be privileged to take your places among the leaders of our country. Friendships here can last a lifetime. Seize this opportunity. The honour of having a Blackleigh education will be with you always. Thank you for your attendance this morning."

And with that, Alec Morton promptly departed the Houseroom, with PG Ring silently traipsing after him.

The moment the door closed, Sleeth stamped his heel to get everyone's attention. "Settle down… from now on, expect significant changes in the House. This term you'll learn a new meaning for the word 'discipline'."

Tunk looked directly at Bhasin, then casually ran his flat palm across his throat. With a twinkle in his eye, he mouthed, "You're mine, dear boy."

Jim felt a shiver down his spine and lowered his head.

Sleeth spun on his heel and Tunk followed him out of the Houseroom. In the lobby, Tunk tapped Sleeth on the shoulder and said, "My good man… does one of your meanings for discipline include 'torture'?"

In response, Sleeth clapped Tunk heartily on the back and burst out laughing.

The boys in the Houseroom hadn't dared say anything in the presence of the Housemaster and the prefects. Now that they'd gone, the boys were free to express their feelings. A palpable hush permeated the large room. Everyone was uncertain who'd be their friends and who'd be their enemies. Some would likely form an alliance with Sleeth and Tunk, to escape their wrath. As if a shockwave had resided, the boys hurriedly left the Houseroom without making eye contact and headed for their respective classes.

Once Jim and Jonathan were sure they were alone, Jim said, "Where does this leave us?"

"In deep shit," Jonathan replied. "Sleeth and Tunk have it in for both of us. We also know from experience that Croat is a two-faced schemer. To top it off, we also have a new Headmaster."

"What do you hear about him?" Jim asked.

"That's just it," Jonathan sighed, "nobody knows anything for sure. Some say he's a godsend – others say he's worse than Sleeth and Tunk put together."

3

THE HEADMASTER

At one o'clock on the same day, the entire student body of six hundred and fifty boys packed into Blackleigh Hall. All members of the eight Houses, each named after glorious victories from England's past, stood chattering and mingling in their allocated sections. Jonathan wondered why Hastings House, named after a defeat by the Normans, was included as a victory for no other reason than that the school decided to call it one. History evolved at Blackleigh in creative ways.

Prefects supervised from the rear. In the Trafalgar section, Sleeth and Tunk prowled the perimeter, eager to flaunt their new leadership and identify potential troublemakers. Sleeth was immaculately dressed in his school blazer, wearing his Head of House tie and shiny black shoes, spit and polished for the occasion.

Sleeth saw a new junior arriving late without his tie, which was mandatory for the assembly. He sighed and signalled to Tunk, then pointed at the unfortunate boy. Tunk knew what to do. He grabbed the boy by the arm, led him outside and around the corner of the building where they were alone.

Tunk released the wide-eyed offender and got in his face. "What's your name, dear boy?"

"M-Moss," the junior replied, shaking.

"Where's your tie, Moss?"

The boy sheepishly removed the crumpled item from his blazer pocket.

"You must know the dress code, so why aren't you wearing your school tie, pray tell?" Tunk often beguiled his victims with a genteel manner of speaking.

"I-I don't know how to tie it, sir."

Tunk allowed a pleasant smile. "Alright, Moss, hand it to me and I'll show you, if I may."

The prefect looped the tie around Moss's neck and proceeded to tie a Windsor knot, explaining each step as he went. When the knot was in place, Tunk explained the final move: "And then, Moss, you simply tighten it." With that, Tunk grabbed the knot with his left hand, and with his right he pulled hard on the short end of the tie, exerting more and more pressure until he was choking the boy.

Moss began flailing his arms and gasping for air as he tried to fend off Tunk, but the prefect was too strong. Soon, Moss's face was turning blue and his eyes were practically popping out of their sockets. He tried, in desperation, to unravel the knot, and was finally able to loosen it. Moss looked up, wondering what Tunk might do next.

To his surprise, Tunk's voice became soft; but his words were hardly soothing. "Now, go right back to Trafalgar. Don't let me see your ugly face again until you've learned to tie a proper Windsor."

With that, Tunk dusted his hands on his trousers and headed back inside the hall.

There, he made eye contact with Sleeth and gave a casual nod to say, *All is under control.*

Rays of light shone from the glass in the high dome and filtered down to the open centre circle and onto the marble floor where the new Headmaster, Dr Macleod, would address the waiting assembly.

Jonathan Simon and Jim Bhasin stood near the edge of the circle. Both were still reeling from the shock of the changes in the Trafalgar power structure.

The rumour mill had worked overtime on the new Headmaster, the man with the absolute capacity to make the boys' existence at Blackleigh better or worse. Talk abounded that Dr Macleod's left hand was mangled from a mortar shell at Dunkirk, before he was rescued on a coal-boat. Later, it was believed that as an intelligence officer, he spent a year as a codebreaker, serving with distinction at Bletchley. Others spread the word that for a year he'd served in a clandestine mercenary unit hunting down dangerous Nazi war criminals and summarily executing them.

Now in in his early fifties, it was known for sure that the Scotsman had been the Head of two difficult public schools, his last appointment being in Aberdeen, where Dr Macleod gained a reputation for addressing disciplinary problems with an iron fist.

Blackleigh's former Headmaster had abruptly stepped down, due to ill health. On short notice, the school's Board of Governors clamored to find a replacement. Here, the rumour was that Dr Macleod's manner of discipline had resulted in several parents removing their sons from Aberdeen. Even so, the Blackleigh Governors could find no other qualified candidate and settled for Dr Macleod on a trial basis.

The main double doors opened and the new Head Boy, Mark Evans from Waterloo House, walked to the podium. His footfalls echoed over the murmurs of those gathered round him. Attendees hushed as the tall, fair, handsome young man waited for silence.

Once quiet, Evans announced, "Greetings… First off, I welcome our new juniors to your various Houses." Scattered applause followed. Evans went on, "And of course, we welcome back those in your second year." A more confident cheer arose. "Finally, welcome back seniors." A louder cheer. Once the assembly was quiet, Evans concluded, "And now let's give a special Blackleigh welcome for our new Headmaster, Doctor Robert Macleod."

To mild and uncertain clapping, the Headmaster entered, wearing a black gown and carrying a mortar board. He walked briskly, acknowledged Evans, and took over at the podium.

Macleod was a tall, unsmiling man with craggy features, a receding grey hairline over a furrowed brow and bushy eyebrows. He had a prominent nose, rimless glasses, and wore a leather glove on his left hand.

The Headmaster cleared his throat and spoke. "I'm not one for protracted speeches," he began in his Scottish brogue. "With a new Head, you can count on an approach that differs from his predecessor. We'll get along fine if you respect that I value discipline and a firm commitment to the high standards I expect from those at Blackleigh.

"I ask each of you to reflect on the meaning of education. Is it simply a means to attain the knowledge and skills to achieve a prominent place in society and earn a good living? Or does learning have a greater significance in your life? This question goes to the heart of what each one of you will make of your time at Blackleigh.

"As a start, I'm instituting certain changes. I'm a stickler for physical fitness. You'll rise two hours earlier at 5:30AM every Wednesday morning for a House run. All of you will participate in this mandatory activity, supervised by the prefects in your Houses. Afterwards, and before breakfast, you'll each take a cold shower.

"Also, on Wednesday evenings, before supper, there will be an additional mandatory chapel service."

A murmur of disapproval reverberated throughout the assembly. The doctor slammed his fist down on the podium. "Silence!"

The room quieted immediately.

Dr Macleod went on, "I run a tight ship and have no patience for those who don't measure up in either their behaviour or in their academic work. The purpose of discipline is to turn you into better versions of yourselves.

"And last, a word to our prefects. For the time being, there will be no change in Blackleigh traditions. You retain autonomous authority to reprimand your House members for any lapses in their behaviour or academic work. Thank you. That will be all – for now."

The doctor promptly left the podium and exited the Hall.

Jim turned to Jonathan. "Excuse me for saying, but is this a public boarding school or a reform school?"

★ ★ ★

After lunch, on their way back to Trafalgar, Jonathan and Jim were joined by Peter Wynn, a good-natured junior from Johannesburg. Peter had a large head, a deep tan, and swept-back brown hair. His father was an old Blackovian – an old boy, who was long ago at the school. Jonathan appreciated Peter's casual manner and positive outlook.

"I'm more confused than ever. I can't tell how life will be at Blackleigh this term," Jim remarked.

"Well, for one thing, as prefects, Sleeth and Tunk now have a free rein," Jonathan said.

He decided to confide a pressing concern to his friends. "Do either of you know anything about a thug in my new dorm? Who is this Rodge?"

Peter Wynn nodded ruefully. "I had a run-in with him last term. Avoid him like the plague. His parents are filthy rich – they live in Sevenoaks. Miller's an only son and heir to a large scrap metal firm."

"What happened with you and Miller?" Jim asked.

Wynn let out a heavy sigh. "Last term, after a breakfast, Flicker told me to go up to the Middle dorm and bring him down his notebook. He'd left it there on a chest of drawers while supervising lights-out, the night before.

"When I walked into the dorm, Miller was there alone, lying on his bed reading a book. I saw Flicker's notebook and was just about to take it when he surprised me, grabbing me from behind. He'd moved so fast I didn't see him coming. You won't believe what happened next..."

Peter blinked his eyes and continued, "Miller lifted me off the floor in a bear hug. He growled in my ear, 'Wot's a foreign bugger like you doin' in me dorm?' He then carried me over to an open window."

Jim shook his head in disbelief. "What did you say? What were you thinking?"

"N-Nothing," Peter stammered. "I was in shock – couldn't believe this was happening – I was scared shitless as to what Miller was going to do. Then somehow, he flipped me around and the next thing I know, he's holding me by the ankles and dangling me out the second-floor window. It was the scariest moment of my life! Croat was passing below, but Frog pretended not to see me."

"No surprise there – that coward," Jim said.

Peter went on, "As he hung me upside down, Miller said, 'If you scream, I'll drop yer.' I knew he meant it, so I begged, 'Miller, please bring me back in.' He replied, 'Not till you pee in yer pants.' I had no choice. After I finished, Miller hauled me back inside and barked, 'Now, get the fuck out-o-here!' I ran like hell and grabbed the notebook on my way out."

"Did you still tell Flicker what happened?" Jim asked.

"You must be kidding. You know the rules in this crazy place. Snitching would make things worse for me," Peter said, then turned to Jonathan. "So why do you ask about Miller?"

"Whitey told me that Miller will plan an initiation for me," Jonathan replied, "just because I'm new to the Middle dorm."

"Do your best to steer clear of him," Peter advised. "And another thing, every time Miller opens his mouth, he murders the Queen's English. But no one dares to tell or correct him."

"Why?" Jonathan asked.

"Because he's too good a boxer and his family's too rich," Peter replied.

Jonathan tensed up when he felt a firm hand nudge his shoulder. He turned to see Gabriel right behind him.

"I couldn't help overhearing," Gabriel said. "You must be really thick in the head, Simon. Don't you know you can't steer clear of Miller?" Gabriel cocked his fist.

"I'll tell Miller what both you and Wynn think of him. He'll probably come looking for you. Also, only my friends call me 'Whitey'." Gabriel faked a punch to Jonathan's face, and he flinched. As Gabriel walked away, he said over his shoulder, "Now, you can worry about me too."

4

TUNK

William Croat, proudly adorned with his new prefect's tie, hesitated before he knocked at the door of Tunk and Snell's study. He usually avoided this smelly domain with its clutter and daunting occupants. This time he didn't have much choice. Tunk had left him a handwritten note, pinned to Croat's study door. "If it's not too much trouble, old boy, see me in my study, Tunk, Prefect."

Croat couldn't tell if the missive was a harbinger of good or bad news. One thing Croat knew for certain, though, now that Tunk held the powerful position of a prefect this term, he'd rachet up his devious shenanigans.

The development was definitely bad news for juniors. Tunk had a warped mind that could conjure up wickedly creative methods of humiliation and torture, which Croat had often witnessed. For example, it was Tunk's idea in their first year to make Jonathan and his friends, Ian and Arthur, strip naked and dip their heads in an outdoor loo – not once but three times.

Norman Snell, Tunk's study mate, was another bizarre character, known by the few who associated with him as "Moth". Snell had a pale, cadaverous appearance, looked older than his sixteen years, and had a love for asphyxiating butterflies – to add to his extensive insect collection.

Croat would always be grateful to Flicker for helping him become a prefect. But among the other House prefects he felt the odd man out. He knew Sleeth detested him, as Croat had always aligned himself with Flicker's ambitions. With Tunk, Sleeth's junior partner in crime, he generally had a civil relationship, but Croat knew to be constantly on his guard. Tunk could be kind and civil one moment, then turn rabid dog the next.

Croat took a deep breath, knocked on the study door and walked in.

He found Snell alone, bending over a wooden table, laden with glass jars of different sizes and a pile of round metal lids; plus, an ancient-looking microscope, a pair of binoculars, a butterfly net, and a heap of insect pins.

"Take a pew," Snell croaked in his throaty voice. "Tunk will be here soon." Snell sat back and looked Croat up and down, his long fingers pitched together as if about to say a prayer, a habit he'd adopted from Tunk.

Croat dropped his hefty bulk onto a flimsy wooden chair; it wobbled, and he had to grab on to a side table to stop himself from falling. In so doing, he knocked over an empty glass killing jar, which fell on the floor, fortunately without breaking.

Snell barely moved but glared at Croat with disapproval. "Don't touch that jar. Leave it there," Snell snapped. "I'll examine it for cracks later."

He noticed Snell appeared to mouth the words, *Frog is hopeless.*

Croat tried to relax and remain still. With each inhalation, he could smell the stench of some odious chemical Snell was using in his insect research. He looked around the bare, untreated walls of the small study. "What are you working on, Moth?" he asked for want of something to say.

"The butterfly has many natural predators, *like all living things*," Snell emphasised, staring unnervingly at Croat. "I'm putting together a small representative collection of wasps, horseflies, and other voracious insects that bite or sting. My experiments involve the various toxicity levels of insect bites on the human species." Snell muttered to himself, "If only I could get my hands on a live scorpion."

"How fascinating, Snell," Croat replied, attempting to show interest despite his cloaked disgust. *Could Snell possibly be any creepier?* Croat was startled when the door opened and Tunk stepped in.

His fellow prefect gave Croat a Cheshire Cat smile then sat himself down in an armchair. Tunk looked at Snell and tossed a thumb towards the door, a signal for his study mate to leave.

Snell ran a hand through his premature thinning hair and frowned at being asked to abandon his work. But he was outranked by Tunk, so he left, closing the door behind him.

"This is such a pleasure!" Tunk commenced, flashing his signature gap-toothed pseudo-smile. "While I'm surprised by your appointment as a prefect, we're now on the same team. As a fellow prefect, it's good to see you, Bill, and know we're not adversaries this term."

"Well, I suppose that's so," Croat replied cautiously.

"And I must say, Bill, how dapper you look in your new prefect's tie!" Tunk leaned forward, raised his hands and placed the tips of his fingers together in his dramatic pose. He looked to the left, to the right, and spoke in a lowered voice, although he knew no one could overhear. It was his oblique way of conveying to Croat the importance of what he wanted to discuss. "I had a meeting with Sleeth this morning. Our esteemed Head of House is keen to move on two key projects."

Croat remained silent, waiting to hear what the two scoundrels were planning, this time.

"As you know, Hugh Sleeth takes an abiding interest in education and discipline."

This was the first time Croat heard that Sleeth had any interests apart from his all-consuming involvement with running the corps and other perverse activities to make juniors' lives a living hell.

"Go on," Croat said, sure he wasn't going to like what he was about to hear.

"Obviously, there can be no enduring education without discipline," Tunk went on. "This, Bill, is where *you* rise to the challenge."

Croat started to roll his eyes, then stopped himself.

"Hugh Sleeth is introducing a new and creative approach to punish… er," Tunk corrected himself, "to improve disciplinary measures, sorely needed in our House. Let me share his vision and creativity with you. For anything but a serious offence, for which there's a caning, six of the best, the offender will receive a 'warning' to be marked down in a disciplinary ledger. This record of offences will be kept in *your* study."

Croat didn't like the sound of this but kept quiet and listened.

"Upon the same offender receiving a second warning, the unruly boy will be required to participate in a strenuous physical exercise programme, lasting at least fifty minutes," Tunk said. "This will consist of no ordinary exercises, but those designed to elicit pain. It will be held every other week on a Friday afternoon in the forecourt of the House, in full view of others. Upon satisfactory completion of the session, the offender's slate will be wiped clean. Unsatisfactory participation will mandate a repeat of the intense programme."

Tunk paused and took in Croat's expression to gauge the impact of his words. He was pleasantly satisfied to see Croat's shocked reaction.

"Sounds like torture to me – this will be deeply unpopular," Croat protested.

"You're thinking small, Bill. Consider the big

picture," Tunk said. "Just imagine, it's four o'clock on a Friday afternoon. Seniors, in their studies facing the forecourt, are about to have tea…"

"What?" Croat broke in, totally confused as to where this description was heading.

Tunk ignored him and, with a faraway look, became almost euphoric. "…like Romans in the Coliseum, the fortunate senior study holders will be entertained outside. They will get to observe the unfortunate plebs, with two warnings, shagged out and half-dead, drilled with back-breaking exercises by two prefects, who persistently threaten slackers. I like to call the stimulating experience for those watching, 'Tea and Sympathy'."

"It's so harsh!" Croat exclaimed, and then the realisation hit him. "With the disciplinary ledger in my study, everyone will identify the programme with me."

"You're a prefect, William. This appointment requires you to undertake appropriate responsibilities," Tunk said calmly. "I assume you wish to remain a prefect?"

Croat knew that Sleeth, as Head of House, had the power to demote him. Still, he wanted to negotiate better terms. But, before he could say anything, there was a knock at the door.

"Enter," Tunk called out.

A small dark-haired boy walked in, looking shy and lost. "S-sorry to interrupt," he stammered in a high-pitched voice. "I'm supposed to see… VH Tunk."

"At your service. He's sitting here in the flesh," Tunk said, grinning benignly, the gap in his front teeth prominent.

"I'm Tim Bell, sir. I've been assigned to clean your study… twice a week, I'm told." This was a standard policy for new juniors.

"Ah, Bell," Tunk said, "thank you for stopping by. But this is not a good time. Return in one hour, prompt. But of prime importance, keep in mind that there are rare insect specimens in this room. You can only perform your duties either when I or my study mate Snell are present. Do you understand?"

"Y-yes, sir, I'll come back," Bell replied in a hurry to leave.

Tunk dismissed the intruder with a flick of his wrist, then turned to Croat. "That inexperienced mouse will need intensive training. Now where were we, my dear fellow?"

Before Croat could reply, Tunk forged ahead. "Ah yes, there's one more item, Bill. It's sensitive and must remain between these four walls." Tunk was clearly relishing his role as a messenger of doom. "Remember last term when we were at the Blackleigh annual fair, open to the public?"

Croat nodded, wondering where this was heading.

"Good, then I'm sure you recall that you were next to me when I was playing at a coin-toss booth. I won several times, fair and square, but then the lowlifes from Enderby running the booth, one an ex-boxer, accused me of cheating…"

"As I remember," Croat couldn't help himself and broke in, "you did cheat… you placed coins by hand on winning numbers when the backs of the booth owners were turned."

"Well, the Williams brothers were running a rigged game," Tunk countered. "I was just evening the score. But I didn't cause the trouble. I merely told them that if they didn't like the way I played, I'd go elsewhere. Anyway, how would you know? As soon as the fight broke out, I didn't see you for dust."

Croat shook his head. "Come on, Tunk, I was there. You and I both know what happened."

"Be that as it may, Bill, my point is Simon and Bhasin claimed they were watching us, and later they went to the police to vouch for the booth owners – told them that the two men were wrongly arrested, instead of standing up for you and me. As a result, the Williams brothers were released from jail, and the blame shifted to us."

"I backed you at the time," Croat reminded Tunk.

"You backed me in your mind, but no more. Fact is, Simon and Bhasin showed total contempt for the Blackleigh code of conduct, which mandates no snitching on anyone enrolled at our school, under any circumstances."

"Yes, I know about our unwritten code. But…"

"Let me finish," Tunk cut him off. "You always jump the gun. Fortunately, the whole matter was dropped after the two local men were released from custody. But can you imagine the consequences if *we'd* been arrested? We'd have permanent black marks against both our names, now and in the future, all because of those two traitors."

Croat knew he couldn't argue this point.

"You do remember also that I was away for much of last term on medical leave…"

"Yes," Croat jumped in, "after the incident at the fair, we heard that while on a nature walk, you were set upon from behind by three thugs from Enderby."

"That's only partly true," Tunk said. "I fought them off as best I could, but one of them was the older Williams brother, a semi-pro boxer. Bhasin happened by, but the little coward took off running, leaving me to defend myself alone."

The true story… Tunk had been stalking Bhasin in the woods and was about to beat him to a pulp. The irony was, Williams, all by himself, had been following Tunk. He stepped in between Tunk and Bhasin, told the junior to go, so there'd be no witnesses, then proceeded to work Tunk over with his fists. From his hospital bed, Tunk had made up the "three men" story to make himself look like a hero.

"So, what do you want *me* to do?" Croat asked facetiously. "Write Bhasin's name in the ledger without an offence to back it up?"

"No, Sleeth has something more radical in mind – especially for Simon."

Croat groaned. "Why include me in Sleeth's and your revenge?"

"You know the answer," Tunk said. "You were the one who set up the scheme to have Rayner and Simon entrap Sleeth into making a romantic pass at Rayner. And it worked. The two juniors then threatened Sleeth, said they'd make sure the whole school knew he was queer unless Sleeth dropped his campaign to become Head of House. That was *your* doing William, and you can't deny it. Fortunately, by a twist of fate, Flicker's gone and Sleeth is our unchallenged Head Prefect anyway."

The sheepish look on Croat's face told Tunk he'd guessed right.

Tunk shook his head in bewilderment. "Rayner is hands-off. For the life of me, I can't understand why Sleeth still has the hots for him. But Simon is another matter. Hugh wants a payback in spades."

Croat sighed in resignation. "Okay, what do you and Sleeth expect me to do?"

"I know you'll come up with some imaginative ideas," Tunk winked, "like you so often did for Flicker."

"I may need help," Croat said hopefully.

"I leave that to you, but get clearance from us first," Tunk replied. "As a start, I separated the two boys by placing Simon in the Middle dorm – where we can better keep an eye on him. And Bhasin is in the Junior dorm."

"What do I get for doing this?" Croat asked, ever the opportunist.

"You'll remain a prefect. How about that?" Tunk smirked. "Let me first see how 'lethal' you can be. Tell me, Bill, do you have any interest in the stock market? I'm talking stocks and shares. They are an ongoing interest of mine."

"I don't know anything about stocks."

"Well, I'll explain. Right now, your stock as a prefect is high. I'd hate to see both it and you go into a sharp downward reversal."

With a chipper expression, Tunk concluded, "Thank you for coming. Always a pleasure, Bill. In the words of the new Headmaster, 'That will be all for now!'"

Croat left the study in a sweat. Ever since the day his parents had enrolled him at Blackleigh, he'd wanted to be a prefect. He had no doubt that Sleeth could take the precious title away from him. To prevent that, he'd have to come up with something especially malicious for Simon and Bhasin to satisfy the ruthless Sleeth.

5

DR FRANK

On Friday, at the end of the first week of school, Jonathan, against his better judgement, headed to the school sanitarium to get treatment for a boil on his thigh. He usually tried to avoid the san, remembering his bad experience with the school doctor when he'd gone for his physical at the beginning of his first year.

The san building, single-storey, pre-fabricated with a flat roof, was located behind the classrooms. The temporary structure looked out of place and a poor relation among the school's brick and stone building architecture, where exterior facades were designed with wide steps and imposing columns.

The san housed the school doctor's offices, a waiting room, and a dormitory for about twenty-five boys, who were sick beyond the capacity of House matrons to care for them. There were also two extra rooms for emergencies. The san was not a hospital, but as ill boys stayed for short periods, one or two 'so-called' nurses were always on duty.

Jonathan stood in the small, white lobby, and gave his name to a preoccupied woman, with mushy hair, sitting behind an open window. She held an over-stuffed sandwich in one hand and a phone in the other. As she chewed, the woman checked for his name on a list, then nodded and pointed a finger to indicate that he should go into the waiting room.

Inside, he came upon David Gold, his gangly Jewish friend from Plessey House, also waiting to see the doctor. Jonathan smiled and sat next to him. David was immaculately dressed, as usual, in his formal school uniform comprising a black blazer with an embossed gold "B" on the pocket, grey trousers and shiny black shoes.

At the beginning of their first year, Jonathan and David had gone to Enderby together and were returning to school when they were racially mocked and physically attacked by Sleeth, then a senior, with some of his cronies. David had surrendered his watch and money to placate them.

"I tried to reach you over the holidays," Jonathan greeted him. "What's happening?"

"We were away in Spain, then had an out-of-town visitor."

Jonathan knew that when David gave a vague answer, he was holding something back. He pressed further. "'Out-of-town visitor'…?"

"Well, yes," David admitted. "Anthony Summers came to stay for a week. You know how it is."

"I don't, but then…" Jonathan had second thoughts and held back. If David was happy entertaining his handsome friend, then it was David's business. He didn't categorise David as queer, but knew he was overly friendly with Summers, one of Blackleigh's star athletes. Jonathan knew that most nights in the dorm, boys climbed into bed with other boys. But in Jonathan's mind, this was just because at Blackleigh there were no girls – so they made do.

Besides, Jonathan's own knowledge of sexual relations was limited, so he avoided the subject, even though other boys were constantly talking or speculating about the mysterious topic.

Jonathan found David to be entertaining company. "What are you doing here?" he asked. "It's the last place I expect to see you." *Does David realise I'm joking*? Jonathan knew David was no hypochondriac, but that he availed himself of becoming "medical" to avoid House runs, rugby practice and any demanding physical activity.

"Quite so," David answered with a frown, "but lately I've developed quite a pressing sinus condition. You may be interested to know it's quite debilitating."

"I imagine it is," Jonathan said, knowing what his visit was really for. "But with a medical chit from the doctor, it'll spare you participating in upcoming sports for at least two weeks."

"Precisely." David let loose a self-satisfied smile. "And I'm sure I'll be missed. Say, Jonathan, maybe we could get together this Saturday? Anthony will be out of town with his parents. How about we take the bus into

Enderby like we did last year? We could have lunch and see an early film at four. They are showing *The Cruel Sea*, with Jack Hawkins and Donald Sinden, at the Savoy Cinema – I'll try not to get seasick," David joked.

"Great, but they won't give you a medical chit after seeing a film." Jonathan laughed. "Let's meet eleven o'clock at the bus stop."

David proffered a hand and they shook on it.

"So, what's the latest in Trafalgar?" David asked.

"Haven't you heard the news? Sleeth is our new Head Prefect."

"Thank God I'm in Plessey." David mimed wiping sweat from his brow. "That loony should be locked up for the way he treats people."

An elderly nurse came out of the inner room holding a clipboard. She looked up and called, "Gold." David stood, winked at Jonathan and slipped inside.

While he waited, Jonathan picked up a year-old copy of *The Illustrated London News* sitting on a side table. He discarded the magazine after discovering most of the pages stuck together by globs of sticky tea stain.

Fifteen minutes later, David came out of the inner office in triumph. He clutched a medical chit as if he was holding an Olympic gold medal. "See you Saturday. I'm medical for two weeks," he said with a sigh of relief.

Two apprehensive boys wandered into the waiting room and found seats. The nurse reappeared and called, "Simon." He followed her into an exam room and was told to sit in a chair.

The woman looked ancient, starched, and rigid. She wore bright red lipstick, a white uniform, free of creases over a stiff dark blue outfit with a large red cross on it, and a prim white nurse's cap in the style of Florence Nightingale. The nurse took his temperature, checked his blood pressure then his weight.

"What brings you here?"

"I have a painful boil on my thigh," Jonathan answered.

The nurse made a notation and said, "The doctor will be with you shortly."

Ten long minutes later, the doctor came in reading Jonathan's chart.

Dr Frank, in a white coat and stethoscope round his neck, was a tall, overweight man, bald-headed except for a ring of short grey hair round the back. He looked at the young boy over his half glasses. Without so much as a greeting, he barked, "I'll examine the boil, Simon. Unfasten your belt and lower your trousers, below the knees."

The doctor wasn't one for small talk, and Jonathan's memory of his last examination made him hesitate.

Dr Frank repeated, "Below the knees. Don't you understand English, boy?"

Jonathan slowly complied. Dr Frank pulled on a pair of surgical gloves, then crouched down to examine the inflamed boil. He poked it with his forefinger. "Does that hurt?"

Jonathan winced. "Yes, it does."

"I thought it might," the doctor said. "You know, it's probably best if I don't lance it at this point. I'll have the nurse give you an ointment. If it's not better in a week, come back and see me."

"Thank you," Jonathan said. When the doctor didn't move out of his way, he asked, "Can I go now?"

"Not so fast. While I'm down here," Dr Frank chuckled at his own joke, "I might as well check for a hernia. Underpants down, Simon."

"W-what?" Jonathan said, taken aback. "I'm sure that I'm fine. Same as last year."

During Jonathan's requisite first-term physical, he'd experienced first-hand Dr Frank's reputation for dealing with every boys' medical complaint, even a sinus problem, by fondling their genitals, under the guise of a hernia exam.

"I'll be the judge of that." The doctor grabbed the elastic on Jonathan's underpants and started to pull them down for him.

Without thinking, more as a reflex, Jonathan shoved the doctor away. Dr Frank teetered over backwards and landed hard on his ass.

Jonathan couldn't believe what he'd done. He yanked up his trousers, headed for the door, fastening his belt on the way.

Dr Frank, his face red with fury, yelled after him, "How dare you treat a leading medical practitioner this way. If you know what's good for you…" The doctor stopped, realising he was talking to a closed door, then clambered to his feet and went directly to the phone.

★ ★ ★

William Croat stared enviously out of his window in the newly painted light blue study he used to share with Flicker. It was mid-afternoon. On the forecourt, the other House prefects tossed a rugger ball to one another. He hadn't been asked to join them for obvious reasons: he was poor at sports, overweight, and slow. Not even his usual pick-me-up of tea and two raspberry jam doughnuts had helped elevate his mood. Unable to take it any longer, he left his study and wandered into the Houseroom.

As Croat entered, the Housemaster, Alec Morton, stuck his head out of his office and looked around. He spied Croat and called out, "William… phone call… in here," then ducked back into his office.

Croat entered the study, looking confused. "Who wants to talk to me, sir?"

"It's Dr Frank on the line." Morton held out the receiver. "He doesn't want to speak to you specifically. He needs to talk to a prefect about some Trafalgar student who's crossed the line. Dr Frank knows, of course, it's for the prefects to impose the proper reprimand."

Croat took the phone, identified himself, and listened. He nodded, along with, "I see… Uh-huh… Simon did what?! …Alright, Doctor, I assure you that this will be handled in the appropriate manner," and hung up.

He made eye contact with the Housemaster, who said nonchalantly, "You deal with this. I don't want to know."

Croat left the office and walked back into the Houseroom just as Jonathan came in, looking shaken.

Croat approached him and said, "I just spoke with the doctor, Simon. My study… Now!"

Jonathan let out a deep sigh and followed him. He entered Croat's study and shivered at the memory. It was the first time he'd been here since last term when, in Flicker and Croat's absence, his friend Arthur had accidentally set off a small fire. Jonathan and his other blood oath friend Ian arrived in time to douse the flames. Ian subsequently took the blame, which led to another accident – Ian's death during his punishment – a case that remained unsolved to this day.

Croat, in fact, was trying to decide whether to follow the doctor's order and punish Simon or let him off with a stern reprimand. He and Simon had a history. The previous year, Croat engaged Jonathan and Keith Rayner to discredit Sleeth, so that Croat's then study mate, James Flicker, would be a shoo-in for Head of House. It worked. Then Sleeth sought revenge but was thwarted by Simon with help from Flicker. So, in effect, Croat owed Jonathan more than a favour, and they both knew this.

"I haven't forgotten what you did for me last term… but as a prefect, I'm duty bound to dole out a punishment," Croat said, with a self-important smirk on his face. Jonathan knew that Frog, forever the schemer, would be trying to work the situation to his advantage. Croat seemed to go into a trance of indecision. Moments went by, Jonathan tired of waiting, pushed the issue. "What are you going to do?"

"Uh, well, I need to think about this." Croat waved Jonathan out the door. "That'll be all – for now."

Jonathan left the study.

On his own, Croat's eyes lit up, after catching himself saying the words that Tunk had repeated from the Headmaster's speech. *Sleeth and Tunk would be thrilled to see that the first entry in the Discipline Ledger is the number-one object of their hatred: JONATHAN SIMON.*

Croat went to his desk, opened the top drawer, and removed a brand-new, hard-backed notebook. On the first page were the headings "Date", "Culprit", and "Offence".

He hesitated a moment out of guilt, took out his pen, and wrote Simon's name with a flourish. Then he put the warnings book and his pen away in a drawer.

With the decision made and the task accomplished, Croat went straight to the food cupboard. He felt an urge to celebrate, tore open a fresh bag of sticky jam doughnuts, and stuffed two in his mouth.

6

OLIVIA

Saturday afternoon, Jonathan and David Gold sat together in a coach on their way to Enderby. They passed by a new brick housing development and were soon enveloped in the timeless beauty of the Yorkshire dales. Jonathan gazed out of the window. He was, as always, awed by the tranquility and beauty of the scenery; so many shades of green melding under a blue and cloudy sky.

A lush carpet, with hues of green and yellow, covered the hills, reaching out of sight. Fields were bounded by hedges or the grey of ancient stone walls. The bus went by fields, where sheep grazed near limestone rocks, and by isolated stone cottages with thatched roofs. Jonathan heard the engine groan along the narrow potholed route bounded by tall trees, each bend in the road offering awesome vistas.

For Jonathan, it was a journey back in time, a hundred years and more. Little reminded him that it was 1956, except for an occasional TV aerial on the roof of a house as they approached Enderby. Enclosed farms, barns, stone bridges over small streams, and fields with cows and sheep grazing, sped by his window. At frequent intervals, he noticed dull silver milk containers, at the side of the roads, left to be collected. On the outskirts, they passed a public house and inn, appropriately named The Horse and Plough.

They reached the town centre, where most streets were cobbled. A small hotel and garden bore the distinguished name The Golden Harp Hotel, next to the Savoy Cinema. Jonathan noted that the local shops included: a post office, fishmonger, butcher's shop, Boots chemist, a bank, a hardware shop and a bicycle shop. The vehicle turned into a newly asphalt-surfaced car park where Jonathan and David stepped down from the bus platform at the stop.

"You're quiet. What are you thinking?" David asked.

"That maybe, in a few years, with so many changes, we may not see a countryside this beautiful," Jonathan replied. "I want to remember how it is. And you… what's on your mind?"

"Truthfully," David answered, "I'm thinking that after lunch, and before our film, there's a football match. Arsenal are playing Liverpool. I expect there'll be a TV showing the game in the High Street appliance shop window, where I plan to watch. Did I tell you that my father gets complimentary tickets for Arsenal's home games at Highbury?"

"Yes, many times." Jonathan was uncomfortable with David mentioning his father's good fortune after his own father had died so young. "How about we go to the café across the street, the one where we went before?" Jonathan gestured.

David agreed. They crossed and entered Janet's.

The place was just as Jonathan remembered, small and inviting. David, in an expansive mood, having just received a five-pound note from his parents, ordered lavishly for them both: two roast beef sandwiches, two slices of walnut chocolate cake, and an extra-large puffy cream-filled meringue for himself, after Jonathan declined, and tea for two. "It's on me," he proclaimed grandly. "You pay for the film."

The door opened and in walked two teenage girls. They took off their coats and scarves and sat at an adjacent table. Jonathan surmised they were slightly older than David and himself.

David droned on and on about Arsenal's prospects in the football season, while Jonathan half listened. He was much more interested in the girls' animated conversation. They spoke in French and were laughing. Even though David often boasted of having natural skill in learning languages, he made no comment and continued to pontificate about First Division team line-ups.

The dark-haired girl was vivacious and exceptionally pretty, but something about her companion, with glinting blonde hair touching her shoulders, was more appealing to Jonathan. He'd have liked to gaze directly at her but didn't have the nerve. However, a sideways glance revealed that she had dazzling light blue eyes, a lovely face, perfect lips, and a light tan. He was at loss for words and frustrated by his own inexperience at a boy's school; add to that, he'd never had much to do with girls.

Should I try to speak to her, he wondered, *or maybe get David's help?*

The girls appeared to be French. He rationalised that if they didn't speak English, there'd be no point in him saying anything. They wouldn't understand him anyway. He strained to hear their conversation for something that might reveal more.

Lunch was served by a waitress who looked like she was having a bad day. David dove right into his beef sandwich. Jonathan picked up his, put it back down, and shifted it around on his plate, keeping the girls in his peripheral vision. He was too nervous to eat while the girls perused their menus.

Jonathan removed the top slice of bread, grabbed the pepper pot, and was so entranced by the blonde girl, he started absently shaking it… and shaking and shaking.

He noticed the blonde girl glancing at him. She made an eye movement to indicate, *You may have put enough pepper on it.*

Jonathan put down the pepper pot and pushed the beef sandwich aside, having rendered it inedible.

He almost choked when the blonde girl spoke to the waitress in a soft American accent. "We'd like to share a mushroom omelette… and two coffees." After the waitress took their menus and left, they reverted to French.

The swift change in speech befuddled him, but Jonathan now had no excuse to avoid making contact.

He reconfigured his campaign. *Should I say a casual hi or a more formal hello?* He pondered the earth-shattering decision. A remedy to his chronic shyness came to him, even though it meant no turning back.

"David," he whispered, "those two great-looking girls speak French. With your language skills, how about you say something?"

"I shouldn't interrupt them," David protested. "What would it look like?"

"Go on," Jonathan urged him. "For Arsenal and England. You can do it!"

The appeal worked. David turned to face the girls and said in heavily British-accented French, *"Etes-vous Francaises?"*

The dark-haired girl turned to David. She laughed and replied, "No, we live in Switzerland, near each other."

Jonathan felt his head swimming when the fair girl looked right at him.

He managed to overcome his fear and blurt out, "We go to Blackleigh School. What are you two doing, so far from home?"

The blonde girl explained, "I'm at St Claire's for a year. My girls' school is a short bus ride from Enderby. Paula here came up from London for a weekend visit."

Jonathan managed to ask, "What's your name?"

"Olivia, and yours?" She flashed a radiant smile.

"Hello, Olivia. I'm Jonathan Simon and this is David Gold. We came to Enderby for the afternoon. I like your name. There's a girl called Olivia in Shakespeare's *Twelfth*

Night. We're reading that play in my English Literature class."

At this point, David coughed to indicate that he felt left out of the conversation. He broke in and said dryly, "I'm glad for a chance to practise French. My parents holidayed in Paris last year and stayed at the Hotel de Crillon."

Jonathan felt like rolling his eyes. *What a typical David boast,* he thought. *This is the first time I heard that David's parents were in Paris.* He so wished he was alone with this golden girl and get to know her better.

"How are your teachers," David asked, "by and large?"

"We're taught by nuns," she replied.

"You don't say? I never knew nuns taught school," David said, then stuffed a greedy helping of walnut cake into his mouth.

"Believe me, they do," Olivia said with a laugh. The girls' lunch was served.

"Well, nice talking to you," David said and turned back to Jonathan. "Must be a Catholic school," he commented loudly. "Did I tell you my parents were in Rome recently, and given an exclusive tour of the Vatican? My father has important contacts there."

What contacts can they possibly have among the cardinals? Jonathan mused. *David's parents are Jewish. Next, he'll say his father is the Pope's accountant.*

"Please don't go on about the Vatican," Jonathan pleaded to David in a low voice, hoping the girls didn't overhear.

David shrugged and reached for his cream meringue.

Jonathan was bursting inside with frustration. *Will I ever get a chance like this again?* He shot a quick glance at Olivia. To his delight and surprise, at the very same moment, she was sneaking a glance at him too. They exchanged shy grins and each turned back to their friend.

The waitress left the bill on their table.

David looked at his watch. "Jonathan, you may be interested to know that it's almost three o'clock. The game is about to start." Then he said loudly, to ensure being overheard, "Let me take care of this bill, I insist."

Jonathan thought to remind David that his paying had already been decided, but let it go. He watched as David made a performance of removing his wallet and opening it to reveal several notes. David licked his thumb before extracting the right amount, including a nice tip, and placing it on top of the bill.

David was in a hurry to leave and get to the TV in the shop window. He stood and headed for the door, calling over his shoulder, "Let's go, Jonathan. I can't miss the kick-off," and blew out of the door.

Jonathan, on the other hand, was in no rush. He knew that if he didn't get Olivia's phone number, the odds were that he'd never see her again. He mustered up the courage to ask, turned to Olivia, took a breath and…

What Jonathan had failed to realise was that several flakes of pepper had landed on his lapel. And to his shock, he exploded with a sneeze. Simultaneously, Jonathan turned his body so as not to spray the girls.

Now off balance, Jonathan's hand raked across his

table, taking with it cups, saucers, plates, cutlery… and the untouched roast beef sandwich. Red in the face, Jonathan dropped to his knees. He began picking up and putting stuff back on the table to restore some order out of chaos. Behind his back, Paula was laughing. He didn't want to know Olivia's reaction but figured it would likely be disgust.

The waitress appeared at his side, clearly peeved. She shooed Jonathan away, saying, "I'll take care of this. Please… just leave."

Jonathan couldn't bear to look at the girls. He hung his head in shame and disappointment as he hurried outside. After hesitating a moment to get his bearings, he saw David across the street, staring intently at a TV through the appliance shop window.

Just as Jonathan was about to cross the road, he felt a light tap on his shoulder. He turned around to see Olivia smiling.

"I wasn't sure I should do this," she said, "but Paula insisted I go ahead. Would you like my phone number, Jonathan?"

"Uh… yeah… yes… absolutely!"

Olivia produced the waitress's pen and a napkin. Holding the napkin in the palm of her hand, she wrote "Olivia" and her number. She neatly folded the napkin and slipped it into his blazer pocket, giving it a little pat for safekeeping. She reached up, gently pinched Jonathan's cheek, and said, "You didn't tell me that you do slapstick comedy." Then Olivia spun on her heel and disappeared back into the café.

Jonathan joined David at the window, who was transfixed by the game. David made no comment about the girls and asked no questions. But Jonathan didn't care. By comparison, he felt he'd been hit by lightning. He experienced a whole new feeling… touched by magic. He could walk on air, maybe fly. He wanted to run, jump, and swing around a lamppost.

But he didn't. Instead while David watched the game and cheered for Arsenal, Jonathan simply whispered to himself the same enchanting name, over and over: "Olivia… Olivia… Olivia."

7

HARRY BATES

Jonathan waited outside the payphone in the main building until it was free. He'd tried to call Olivia before and was told she was away. He now attempted to reach her again before his Latin class. His hands were shaking so badly he was having trouble reading her small, handwritten number. It took him two tries to get coins in the slot.

"St Claire's," an elderly woman's voice answered in an efficient tone.

"Hello, yes, uh, this is Jonathan Simon. I'd like to – to speak with Olivia," he stammered.

"Which Olivia?" she said curtly.

Jonathan looked at the napkin and saw she'd just written her first name. His only consolation was that she must've been somewhat hurried at the time, too. "Uh, I don't know, but I think she's from Switzerland?"

"You must mean Olivia Crest."

"Uh, yes, probably." Jonathan realised how lame he must sound.

"She may be in the library. You said your name was Jonathan Simon?"

"Yes."

"Does she know you?"

"I hope so." He couldn't believe himself. *Come on, Jonathan, pull yourself together.*

"Hold on, please."

Jonathan bore the unbearable silence on the other end of the line as he waited, his heart beating with anticipation.

"Hello, who's this?" The tentative girl spoke with an American accent.

"It's Jonathan… Jonathan Simon. I met you briefly at Janet's café."

"Sorry? Where?"

"The café in Enderby." Jonathan fretted that he hadn't made much of a lasting impression. "I was there with my friend, David Gold."

No response.

Then Jonathan remembered. "You said you liked my comedy act."

The reserve vanished. "Oh yes, of course, now I know. Sorry, I didn't recognise your voice. You sound different on the phone."

"Your voice sounds as lovely as I remember," Jonathan said, then immediately worried he'd gone too far.

A giggle assured him that he hadn't. "How are you doing, Jonathan?"

"Good," he replied. "Thank you, I'm fine."

"And how is your friend who speaks *fluent* French?"

He heard the familiar laugh in her voice and felt more at ease. "Last time I saw him, he was well – but I don't think his French is as great as he thinks it is."

Ah, that mesmerising laugh again. It gave him the courage to forge ahead. "Um, Olivia, I called because I'd like to ask you out to lunch. Just the two of us this time, at the same place we met before. Next Saturday, if that's possible." Not wanting to run out of options, Jonathan hastily added, "If that's no good, we can always make it another day."

Jonathan's life passed before his eyes as he waited for her answer. He could feel her thinking.

"You know what…" she started, then paused.

"You know what" sounded more like a prelude to "you're not really my type".

"No," she finally said in a voice that had reached a conclusion, then went on, "I don't have anything on Saturday. So yes, I'd like that."

Jonathan's heart felt it was going to catapult out of his chest.

Olivia continued, "I'll ride over to Enderby on my bike and meet you at one. I have to be back at school by four, though."

"Great!" Jonathan exclaimed. "So I'll see you… one o'clock… Janet's café."

"Yes, I'll look forward to it. Bye."

He put the phone down in its cradle. *She said YES!* He wanted to yell out at the top of his lungs for all the world to know, but that would draw attention to himself and questions from boys in his vicinity.

★ ★ ★

All the way to his next class, Jonathan hummed "Young Love", a catchy pop song he'd often heard on the radio, while cleaning his corps boots.

In his Latin class were boys from various Houses. Jonathan was in high spirits as he entered the classroom and plonked down in his usual spot next to Harry Bates. Harry was a junior in Trafalgar whose naiveté had reached epic proportions. Boys would probe him with ridiculous questions, then roar with delight when his inane answers matched their low expectations.

"Hey, Bates… Who wrote Shakespeare's sonnets?"

"Hmmm… was that Wordsworth?" Bates might answer, thinking he'd guessed correctly.

"How could *Wordsworth* have written *Shakespeare's* sonnets, you twit?" would howl the questioner.

"Did I get that wrong?" Bates might reply, completely oblivious that he'd been duped.

One winter morning, Bates wandered into the Houseroom looking dishevelled. When asked, "What happened?", he replied, "I just fell on some frozen ice."

Bates' redundancy "*frozen* ice" was repeated over and over with peals of laughter.

But what sealed his reputation more than anything else, was that at the end of one term, his mother had called the school about his class academic ranking. "I don't understand," she said. "How could Harry come twentieth in a class of nineteen?"

Bates was a tall boy with an oversized head and black hair in a bowl cut. All his life, he'd been regarded as a slow learner. A hundred years ago, he would've been called "the village idiot". These days, his fellow housemates referred to him as "thick".

Bates' parents were in denial. Their attitude was, *One day he'll work it all out… just give him time.* The senior Bates owned a chain of supermarkets. Due to a generous endowment to Blackleigh School, against better judgement, the boy was accepted, even though he hadn't done well in the common entrance exam. In his favour, Bates never took offence or lost his temper, despite the nonstop verbal abuse he received.

Jonathan wondered how Bates was faring in the Latin class, since the language was incomprehensible to most boys, including himself. But most students of Latin availed themselves of crib sheets, posted to them from a bookstore in London. If they weren't available, an enterprising senior would resell one or more of his old cribs to juniors at an exorbitant price.

The crib that Jonathan obtained translated *The Aeneid*, a favourite among Blackleigh teachers. Typically, boys sat at their desks, with the original in Latin, and the English version on their laps, and made ready to come up with the right translation. Clearly this was cheating, but if the masters were aware, they must have turned a blind eye to the practice, as no one was ever called to task.

Today's class began punctually under the tutelage of the grey haired and bespectacled Mr Paul Wood. He was a kind man who spoke with a genteel voice and was aware of the difficulties Latin students faced. Clad in his master's robe, he was a stickler for learning and commanded respect, though he rarely raised his voice.

Unfortunately for Bates, he was unaware of crib sheets. On the rare occasion Mr Wood called upon him to translate a chunk of Latin, Harry was invariably at a loss.

Jonathan tracked Mr Wood's eyes as he searched the class for his next "volunteer". He kept his fingers crossed, hoping Mr Wood's eyes wouldn't settle on him.

"Now let me see," Mr Wood said, his head swivelling and came to a stop. "Yes, Bates, I don't believe we've had the pleasure of hearing from you of late. Would you please continue with our translation? Yesterday, we left off at line forty. The Greeks were pitching their *tents*. What is the Latin word for 'tent'…? We are waiting to hear?"

By now the class was on pins and needles waiting for Bates to answer.

"Yes, carry on," Mr Wood prompted.

In the silence that followed, Jonathan exhaled with relief that he wasn't on the hot seat. Yet he pitied poor Bates, sitting with all eyes cast upon him. The blank expression on Bates' round face had the other boys at the ready to erupt in laughter at his expected inane response.

Jonathan didn't think about it; rather, he felt what he had to do, and "accidentally on purpose" dropped his pencil. As he bent down to pick it up, he slipped his crib sheet onto Bates' lap.

Harry looked down.

"I need the Latin word, Bates?" Mr Wood pressed. "Speak louder… We can't hear you."

Harry looked up, blinked, and said, "*Tabernaculum.*"

Mr Wood's jaw dropped, and he stammered, "Well, uh, yes, Bates, thank you, that is correct…"

The class was frozen in disbelief, shock, and disappointment.

Bates just smiled like the cat who ate the canary.

Forty minutes later, the bell ending class rang. Jonathan joined Peter Wynn as the boys streamed out of the door, and the two headed down the path towards Trafalgar.

"Ever get the feeling that there are days when everything goes right?" Jonathan said, feeling emboldened after saving Bates from his usual role as a laughingstock. That and the upcoming date with Olivia.

"Not in this hellhole, Jonathan," Peter replied.

"Well, I'm feeling daring today. Watch this…" Jonathan stepped off the path and walked on the well-manicured lawn. This was strictly against school rules. The gardeners had even posted a "Keep off the Grass!" sign as a reminder.

"What the hell are you doing?" Peter said, tossing his hand in the air.

"Just taking a shortcut to the House," a carefree Jonathan replied. "Want to join me?"

"This isn't one of your best ideas, Jonathan," Peter called out.

But Jonathan proceeded to step one foot after another on the precious grass.

"Simon!"

Jonathan recognised Tunk's voice coming from somewhere behind him. He turned to see the angry prefect stomping down the pathway. "Come here! Now!"

Jonathan retraced his steps.

"Oh, you've done it," Tunk sneered with glee. "This transgression will cost you a warning. I believe you now have two, if memory serves."

"Two?" Jonathan echoed, confused.

"I heard your little stunt at the doctor's office was number one."

Jonathan couldn't believe it. His so-called friend Croat had let him down and turned against him.

"Next Friday afternoon, at four o'clock, kindly turn up at the forecourt of the House, where you will be subjected to appropriate punitive measures. I promise you an afternoon to relish and remember. Try to keep out of trouble for the rest of the day." And with that Tunk strode on.

Jonathan joined Peter, who was shaking his head.

"There has to be a lesson in this," Jonathan reflected.

"There is, Jonathan," Peter said. "At Blackleigh, you can't let your guard down for even one lousy second."

Peter would later learn to heed his own advice, when he faced a situation he could never have imagined.

8

CABAL

Sleeth called the planned meeting for eight o'clock in his study – at a time when the rest of the House would be preoccupied with evening prep. He'd neatly arranged four wooden chairs in a semi-circle and set a wooden table in the centre. On it he'd placed a tall candle, along with a small sheet of white paper, a cigar box, a fountain pen, and an empty bronze bowl.

He needed one final implement. Sleeth opened the bottom drawer of his desk and removed an object wrapped in newspaper. He opened the package to reveal a short steel rod to which was soldered a small white medal, a cross with a gold rim. In the centre of the medal was a crown encircled by a faded green wreath. Sleeth placed the gadget on the table next to the candle.

The few decorative changes he'd made to the study since becoming Head Prefect were to install a khaki-coloured carpet and paint the walls off-white. He relished his exclusive use of the space. As Head of House he wasn't required to share a room with a study mate. The only "art" on the walls was a framed black and white seated portrait of his stern, unsmiling brigadier general father in martial uniform.

Sleeth had carefully selected his guests. If anything went wrong, he had enough on each of them to destroy their credibility and protect himself. He'd boned up on their backgrounds, knew their histories and their uncomfortable secrets. Still, he wasn't going to take any chances – hence the rod that would come into play at the end of the meeting.

Sleeth's only closely guarded secret was the sick gratification he took in sexually abusing juniors. Afterwards, he made sure his victims, now totalling eight, were too terrified to speak out. Sleeth accomplished this by threatening to take revenge on their families if he were ever exposed.

None of Sleeth's four guests knew the reason for the meeting. He had invited Tunk, his partner in crime, and Rodge Miller, whom he regarded as a tough son of a bitch with leadership qualities. Add to that, the brute-sized boxer possessed the admirable characteristic that almost all the juniors feared him.

Sleeth also invited Norman Snell. He knew that Tunk's strange study mate caused the juniors' flesh to creep. Moth would add an interesting element to the coming discussion. Sleeth regarded both Snell and Miller as potential prefects who'd take over at the helm and continue to menace and terrorise unsuitable juniors after he and Tunk left the school.

Finally, he'd invited Croat, the only member he thoroughly despised and trusted the least. Sleeth considered him a loose cannon but was paying heed to advice his father often espoused: "Keep your friends close… and your enemies closer." By the end of the evening, Sleeth would neutralise any possible threat that Croat might pose.

Sleeth set out drinking glasses on the table and waited. He checked his watch and recalled a favourite quote from *Macbeth*, which he'd studied for A level English: "By the pricking of my thumbs, something wicked this way comes."

A knock at the door and his four prospective conspirators trooped in.

Tunk, Croat, Snell, and Miller sat on their allocated chairs, and Sleeth offered them Coca-Colas.

The Head Prefect began by his asking Miller, the youngest, to introduce himself. Miller, he knew, was seldom happier than when recounting his own achievements.

The tall, muscular figure had a five o'clock shadow and a face pocked with acne. He lapped up his moment.

"You all know me… Rodge Miller," he announced, leaping to his feet. "There's nuffing wot happens around ere that I don't know about. I'm not just a pretty face. Me *faver* is on the school's Board of Governors. I don't take shit from no one." Then, with a defiant look, Miller dropped back and slouched in his chair.

"Thank you, Rodge," Sleeth said. No sitting for Sleeth, who had purposely left out a chair for himself. By standing, while the others sat, he'd maintain command of the room and the meeting.

"Let me tell you in part why I asked you here," Sleeth said, getting down to business. "Tunk and Croat are already prefects. I regard you other two," Sleeth indicated Miller and Snell, "as future leaders of our House."

Miller sat up straight. "If I hear rightly, yer callin' me a future prefect… I likes the sound ov that," he gleamed.

Sleeth smirked and said, "As Head of House, my nomination carries a lot of weight with the Housemaster."

Snell showed no reaction, other than to continue to examine his bitten-down fingernails.

"Next," Sleeth continued, "I want to bring up the name of a junior who is a blight on the House. Jonathan Simon disregards the Blackleigh code of conduct. He's a snitch and a major troublemaker. Last term, he accused my good friend Tunk of cheating at the Blackleigh fair – even went so far as to report him to the police."

Tunk chimed in. "You're so right, Hugh. Simon is a compulsive liar and a bumptious brat."

Sleeth concluded, "Further, Simon was also insubordinate in the corps and would have been punished severely for his offence had that bugger, Flicker, not intervened. But this time, I intend to see that Simon gets what's coming to him."

Miller by now was all eyes and ears, practically licking his chops at the prospect of hearing whatever creative retribution Sleeth was planning.

"I want us to work together," Sleeth said, "in getting Simon thrown out of the school…" he paused for emphasis, "but not before we've made his life a living hell."

"Wait a mo'." Miller leapt to his feet again. "Let me have a say. I've also got a grudge against an obnoxshus foreigner name ov Wynn. How 'bout we get rid ov him too?"

Tunk rose to his feet. "If I may have the floor. In addition to those two, I want to nominate for expulsion a lowlife from India, Jim Bhasin."

Sleeth had only intended to target Simon; and to his surprise, his enterprising minions had upped the ante. This was going to be even more fun – albeit more challenging than he'd anticipated. Sleeth glanced at his father's portrait and then said, "Thank you for your suggestions. In the army, we would simply have Simon, Wynn and Bhasin court-martialed. Since that is not an option available to us, any ideas how we should approach this? …Snell, I've yet to hear from you."

"Thank you for including me," Snell said with a note of sarcasm. "May I briefly digress. When I stalk butterflies, I study their movements and observe the flicker of their wings before I net a specimen. After waiting patiently, I spring! Once in my grasp, poison jar at the ready, there's no escape." He said in a croaky, breaking voice, "'Come into my parlour, said the spider to the fly.' That's how I'd also snag a human specimen."

"I've no idea what you're on about, and how's this butterfly crap got anyfin' to do wiv us?" Miller spat. "We want the three pricks expelled, not pinned on a board."

"That's what I'm advising," Snell went on. He shot Miller a look of exasperation. "Learn more about these three. Once they establish a kind of pattern, they'll be ripe for plucking. We set a trap, they walk into it unwary, and we screw down the lid, so to speak, before they realise what's happened."

Tunk, who'd rarely heard Snell, his study mate, talk so much, was impressed. "Moth, you're a source of wisdom!"

Croat was thanking his lucky stars that Sleeth hadn't called on him to come up with a scheme. He'd been uncomfortable with this meeting from the very moment he walked in. For a start, he couldn't figure out why Sleeth had chosen him to be part of this vengeance pact. Was this a kind of reward – for entering Simon's name in the Discipline Ledger? Or a punishment – for plotting against Sleeth last term? Croat figured his best approach was to be careful of what he said and pretend to go along with whatever Sleeth had in mind.

After contemplating Snell's idea for a moment, Sleeth nodded, then restated it in plain English. "Okay, for now, here's my plan. I'll work out shifts for keeping a close eye on them. Be cautious about this – they can't suspect anything."

"What we lookin' for?" said Miller. "Can you 'elabruate'?"

"Primarily a time and a place where they are usually alone. We can't have any witnesses. Despite the 'no snitching' code, I want to hurt Simon badly. And, if someone were to see what I did to him, the witness might feel obligated to come forward. Understand?"

"What do you 'nintend?" Miller asked, hoping for pointers.

Sleeth replied, "That part is still in the planning stage. My second, Tunk here, has a brilliant-wicked mind for this sort of thing. Between the two of us, I'm sure we'll come up with something. Now, can someone watch the three on weekends?"

"Easy, boss," Rodge said, his eyes gleaming. "I'll handle that."

Croat broke in, "I know Wynn goes to the shop like clockwork after lunch on Thursdays to stock up for the weekend. I'm usually there at the same time and I could keep an eye on him."

"We can do better still," Sleeth replied. "On the pretext that we're looking for a thief who's been stealing from the shop, we can do a spot-check on Wynn's purchases to make sure he's paid for everything. We probably won't find anything, but we'll turn up the heat. In fact, we can do spot-checks on all our three victims. What do you think, Tunk?

"Sounds ingenious," Tunk replied with a strange smile. He couldn't wait to prove his value to Sleeth.

"Now, I want to commemorate our understanding with a symbolic ritual – then we'll all swear an oath of allegiance to each other," Sleeth said.

He had originally planned to write only one name on the blank sheet of paper. Now there were two more victims. Sleeth picked up the sheet, tore it into thirds, and placed them back on the table. "I want each of you to write down the name of your victim."

Sleeth lit the candle and ordered Croat to turn off the lights. Sleeth wrote "Simon" on a strip of paper and passed the pen to Miller, who wrote "Wynn". Tunk took the pen and, in near-perfect penmanship, printed "Bhasin".

The Head of House held his slip over the candle flame until it caught fire. Tunk and Miller followed suit, and the small flames illuminated their faces. While the slithers slowly burned, Sleeth led the group in their oath.

"We vow to do all in our power," Sleeth said solemnly, "to purge our school of Simon, Bhasin, and Wynn, by fair means or foul."

The group repeated the oath, then the three dropped the burning slips into the bowl. They watched the papers fade to black and become nothing but ashes.

"Our oath is sworn in fire," Sleeth said. "I want Simon, Bhasin, and Wynn to disappear like these ashes. Our mission is clear. Croat, turn the lights back on."

Sleeth then held up the rod: a makeshift branding iron. "I now want a final gesture from each of you to solemnise your commitment. On this rod is affixed a DSO combat medal from the Second World War. It was awarded to my father for gallantry. He gave it to me, when they made me an officer in the Blackleigh corps.

"Take off your jackets and roll up your left sleeves. Branding identifies us all as allies. If one goes down, we all go down – so we must protect one another. No one can opt out or claim they weren't involved."

"What's going to happen?" Croat shuddered.

"Just do what you're bloody told," Sleeth snapped.

Sleeth held out his bare forearm, heated the medal in the candle flame, gritted his teeth, and branded himself first as a gesture of his commitment. The small imprint of the medal sealed against his skin with a sizzling sound, and a wisp of smoke. Croat pinched his nose to ward off the burning stench.

Sleeth handed the iron to Miller, who reheated it and branded himself. "Aach… blimey!" Miller let out a roar of defiance.

Miller reheated the iron over the candle and passed it to Tunk.

In stoic silence, Tunk impressed the outline of the burning medal on his bony inner forearm without showing any reaction and handed it to Snell. "I believe it's your turn, dear boy. Burning time!"

Snell, well accustomed to Tunk's warped sense of humour, replied, "You're too kind," as he accepted the iron.

Snell branded himself, heated up the iron and passed it to Croat, who didn't want to take it. Miller grabbed Croat's hand and forced the heated branding iron into it. Croat's whole body shook in abject fear as he held the iron two inches above his forearm.

Seconds went by. Tunk, tired of waiting, snuck up behind Croat and gave a hard tap to the butt of the rod, driving it into Croat's arm. Croat screamed in agony as the pain seared through his body. He let go of the iron, and it clattered onto the floor.

Sleeth glared at Croat. "Pick that up! How dare you disrespect my father's medal!"

Croat did as he was told and placed it on the table.

Everyone's eyes were fixed on Sleeth. The only sound came from Croat, in pain, as he clutched his forearm; and there was an odious stench of burnt flesh.

"One more thing…" Sleeth said with a clever smile. He opened the cigar box on the table and removed a tube of antiseptic healing ointment and five plasters. The last thing he wanted was for them to get infections and go in to see Dr Frank at the same time. *That* would raise suspicions.

He squeezed the white salve onto his finger, then coated his burn. After, everyone did the same, Sleeth handed each one a plaster. When the plasters were secured, Sleeth said, "Thank you for coming, gentlemen. You may leave now."

Alone, Sleeth mused, *When Simon finds out what's in store, death would be preferable.*

On his way back to his own study, Croat was in a quandary. *What should I do?* Whatever Sleeth and his group had in mind, their wicked plans were dangerous with unpredictable outcomes. Croat needed insurance in case things veered out of control, and he had to escape the trap in which he found himself.

Frog went along to the study occupied by Ben Winkler and his study mate Archie DeWardener. He heard voices inside, knocked at the door, and went in.

9

TEA AND SYMPATHY

September, 1956

On a chill Friday afternoon, ten forlorn boys, dressed in T-shirts, shorts, and running shoes, gathered in the House forecourt. The participants nervously chatted amongst themselves, unsure what to expect from the first Trafalgar punishment session for those with two disciplinary warnings. Among them were Jonathan and Jim.

The sky grew overcast. One by one, lights came on in the downstairs and upstairs studies facing the forecourt. Several seniors at the windows held mugs of tea and nibbled toast as they looked at the unusual activity outside evolving before their eyes.

Jonathan was taken aback when he heard a familiar voice call to him, and David Gold turned up, looking worried. David wore an impeccable light-blue track suit and spotless white tennis shoes. This attractive attire couldn't conceal the fact that David, with his long, stringy body, was nowhere near the definition of an athlete.

"David, what are you doing here?" Jonathan asked, blinking back his surprise. "This is a bad time to come. Tunk has concocted some demented torture for us."

"There's been a terrible miscarriage of justice," David replied. "Grant, the Head Prefect at Plessey, called me to his study last night. He said that I've had too many medical chits excusing me from sporting activities. I don't know where the twit got such a loony idea. He ordered me to join your punishment group this afternoon and couldn't have cared less when I told him about my sinus condition."

"Well, as long as you're here," Jonathan said, "say 'hello' to my friend Jim Bhasin. He's in this sinking lifeboat with me."

David and Jim and formally shook hands.

Jonathan gestured to the other boys. "You also may know some of Tunk's other victims. That's Harry Bates over there. He was twice late for breakfast. Then there's Peter Wynn, who somehow got two warnings after arguing once with Croat. The rest are juniors. The pudgy one is Ronald Clegg. I don't know the others or why they're being punished."

David asked, "And, if I may ask, what was your heinous crime, Jonathan?"

"I had a sort of disagreement with Dr Frank on the day I saw you at the san. And," Jonathan added sarcastically, "akin to the crime of murder, Tunk caught me walking on the precious grass in front of the classrooms."

David shook his head and couldn't help smiling.

Jim pointed and said, "Look, here comes Tunk, along with Miller. What's Miller doing here? He's not…"

Jim was cut off by Tunk's usual polite voice as he called out, "Greetings, boys." Tunk wanted to cherish this special moment before addressing the dispirited group. His idea of a joke by referring to the ordeal as "Tea and Sympathy" was meant to appeal to the watching seniors, whom he expected to delight in the coming spectacle.

His voice was calm as he addressed the group. "From now on, no talking. You boys know why you're here. Endure your punishment without protest and your slate will be wiped clean. Fail to keep up, or complain, and you'll be back here next week."

Tunk rubbed his hands together. "Let's get started, shall we? I'd like you to form two lines with plenty of space between you, if you will."

When the boys had formed rows, Miller took up a spot at the rear. Tunk pulled out a sheet of paper and read off each boy's name. "Here," was called out in response every time.

When Tunk finished reading the roll call, he said, "I've asked my good friend Miller to assist in monitoring your activities." The plan Tunk had worked out with Miller was for himself to give the directions. Miller's job was to supervise from the rear and berate the boys who became tired and slowed down.

David whispered something to Jonathan and Tunk spied him talking. "If our guest from Plessey opens his mouth-trap again, he'll be sorry."

Miller walked up behind Peter Wynn and sneered, "I've got me eye on you."

Tunk began barking orders in rapid succession and the group complied. "Stand at attention… Lie down on your backs. I want to see your legs bicycling as fast as you can."

"Faster… faster," Miller growled inches from Wynn's ear, and as Peter slowed, he not only yelled louder, but pinched Wynn's earlobe.

"Now, stop!" Tunk ordered. "Next, squat down on your haunches."

"Get on, move it!" Miller spat, crossing from one boy to the next.

"Raise your arms straight out to your sides," Tunk ordered. "Make small circles. After fifty small circles, I want to see fifty large circles."

Miller went over to Ronald Clegg, taking a brief rest. He got right in the young boy's exhausted face. "Listen, fatso, take it easy again and you'll repeat."

Ronald attempted the calisthenics as best he could.

"Now, on your feet," Tunk ordered. "All of you sprint around the House. The last five back will run again. Then, from those five, the last two will repeat while the rest stand in place on one leg and wait for them."

Jonathan looked over at David and saw he was ready to collapse. David was panting heavily and making loud, dramatic groans as he slowly and valiantly tried to pull himself together.

Miller roared at him, "Pick up yer pace, boy!"

The selection of exercises increased in their velocity and sadism, yet somehow David managed to prolong his periods of inactivity.

Harry Bates was heaving with exhaustion, his T-shirt and rotund face dripping with sweat. Finally, Harry expelled a sigh of surrender and collapsed on the ground.

Miller bent over him. "Get up, spaz!"

Bates was too spent to react.

Tunk called out, "Stand up, Bates, or you'll be here next week."

No response.

Tunk removed the roll sheet from his pocket and wrote down with satisfaction "repeat punishment" alongside Bates' name. He then beckoned Miller to join him at the front. Tunk whispered to Miller, "I deliberately started with exercises to tire them out, so they'll be unable to complete the final challenge."

He then addressed the group as Bates revived. "For your 'Grand Finale', you boys are going to form a human pyramid. Four on the bottom, three over them, then two, and finally one at the very top. Get moving!"

With no instructions as to who was to occupy which row in the pyramid, four boys randomly planted themselves, hands and knees, on the ground. Three more wobbled up on top of them. As the next two were climbing on top, one of the boys in the three-man row buckled, and the pyramid collapsed in a heap.

Having worn the boys ragged with exercises, this was exactly what Tunk expected. All the same, he couldn't help but laugh uproariously at the disorderly sight.

Miller was so surprised by the cave-in, he clapped his hands and jumped up and down with glee, pointing at the boys in the pile and laughing like a hyena.

"Repeat again!' Tunk ordered between gulps of laughter.

The boys attempted the pyramid again in the same order. This time, they got four, three, and two, but when the portly Ronald Clegg got to the top, his fourteen-stone body caused the pyramid to collapse on itself again.

It was even funnier this time to Tunk and Miller, and they doubled over with laughter. They were so busy congratulating themselves that they weren't paying attention to the pile of boys. Jonathan, in the middle of the pile, suddenly had an idea.

"Gather round," he said under his breath. Most of the boys inched nearer; those out of breath turned an ear in his direction. "We're going about this the wrong way. Here's what we need to do…"

Eventually, Tunk noticed something going on. "Hey, no talking, Simon. Let's do it again. Jump to it."

This time the four heaviest boys, including Ronald, formed the base. A lesser weighty set of boys formed the three-man row. Two light boys climbed on. And finally, Jim, the lightest of them all, scampered to the top.

What Jonathan had realised was that the most tired boys – who were also the heaviest – were going last. All they had to do was to reverse the order – heaviest *first*, lightest *last* – and they stood a better chance of succeeding.

And now the pyramid perched solid like the Rock of Gibraltar, and the boys were staring defiantly at Tunk and Miller, as if sending the message, *We can stay here all day… and all night, too, if we must.*

Miller waved his arms and shouted profanities at the boys to try and spook them into a collapse, but to no avail.

Tunk, realising he'd been upstaged, barked out new orders: "You boys will do it again, only this time…"

Tunk stopped talking when he saw Ben Winkler, a fellow prefect, and Ben's study mate, Archie DeWardener, walking towards him.

Ben was tall, bespectacled, with black hair, neatly parted. He had a studious air and rarely involved himself in matters of House discipline. As a wiz in maths and science, the quiet, modest young man was regarded by many as having a great future. Others who resented his success called him "a swot".

DeWardener was a young aristocrat: tall, lean, with fair curly hair and an uppity-class accent. He was a posh, benign presence in the House. Jonathan and he had barely spoken, yet Jonathan easily imagined him residing in a stately home where he'd be served a lavish English breakfast daily. Jonathan could see DeWardener sitting at a long dining table, with a neatly folded copy of *The Times* beside his nourishment, and say to his equally aristocratic and somewhat eccentric parents, "Kindly pass the marmalade."

Ben Winkler looked at Tunk, his fellow prefect, in the eyes and said in a clear voice, "You can't start something new." Ben had the same authority as Tunk. Ben turned to the pyramid and said, "All of you can climb down now and go and shower."

"Nobody move!" Tunk yelled at the boys, who simply looked on with curiosity as to how the stand-off would be resolved.

Archie spoke up. "I say, Tunk, steady on! You need to stand down, man."

Tunk ignored Archie, turned to the pyramid, and started to give an order.

Ben cut him off before he could speak. He moved in close to Tunk so that no one else could hear him. "Before you say another word, let me point out that you've involved Miller in handing out punishments. This is a violation of our school code because Miller isn't a prefect. Only prefects have the authority to discipline. End this now, or you'll force me to report this outright breach of conduct to the Housemaster, and you'll have to deal with him."

Tunk paused in thought, then stepped away from Ben. He gave the boys a frustrated look and reluctantly said, "All of you, get out of here... The session is over!"

Miller, not privy to the conversation between Ben and Tunk, threw up his hands. "Wot's happenin, Tunk? We didn't get to..."

Tunk grabbed Miller's arm and gave it a yank. "We're done here. C'mon, let's go."

Miller followed Tunk but kept looking over his shoulder in disappointment. "Just when it was getting to be fun," Miller complained.

The boys, still in pyramid formation, could hardly believe their luck.

Ben turned to them and said, "What are you waiting for?" Then he patted Archie on the back, who said, "Damn good show, Ben," and the two walked away.

Jim hopped down from the top, then row by row they disassembled and stood on their feet. The squad let out a spontaneous cheer, then broke up in groups of two and three, and headed for the showers. Jonathan and Jim remained behind with David.

"You made it!" Jonathan said. "Well done!"

"Naturally," David replied, brushing off one arm of his jacket, then the other. "How fortunate to have me as the cornerstone at the base of the pyramid. I should send you my bill."

Jonathan laughed, then bade him goodbye. But Jonathan's joy was short-lived, for he knew Tunk, having been bested, would thirst for revenge.

10

JANET'S CAFÉ

Jonathan stepped down from the bus in Enderby a few minutes before his one o'clock lunch date. He was eager to see Olivia and didn't notice a boy in a hooded duffle coat get off the bus shortly after. The boy's eyes locked on Jonathan.

In Janet's Café, it was more crowded than Jonathan expected, and he stood in the entry looking for a table. Jonathan had hoped to enjoy lunch in a quiet atmosphere. The same waitress who'd waited on him and David previously walked up.

"Hello," Jonathan said apprehensively. "Last time I was here, I'm really sorry about knocking over the food onto the floor."

"No problem." She flicked her wrist. "I was having a bad day. Did the girl give you her phone number?"

Jonathan was taken aback. "How did you…?"

"She borrowed my pen to do it."

"Yes, she gave it to me. In fact, she's meeting me here today. Table for two, please."

The waitress smiled and led him to a secluded table, set for two, by the window.

The hooded boy stood outside, uncertain what to do next, until he saw Jonathan taking a window seat, then made his move. He went over and sat on a bench outside the restaurant. Here he could keep an eye on Jonathan through the window by occasionally glancing over his shoulder.

As Jonathan waited, he nervously re-checked his wallet to ensure that he had enough money. Once satisfied, he began to wonder if he should greet Olivia with a kiss. Then he worried that having never kissed a girl before, if he'd be a big disappointment to her? *After all, how do you practise a first kiss with a girl?* These and other endless questions bombarded him. *Maybe I'm not cut out for this romantic stuff? It takes too much out of me.*

Jonathan checked his watch: 1:15PM. He looked at the menu for the second time and decided against his first choice of eggs, chips, and baked beans. *Too basic for such a special occasion.* He hastily searched for something with more of an exotic flair of foreign places.

Another watch check. Thirty minutes had gone by. No Olivia. *How long should I wait?*

A short while later, the waitress came over to his table and asked if she should clear the other setting. She could recognise a boy who'd been stood up when she saw one. And moving the other setting away would look to the other customers that the boy was just eating alone, thus saving him any embarrassment.

"Not yet," Jonathan said, holding out hope.

After adjusting and readjusting his empty plate, cutlery, and water glass, Jonathan looked at his watch again. She was now forty-five minutes late. He was heartbroken and got up to leave. As he did, he felt all eyes in the restaurant were upon him, so he walked as fast as he could to the door. He opened it, hurried outside, and almost crashed into Olivia, rushing toward the door from the opposite direction.

They grasped each other's hands to break their momentum. Both were blushing and began apologising to each other.

"I'm sorry," Jonathan said, "I thought you weren't coming and…"

"I know I'm late… really sorry," she said. "My bike had a flat tyre, so I had to rush around and find another one to borrow."

Jonathan paused, realised they were holding hands for the first time, and felt a rush of adrenaline. "Shall we?" he said, gesturing to the restaurant door, then opened it for her.

She took off her coat and hung it on a rack by the door.

The waitress flashed Jonathan a big smile and said, "Ah… you're back." She then led them to the same table where he'd been sitting.

The hooded boy watched the two of them with keen interest from his position on the bench. A short while later, he too entered the restaurant, went to an adjacent table that happened to be free, and sat with his back to

Jonathan to listen in on their conversation without being obvious.

Today, Olivia's shoulder-length blonde hair was tied in a ponytail. She wore a light blue dress, pink lipstick, and glossy stockings. Almost too much for him to take in, Jonathan could feel his heart pounding.

The waitress returned and Olivia ordered a chicken salad and coffee. Jonathan chose spaghetti with an Italian meat sauce called Bolognese. In the momentary silence, he sat in awe of her, trying not to stare, but couldn't help gazing into her clear blue eyes.

Olivia adopted a slightly teasing manner and Jonathan wasn't sure how to respond.

"Do you often meet girls in restaurants?" She grinned.

"Only on Saturdays," he said.

"Touché!" she replied and laughed.

"Tell me, how you've been?"

"I've had a crazy two weeks," she said. "After we met, I had to return to Zurich for a week to attend a family thing… Don't worry, nothing serious," she said when Jonathan blanched. "When I returned, Paula came up again from London. Thank goodness things have settled. How about you?"

"I don't travel much apart from shunting back and forth from London for school." *Who lives like she does?* he wondered. Olivia's travels only added to her appeal and mystery.

Lunch was served. He had trouble eating the spaghetti while talking, which slipped and slid from his fork. The soggy meat sauce also ganged up on him and threatened to splash brown dollops on his white shirt. *Next time, I'll order salad.*

"How's school?" Jonathan asked.

"It's good," she replied. "They have lots of music courses, which I really like, and the nuns are not as strict as the stereotype."

Jonathan couldn't imagine what kind of school she attended. The only nuns he knew of lived in monasteries. Then again, he wondered if it would matter to her that he was Jewish and resolved not to probe further.

"What's it like to attend an all-boys school?"

"I'm in my second year, so it's not as bad as last year. I'm still getting used to it. There are eight Houses at Blackleigh and I'm in the one called Trafalgar. Most weekends I…"

Olivia's eyes lit up and she interrupted him. "Trafalgar? Really? My cousin was in Trafalgar. That's one of the reasons my mother thought St Claire's would be a good school for me – because it was near to him. And as a bonus, I must say, the countryside is beautiful. I love to walk in the dales."

"Wait… wait!" Jonathan waved his hands. You said you had a cousin at Trafalgar?" He wondered why she'd said, he "was", rather than he "is" at Blackleigh.

"Yes, James Flicker. Did you know him?"

Jonathan almost dropped his forkful of spaghetti. *What are the odds Olivia would turn out to be Flicker's cousin?*

"Of course," Jonathan said. "When I first came to Blackleigh, he was already a senior. We didn't hit it off at first. But by the end of last term, he saved me from a harrowing situation, and we ended up as friends. He'd have been Head of my House but for what happened to his father."

"Right." Olivia winced. "My uncle's death came as a shock to everyone. I just received a letter from James. He's working in the family business. So, how are you getting along at Trafalgar these days?"

Jonathan wondered how much he should tell her, then decided to be forthcoming. "Blackleigh has a history of bullying. But last term I swore an oath with two friends that none of us would take abuse from anyone, including the prefects."

"Why do the older boys pick on the younger ones?" Olivia asked.

"Sometimes it seems that they don't need a reason. For them it's their warped sense of fun. But in my case, it's because I'm an outsider. Sometimes I feel I belong at the school, at other times I'm sure I don't… but I probably shouldn't burden you with this."

"It's not a burden," she assured him. "I want to know. I'm glad to hear you're an outsider. I sometimes feel like an outsider too. I guess it's because my parents are divorced. My father is in banking in New York, and my mother keeps moving around, can't seem to settle in one place."

"But you look as though you have it all," Jonathan broke in.

"Everyone seems to think I live a charmed life, but I see myself as no different from anyone else."

"I'm not so sure about that," he said.

Olivia let out a sigh. "You know, it's too bad I never got a chance to spend time with James last term. He'd planned to give me a tour of the school." She said this with a hint in her voice, and it took a few seconds before Jonathan picked up on it.

"You know what? I'd love to show you around," he gladly offered. "I have midterm exams this coming week, but the first Sunday of next month is fine. There's an Enderby bus that arrives at Blackleigh around noon."

"Yes, that's great," she said. "I'd really like that. Let's make it a date." Olivia looked at her watch. "Hey, it's getting late. I should be going. I can't be late for choir practice."

Jonathan paid the bill, then asked her, "Where's your bike?"

"I locked it up in the metal rack next to the bus stop."

Jonathan helped Olivia with her coat. They left the café and crossed the road. She collected her bike, then turned around to face him. "Goodbye, and thanks so much. I'll look forward to Sunday." She sat on the seat of the bike and put her foot on the pedal, ready to push off.

"Olivia! You've forgotten something," he called out.

She turned to him with a quizzical look. "What?"

Jonathan stepped up to her. "This…" And he kissed her.

This was totally unexpected. Olivia wasn't all that experienced herself. She'd only kissed three boys in all her fifteen years. But she knew a first kiss when she felt one and wanted Jonathan's to be one to remember. She smiled and said, "Can we do that again? A little slower this time?"

Jonathan happily complied. They touched lips softly, and Olivia held the kiss for a good twenty seconds.

When their lips parted, Jonathan knew something magical had happened. He felt he could do anything. Maybe even touch the sky.

Through the window of the café, the hooded boy never stopped staring at them like a hawk.

11

THE CORPS COMPETITION

Autumn was in the air. Leaves shrivelled then limply fell. On the pathways, Jonathan saw green, spiky casings opened to reveal burnished chestnuts. With each rush of wind, cascades of green, gold, and yellow leaves fell and whisked along the ground.

Shapely rose petals, once drenched in glorious colours of radiant red, crimson, pink, and white, were gone. The pitiless wind tore blooms from bushes; petals drifted and floated away. Now and again, a rose appeared; its singularity only emphasised summer was gone.

Boys no longer practised cricket in the grassy area at the back of the House. They packed and stored away their equipment for next year, including their white-woven V-necked sweaters, batting pads, dark-red leather cricket balls, and expensive bats with facsimile autographs of Dennis Compton or Don Bradman on the face.

The boys now played rugby. When Jonathan looked out of a Houseroom window, he'd often see a leather oblong rugby ball spiral through the air. He'd follow its flight to the next window along and watch it be caught in a pair of outstretched hands.

Jonathan reflected on the days ahead. He sensed change and unease in the House. Discipline was on the increase. Jonathan noticed that for some unknown reason Miller seemed obsessed with keeping an eye on him. He could tell that Miller was trying to be discreet, but it was so obvious in Miller's reactions. When Jonathan would look over his shoulder, there he was, several yards back, pretending to be minding his own business. *Let's hope that Miller doesn't join MI5 when he leaves school*, he mused. *He'd make a rotten spy.*

The brightest light was that he'd see Olivia again in a little over a week. The low point was the upcoming corps competition between the Houses. All members of the corps were required to participate. The only exclusion was in the case of a boy who didn't meet the height and weight requirements, such as the diminutive Jim Bhasin.

Sleeth, the highest-ranking officer in the Trafalgar corps, was determined to win the competition and attain glory for the House and especially for himself.

Jonathan never considered himself as a future candidate for a military academy, but enrolment in the Trafalgar section of the school corps was mandatory for all boys after their third term.

Now, every Friday afternoon at the rifle range, Sleeth assembled his Trafalgar squad of about thirty cadets, for another practice drill. Sergeant Tunk rarely attended corps rehearsals, on the basis that it was beneath him, which suited Jonathan just fine.

The date of the corps competition was approaching fast, and with every passing day, Sleeth became more demanding. Each cadet had to be fully dressed for every practice with their boots spit and polished, corps uniform neatly pressed, belt buckles shining, and equipped with a bolt-action rifle, always unloaded and for show only – but thoroughly cleaned and oiled all the same.

Jonathan snuck a glance at his watch, relieved that only a few minutes remained of the day's practice drill. The squad was standing at attention, shoulder to shoulder, in three rows of ten. Officer Sleeth at the front, accompanied by Sgt Miller, ordered, "Atten-shun! ...Pre-sent arms... Order arms."

After completing Sleeth's commands, Jonathan, at the far end of the second row, stood ready to march, his rifle butt supported in his left palm and the barrel over his left shoulder. Directly behind him, in the third row, cadet Gabriel also waited for orders before the welcome command of, "Squad dismiss."

Officer Cadet Sleeth shouted, "Squad, left turn... Forward march!"

As Sleeth had instructed him earlier that day, Gabriel deliberately shot out his left foot and clipped the back of Jonathan's heel.

Jonathan stutter-stepped, and in trying to maintain balance his rifle fell out of his hands and hit the ground with a clatter.

Officer Sleeth screamed, "Squad halt! Cadet Simon… break formation… to the front, now! Leave your rifle."

Jonathan knew that snitching on Gabriel would be inexcusable. There was nothing he could do but accept Sleeth's reprimand.

Sleeth wasted no time in tearing into Jonathan, in front of the squad. "The competition takes place in five days. A cadet *in my squad* cannot fumble around and drop his weapon. Such a soldier is a liability to the others."

Sleeth went on, "Cadet Simon, you're a hopeless case. When I see you march in formation and column o' route, you're out of step. Your right arm doesn't shoot forward at the same time as your left foot. After I give you a simple order such as 'About turn', your feet get tangled up. Then there's your rifle drill, which is totally spastic. What do you say for yourself?"

None of this was true, but Jonathan knew better than go on the defensive. "Sir, I'll practise an extra hour on my own each day until the competition."

"You need far more than extra practice."

The final criticism came like a dagger to Jonathan's heart. "You are a pathetic excuse for a soldier. You're not cut out for it. I can't allow you to participate in the corps competition," Sleeth barked. "There's just too much at stake."

Jonathan looked into Sleeth's eyes and probed his red-freckled face, topped with a beret. From his aloof and disinterested expression, Jonathan realised the decision to exclude him was pre-planned and accomplished.

"Cadet Simon," Sleeth went on. "You are a disgrace to the corps. Pick up your rifle and return it to the Armoury. Dismiss."

Jonathan, cringing inside, collected his rifle and did the walk of shame past the other cadets. His dressing-down by Sleeth, and the stigma that he wasn't good enough, were going to stick with him. He could tell that some of the cadets felt sorry for him; others were disinterested; but most were happy to see him go and didn't hide it. Several whispered snide remarks behind his back.

★ ★ ★

At bedtime, Jonathan confronted Gabriel in the dorm. "I know you deliberately tripped me. What kind of a person are you?"

"What are you talking about?" Gabriel countered. "You react to Sleeth's orders too slowly. It's your fault not mine that Sleeth won't allow you in the competition."

Jonathan turned away. Trying to reason with Gabriel was a waste of time. His sole consolation was that he was learning who his enemies were.

12

NICHOLAS KRILL

Hastings House was a three-storey brick building on the west side of a landscaped square near the Administration Building. On Sunday evening after supper, Rodge Miller made his way along a path, across the square, to the other side. There, he stood outside Hastings, under a lamppost.

Rodge reflected that he'd already disregarded Sleeth's admonition not to confide in anyone outside the branded group. But he and Sleeth had different goals. For him, Sleeth was a means to an end. *Flatter Sleeth now and, if necessary, screw him later.*

He waved at the new first-term junior exiting Hastings, walking towards him, with a lilt in his gait.

Jeez, thought Miller, *Nick Krill looks as innocent as a lamb.* They shook hands as old friends.

"Say, Rodge, is that a real gold bracelet you're wearing on your wrist?" Nick asked, noticing the gleam in the lamplight.

"Yes, Dad bought it from a jeweller on Old Bond Street. Must've cost him around five hundred quid. He gave it to me when I was made captain of the boxing team."

"Phew! No kidding. That's big money!" Nick said, clearly impressed.

"Next summer, I'll have me initials engraved on it," Miller said, eyeing his bracelet with pride. "Tell me 'bout you, how's it goin'?"

"Can't complain," Krill replied. "By the way, I finally wrote a letter to your dad, like you told me, thanking him for getting me into Blackleigh."

"Lucky break for you that he's on the board," Miller said.

"So far, I've had no problems here, other than with John Berge. He's been at Hastings for a year and wanted my Houseroom locker, claiming seniority. He tried to give me a hard time."

"Wot happened?"

"Berge changed his mind when he found a dead rat in his bed," Nick said casually. Miller was amazed how the blond-haired boy looked so guiltless and trustworthy, and appeared more youthful than his thirteen years. Nick's beguiling smile said, "Believe in me," and took the other person off his guard.

"Wot's the latest with yer mum and dad?" Rodge asked.

"They're living it up on holiday in the south of France, Juan-les-Pins. But I know when they get back, they plan to have dinner with your folks."

After a pause, Miller said, "Okay, let's get down to business. Wot 'ave you found out? Did you take care of that matter we talked about last week?"

Krill looked furtively to the left and right. "Let's go somewhere more private."

They walked into the square and sat together, away from any lamps, on a secluded bench.

Rodge put his hand in his pocket and took out a pound note. "Here's a quid for yer first job. If things go as I 'ope, there's plenty more for you. And I'll be made a prefect."

"Thanks. Your confidence is appreciated." Nick took out a pack of Peter Stuyvesant cigarettes, popped one in his mouth, cupped his hands over the cigarette against the wind, and lit it with a lighter. "Want a fag, Rodge?"

"No, thanks, I'm in trainin' for the upcoming boxing match against Millstone School. Problem is they can't find anyone to fight me." Rodge chuckled. "Tell you no lies, Nick, I wouldn't want to fight me eiver."

"I can imagine," Nick said. "Alright then, so here's what happened. I followed Simon last weekend like you told me. On Saturday morning, I saw he was leaving Blackleigh. Lucky me! He headed for the bus stop a good half hour early. It gave me time to disguise myself. So, I went back to the House, grabbed my hooded duffle coat, gloves, and glasses, then returned in time, just as Simon was boarding the bus. When I saw him take a middle seat, I jumped aboard and sat in front."

"That's my boy," Rodge broke in. "Good thinkin'."

"Yes, it was, if I say so myself," Nick boasted. "The bus arrived at Enderby, and as Simon walked by my seat, I bent over to tie up my shoe. But he was in such a hurry he wouldn't have noticed me anyway."

"Alright, enuff with yer life story," Rodge said with impatience. "Get to the point. Wot was Simon doin' in Enderby?"

Nick milked the moment. He took a final drag off his cigarette, flicked it away with his thumb and forefinger, then blew out a lungful of smoke. "He met a girl."

"A girl? Are you kiddin' me?" Miller said in disbelief.

"I wouldn't kid you," Nick said.

"Wacha mean by 'met'? Are you sayin' they ran into each over by accident?"

"No," Nick said. "It was arranged. They knew each other."

"Wot's she look like?" Miller snorted. "No, don't tell me, let me guess, toothy, big and ugly – a troll!"

Nick shook his head. "No, she's not like that at all. This girl is a cracker!"

"What the hell can she possibly see in 'im?"

"Beats me!" Nick shrugged his shoulders. "But you're going to get a chance to see for yourself. I overheard him invite her to Blackleigh – two Sundays from now."

Miller couldn't believe this break. He reached into his pocket and pulled out another quid. "This calls for a bonus, Nick. You've earned it."

"Thanks, I can always use the money," Krill said. "The parents keep me on a tight budget. They have an older people's idea that I'll learn the value of money by barely giving me any."

Rodge couldn't wait to tell Sleeth. Of course, he'd leave Nick's role totally out of it. "Nick, you did good. Say, are you ready to make more money?"

"Sure. Something else with Simon?"

"No, I'll look after Simon from now. Your next target is Peter Wynn, a tall, fair-haired boy from South Africa. Keep an eye on 'im. But do it smartish, like with you did with Simon. Get to know his usual haunts. Find out if there's a time he goes somewhere. He's another I want to see his goose cooked."

"I'm on it." Nick winked.

"One more thing." Rodge gave him a stern look. "This is strictly between us." To emphasise the point, Rodge extended his middle finger and wrapped it tightly over the next finger in his right hand. "As close as this."

"Don't worry. I know which side my bread's buttered," Nick assured him.

As the older boy left, Nick wondered if there was a way to earn more. Maybe he could really impress Rodge by taking his new assignment a step further than his benefactor envisaged.

13

MARK EVANS

Mark Evans, the new school Head Boy, entered the Administration Building, crossed the assembly and turned right as he headed towards the wood-panelled double doors at the far end of a long corridor. He passed through the doors and entered a small lobby.

Mark was eighteen, tall, fair-haired, and self-assured. His life at Blackleigh had begun five years earlier in an unusual way. He was one of the few students accepted by the school on their limited academic scholarship programme. The school boasted about their benevolence profusely, far beyond their actual participation in the charitable programme, which admitted only a few boys on a tuition-free basis.

His family lived in a council flat in York, and Mark had shown exceptional promise in academics and sports while attending a local school. It was to Mark's credit that he also distinguished himself at Blackleigh, where he boarded, despite living so close to home.

Mark was trustworthy and responsible. He loved the school and wanted to overcome many of the serious problems that a hundred years of tradition left in its wake. The previous term, he was voted to his leadership position by the Housemasters with input from the previous Headmaster. As such, Mark functioned as a role model, who represented the school at events, gave speeches at other schools, and oversaw the prefects in their responsibilities.

His weekly meeting with the new Headmaster was scheduled on Monday mornings at ten o'clock. Mark was greeted by Dr Macleod's efficient, grey-haired secretary. She was short, plump, and wore eyeglasses. Mrs MacNally was typing at her desk, on which two phones frequently rang.

"Morning, Mark." She welcomed him cheerfully. "He'll be with you soon. Can I get you some tea?"

"Great, if it's not too much trouble, Mrs MacNally." He sat down in an armchair.

"My pleasure." She smiled, adjusting her glasses, and crossed to an annex next door. She soon returned with a tray of tea and biscuits and placed them on a side table next to him.

"You look busy today," he said.

She gave a short laugh. "You've no idea. It's nonstop. After your meeting, he's seeing prospective parents, and later there's a lunch with some of the governors. He's also attending a Headmasters' conference in York later this week."

Evans drank his tea. The house phone was ringing, and she answered.

"He can see you now," she said. "I'll bring in the tea."

Mark Evans stood, knocked at the Head's door, and walked into a large, wood-panelled, carpeted room, filled with bookcases and photographs. Place of pride on the wall was reserved for a framed, signed photo of Winston Churchill, with a fixed, bulldog-like glare. Next to it, a separate, mounted, glass-framed case displayed three WWII medals. The doctor had removed his jacket and rolled up his shirt sleeves. He rose from his desk to welcome Evans.

"Good to see you, Mark. How are things at Waterloo? New boys settled in?" The Headmaster's stern look evolved into an engaging smile. A handshake, then the doctor gestured to a chair in front of his desk. Both took their seats.

"Yes, it's going well, sir," Mark replied. "We're implementing some of the changes you've recommended."

Mrs MacNally brought in tea and quietly left.

"The good news," the doctor said, "is that we've already streamlined the Bursar's office and are working on a revised and expanded curriculum."

"That's quite an undertaking," Mark said, impressed.

"Yes, if done right. When I started teaching at Farley School in Scotland, the parents of a new boy insisted that their son focus his attention on English History prior to the twentieth century. It happened to be a hobby and special interest of the father. He wanted his son to follow in his footsteps. The son, on the other hand, wanted to concentrate on maths and science."

"How did you handle that?"

"In the most tactful way possible." He grinned. "I explained to the father that the way we teach today is to respond to the interests of the boys being educated as best we can. The father had the benefit of studying what he wanted and now it was his son's turn."

"What did the father decide?"

"The father didn't decide. I'm pleased to say that his son did. Our new curriculum is designed to expand students' choices and encourage them to take chances. This will include an increase in sporting activities.

"It's also gratifying that we have more school applications than we can possibly fill. Many of them come from abroad. Also, I'm seeing some of the governors today about establishing a separate building fund to upgrade some facilities and maybe add a new House."

"Besides these achievements, what else lies ahead?" Mark asked. "I'd like to know how best I can help."

"Yes, I'm glad for our time together. I've given thought to some critical issues. My main concern is how discipline is handled in our school, and the nonexistent reports about bullying activity. I've met with the Housemasters and received conflicting opinions on whether or not there's an abuse of power by some of the prefects."

Mark hesitated, then said, "Well, sir, if you want my opinion, I'd say we have serious problems." Mark elaborated, "Two deaths occured in Trafalgar over the last few years, and little is said about them. They were juniors and both were deemed a 'suicide' in the police reports. However, many question whether the more recent one, Ian Gracey, was actually of his own doing."

"Why is that?" the Headmaster asked.

"He didn't seem the type."

"Mark, what would drive a Blackleigh boy to commit suicide?"

"In both cases, sir, it was common knowledge that the deaths occurred *not* because the curriculum was too tough – rather, another factor was in play."

"What might that factor be?"

Mark hesitated again, then said, "Persecution – both mental and physical – by seniors. Much of the discipline here is based on traditions that have stood the test of time, such as the no-snitching code. Each House handles discipline and punishments in its own way. But in all cases, no one ever reports them."

The Headmaster nodded. "Any time you're up against tradition, you can expect resistance from the powers that be. I can see some of the governors, especially the old boys, shaking their heads and saying, 'It's all part of the experience. What was done to us as juniors, we did to others when we were seniors.' And so, on it goes."

"Any ideas, sir?" Mark asked.

"Yes. I'd like you to speak to the Heads of Houses. Tell them I've requested they each prepare a typed report for me on the ways they maintain discipline in each of their Houses. We can then review this material and take it from there."

"I'll do that, sir. Anything else?"

"Yes," Dr Macleod said. "I've a radical thought I want to run by you."

Mark's interest was piqued, and he sat up straighter. "Yes, sir, what is it?"

Dr Macleod's phone rang, and a light flashed. He picked it up, punched a button, and said, "Yes, Mrs MacNally? …They're here already?" He glanced at his watch. "Alright, please tell them I'm on my way."

He replaced the phone in its cradle, stood up, and shook Mark's hand. "It seems I must dash off to my next meeting. I'll have to tell you about my plan another time."

Mark left the building with mixed emotions. On the one hand, he was eager to find out what new plan Dr MacLeod had in the works. On the other, he knew that at least half the Heads of Houses were up to no good. Sleeth, especially, was adept at covering up his trail of abuse.

14

PETER WYNN

Peter Wynn warned Jonathan that at Blackleigh you couldn't let your guard down. But Peter couldn't have imagined the outcome of his next visit to the school shop.

The shop was a small island of civility in a sea of anguish. The facility, in a separate single-storey structure near the Administration Building, was open from nine in the morning to six o'clock in the evening. On this Thursday afternoon, it was jammed with seniors and juniors alike. They came to stack up on groceries for the weekend, when the shop was closed, except for serving elaborate Saturday afternoon teas in a separate room.

Nowhere else in the school was found such an abundance of civilised food, sweets and snacks. A few non-food items such as transistor radios and clocks also were on display. Visitors to the school were often surprised to come upon a seemingly endless array of treasures, including chocolate bars, toffees, sugared almonds, crisps, bottles of Coke, iced fruit on sticks, and both Walls and Lyons ice cream. Along one wall were such delectable items as a wide variety of frozen foods and vegetables, bottles of Heinz tomato ketchup, tins of Goblin hamburgers and baked beans, OK sauce, Marmite, and chocolate spread.

Jonathan's regular habit was to purchase a cucumber, a loaf of bread, margarine, and a jar of sandwich spread. For his dessert, he'd often buy a Dainty, a rectangular chocolate-covered marshmallow with tiny coconut flakes sprinkled on the outside. He'd return to Trafalgar with his supplies, sit on the outside steps, and relish the opportunity to offset the bland school meals.

Don Fry ran the shop. He was practically a tradition at Blackleigh. With his affable presence and humour, he was always prepared to distribute worldly-wise advice. Don showed courtesy to all who entered, whether they were juniors or old Blackovians who'd left the school and were returning for a day visit. His stringy hair was tied in a knot at the back. Don's long sideburns and his offbeat clothes placed him in another era, where he'd have been equally content.

After lunch, on Thursday, Jim Bhasin joined Peter Wynn, both wearing duffle coats against a sky that promised rain and went on their routine pilgrimage to the shop.

"Why do you always bring that canvas bag?" Jim asked Peter. "They give you paper ones."

"Their bags aren't reliable – they sometimes break," Peter replied.

They reached the shop and made their separate ways inside amongst the throng of boys. Jim noticed Tunk and made a point to keep plenty of distance between them. He almost bumped into Croat, who was stocking up on donuts, and quickly veered away.

Jim found a few items and waited in the queue to pay. He purchased three tins of hamburgers, a packet of frozen vegetables, a cucumber, bread, butter, milk, and two Daintys. He collected his receipt from Joy, Don's eighteen-year-old daughter, at the lone register. Somewhere in the crowd, he heard "Whitey" Gabriel admonishing a boy for his food selection. "When you make fried bread, buy fat for frying, not butter. Jeez, didn't your mother teach you anything?"

He looked around for Peter and saw him standing in front of the shelving for accessories, surrounded by a crush of bodies. Peter had put his carrier bag on the floor and was still checking out alarm clocks. Each clock stood on the shelf like a soldier on parade, some round and others square. One by one, Peter was trying them all, but returned each to the shelf when he experimented and found the clock emitted a harsh alarm. Various boys who drifted near him reacted with disgust at every unexpected blast of discordant alarm noise.

Peter finally gave up, collected his bag and decided not to buy anything in the crush of bodies. He saw Jim at the front of the shop and joined him. "It's too damn crowded," Peter concluded. "I only needed a couple of things, but there's such a long queue at the register, I'll make do without this weekend."

"I thought you wanted an alarm clock," Jim pointed out.

"Yes, but they're all too bloody noisy. I want to wake up slowly, not with a shock to my system. It's bad enough having to open my eyes and find I'm at Blackleigh."

Peter and Jim left the shop and started back to Trafalgar. They hadn't gone far when they heard a strident voice calling their names. It was Tunk, standing outside the shop with two grocery bags at his feet. He waved at them to come back. Beside him was Don Fry, with a look of concern on his face.

Tunk repeated louder, "Bhasin and Wynn, step back here, if you will."

The two juniors returned to the shop. The last thing Jim Bhasin wanted was a confrontation with Tunk. "What's wrong, now?" he enquired. "Why shout at us in front of everyone? It's so embarrassing."

"Hold your tongue, if you know what's good for you," Tunk snapped. "There've been items stolen from the shop recently, so Sleeth has ordered spot-checks. I'll need to look at what's in your bags."

Jim rolled his eyes knowing this was bogus and Tunk was singling them out simply because he had the authority to do so. "Go ahead," Jim replied defiantly. "Do you think I'm so desperate that I'd stoop to steal a Dainty or a Cadbury's flake?"

There were a couple of tables with chairs outside the shop.

Tunk gestured, "Bhasin, be so kind as to remove your purchases and put them on this table. Then I'll need to see a receipt for your items."

Jim looked at Don, who shrugged as if to say, *Sorry, this is out of my hands.* Jim grudgingly took out the items he'd bought and placed them on the tabletop. He dug into his pocket and retrieved his receipt.

Tunk compared the receipt against the groceries on the table.

"Bhasin, it appears you're in the clear," Tunk said, looking disappointed.

Don Fry spoke up, "Let's drop this, Mr Tunk."

"On the contrary," Tunk replied. "We must stop pilfering, and this is the only way."

Tunk turned to Peter. "Wynn, what about you?"

"I didn't buy anything," Peter said casually.

"Just open your bag," Tunk ordered. "I haven't got all day."

Peter made a grand gesture of dumping his empty canvas bag onto the table. He reacted with a look of horror when two small wallets tumbled out.

Tunk's eyes lit up with delight. "Well, well, what have we here?"

Peter was dumbfounded and turned to Jim in dismay. "Hold on, hold on," he said to Tunk. "I've no idea how those wallets got in my bag."

Tunk made an ostentatious display of opening the wallets to check the contents. "Hmm, Pearl... and

Davies. As I'm sure you already know, Wynn, this wallet belongs to Alan Pearl, a new boy in Waterloo…" Tunk waved it under Peter's nose, then did the same with the other. "And this wallet comes from a junior in Hastings, name of Callum Davies. Okay, Wynn, explain yourself… I'm waiting."

"There's nothing to explain." Wynn shook his head in disbelief, and said again, "I swear I've no idea how the wallets came to be there. This is a frame-up. I'm not a thief."

"Are you suggesting that two different boys from two separate Houses *voluntarily* put their wallets in your bag?" Tunk scoffed.

"I've never seen these wallets before, and I won't answer any more ridiculous questions." Peter turned and started to walk away. Jim, completely confused, remained frozen to the spot where he stood.

"Stop right there, Wynn!" Tunk called out. "This is far from over. Get back here."

Peter let out a heavy sigh and complied.

"Deny this all you want, Wynn," Tunk said, "but I've caught you red-handed. Report to Sleeth's office at 6PM this evening. Try and explain yourself to him."

★ ★ ★

Peter Wynn slammed his right fist into his left palm in frustration as he sat waiting in Sleeth's bare study in Trafalgar. The Head Prefect ignored him while busying himself with paperwork. He wanted to deliberately make Wynn wait to plead his innocence.

Sleeth finally closed the folder he was pouring through, then looked at the accused. He relished the sight of Wynn, seated before him, and hoped the boy would snivel and beg for leniency.

"Wynn, how do you explain the stolen items Tunk discovered in your bag?" Sleeth finally said, feigning a look of concern.

"I didn't steal these wallets," Peter said defiantly. "And I didn't hide them in my bag."

"You're asking me to believe that two boys accidentally dropped their wallets in your bag?" Sleeth exclaimed. "You must know that makes no sense. I'm trying to give you the benefit of the doubt, but I can't understand how you came to be in possession of these items."

"Some evil chappie must have set me up," Peter offered.

"Do you suspect anyone?" Sleeth enquired, curious to find out if Peter knew who his enemies were. "Is there someone who has it in for you?"

Peter considered the question for a moment, then replied, "The only person I can think of is Miller, but I didn't see him in the shop."

"Then I can only deal with facts. The wallets were discovered in your possession, and you're unable to provide a logical alternative to the theft."

Peter wanted to scream in anger, but he bit his tongue and kept his composure.

Sleeth deliberated for a moment, then said, "But maybe there's an option."

"What have you in mind?" For the first time, Peter felt hopeful.

"I could consider leniency if you were to make a public apology to the boys whose wallets you stole. Also, you'd need to perform some type of school volunteer service for a couple of weeks. It has to be something demeaning – to send a message to others."

"But I never stole the wallets," Peter pleaded.

"The evidence says you did." Sleeth threw out his hands. "And if you don't show contrition, and take responsibility for your actions, there's no way I can help you."

Peter knew he had no other option. He pictured himself scrubbing toilets while other boys opened the door to sneak looks at him and snigger. But he weighed that against the consequences for theft at Blackleigh, if a prefect with hard evidence pressed for it. "Okay, okay." Peter resigned himself. "Whatever you say, I'll do it."

Sleeth nodded and went over to a typewriter on another smaller desk. He quickly hammered out a note to the Housemaster, tore it out of the carriage, put the letter in an envelope and sealed it. He addressed it to "Mr Alec Morton" and handed it to Peter. "Please give this to the Housemaster; he's expecting you."

"What have you recommended?" Peter asked. "I assume it's something janitorial."

"Nothing like that," Sleeth said with a poker face.

★ ★ ★

Fifteen minutes later, Mr Morton opened the envelope, scanned the letter, and decided to read aloud Sleeth's recommendation, verbatim.

109

Mr Morton cleared his throat. "Dear Sir, as I informed you last week, lately items of significant value have been vanishing from the school shop. No culprit had emerged until earlier today, when I arranged for one of my prefects to do a spot-check on the contents of boys' bags and compare them to their receipts.

"Prefect Tunk is to be commended. He discovered that Peter Wynn was found to be concealing in his bag not pilfered groceries, but two stolen wallets belonging to boys of other Houses.

"During my questioning, Wynn could not adequately explain how these wallets were found in his possession. Furthermore, I found Wynn to be in complete denial and unrepentant. Therefore, I have reason to believe that in Wynn, we have a career offender. If we allow him to stay on at Blackleigh, his crimes of theft will likely continue.

"I wish it were otherwise, but I am left with no option but to recommend that Peter Wynn be expelled from Blackleigh, not only for this crime, but as an example and deterrent to others.

Respectfully,

Hugh Sleeth, Trafalgar House, Head Prefect."

Peter Wynn gasped at the severity of Sleeth's recommendation and his duplicity. Peter never anticipated that Sleeth would opt for expulsion.

"I'm sorry." Morton looked at Peter with an unforgiving face. "I wish this turned out differently. But, under the circumstances, there is no place for you at Blackleigh. I'm obliged to respect this recommendation and will inform your parents."

"I can't believe this," Peter cried. "Sleeth led me on… said he wanted to help me… and all for something I didn't do. Is this Blackleigh justice?"

Mr Morton was unmoved. "Do you have anything more to say before I dismiss you?"

"Yes, sir, I do. You should know there's a conspiracy of evil here, going on right under your nose. But the current system of justice in this school prevents you from seeing it."

Mr Morton let out a sigh. "Every system has its flaws. But prefects handling punishments have served Blackleigh well for over a hundred years."

"So did the Spanish Inquisition," Peter countered.

"You're exaggerating, my boy."

"Maybe so, but the Inquisition was an abuse of power. And that's what passes for justice at Blackleigh these days."

"You're entitled to your opinion, Peter."

"Ah, sir, but I'm not entitled to a fair trial. One person, Sleeth, declared me guilty, and that was enough."

"That will be all," Mr Morton announced. In his mind, there was nothing more to be said. He gestured towards the door to convey that their meeting was over, and Wynn should leave his study.

★ ★ ★

The following evening, Rodge Miller waited for Nick at their usual meeting place.

Nick pranced up whistling, proud of himself.

Miller was not amused. "I told you to keep an eye on Wynn and report to me. But I never expected you to take matters into your own hands," Rodge admonished Nick.

"I saw a golden opportunity," Nick said casually. "After all, you did say you wanted the bloke gone, and that is what's happened."

"True," Rodge acknowledged. "But the idea was to make him *hurt* first. Feel the pain."

"What's more painful, mate – and embarrassing – than being labelled a thief and kicked out of a top school like this? His crime and the disgrace of expulsion will follow him for the rest of his life. People will know he was sacked from Blackleigh."

"Okay," Miller said with resignation, "you 'ave a point. So, tell me, how d'yer pull it off?"

"I started trailin' Wynn," Nick explained, "and I already knew that every Thursday he went to the school shop to buy groceries for the weekend. So, right after lunch, I got there ahead of him, and sat outside at one of the tables. It began to rain, and I had on my duffle coat.

"Right on time, Wynn and that Indian boy show up. For some reason, Wynn brought along his own canvas bag. The two went into the shop. I waited a couple of minutes and followed them. They separated in the crowd. When I tracked down Wynn, he was testing alarm clocks on a shelf, one by one. He'd placed his canvas bag on the floor."

Miller, as usual, was impatient. "Get to the point, Nick. So how did those two wallets end up in Wynn's bag wivout him knowin' it?"

"Easy. Each time Wynn set off an alarm, one or two boys in the vicinity would be distracted for a moment. The alarms did the trick for me. I turned around and saw Peanut Davies, who's in my dorm. He'd just put his wallet into his coat pocket. Believe me, it happened so fast, Peanut never knew I'd snatched it. Right after, I see Pearl from my history class, and in a moment, I snagged Pearl's wallet too. Then, all I had to do was bend down to tie my shoe whilst I slipped the wallets into Wynn's bag.

"Bingo! After that I bought some gum, so as not to look suspicious, and left the shop. But I tell you no lies, Rodge, I never knew Tunk was going to do a spot-check on both Wynn and his pal. My idea was that Wynn would eventually find the wallets himself and have a lot of explaining to do. Sometimes, you just get a lucky break."

"Phew, Nick, you're somfin' else." Miller looked at Krill differently now. He was unsure whether Nick was an asset or a liability, but the boy certainly had a wicked talent. "You went too far, even though I got no problem with Wynn bein expelled," Rodge said. "But, next time, follow my instructions to the letter. This could 'ave gone so bloody wrong."

"Alright, hold your horses!" Nick replied. "After all, things did work out."

Miller only wished that there was a way for him to take the credit without jeopardising his relationship with Sleeth. But Rodge knew that making himself the pickpocket would be as dangerous as the risk taken by Nick.

Rodge took out a small envelope from his pocket. "There's a pound note in here for trailin' Wynn. And an extra pound bonus for keepin all this just between us. Got it?"

Nick broke into a smile. "Absolutely," he said, placing his hand over his heart. But already the wheels were spinning in his devious mind.

15

OLIVIA'S VISIT

At 1:15PM, on the Sunday Jonathan had arranged with Olivia, the green bus arrived at Blackleigh. He held back, not wanting to appear too anxious. The bus stopped and a few passengers stepped off, two sets of parents, and a junior from another House. Then, his heart skipped a beat… Olivia! She looked so lovely he could imagine her appearing in the pages of a glossy fashion magazine.

"Hey," he called, "Olivia." And, forgetting his vow to remain calm, Jonathan rushed up to greet her.

Olivia wore a dark blue open coat, a light blue cashmere sweater, a white silk scarf tied round her neck, and a white beret. Her blonde hair flowed down to her shoulders. She wore no stockings and had navy blue shoes.

"Hi, Jonathan." She grinned. "Will I see your friend today, the one who speaks French?"

No way, he thought, *I won't share her with David*. "Uh, David's tied up."

"That's too bad," Olivia said, her face feigning disappointment. They both laughed.

"It's good to see you, Jonathan."

He liked to hear her say his name and hoped that nothing would spoil his hope for a perfect afternoon.

"What's our programme?" she asked. "I'd love to see everything."

"Let's start with the Administration Building, then the Assembly, and the Chapel, because they're the nearest," he suggested.

"Look, Jonathan," she pointed, "over there, two squirrels playing. They're so cute."

He turned to see them chasing each other up a tree trunk, flicking their long, bushy tails. He wisely held off telling her how some boys liked to throw stones at "rodents".

His body tensed. Coming towards them, on the same path, was the portly figure of Dr Frank, dressed casually for an afternoon walk. When Dr Frank registered who the boy in front of him was, he made an angry face and was about to say something. But then he noticed Jonathan's female guest. Dr Frank nodded to Olivia, grunted, then walked on.

"He looks moody. Do you know him?" she whispered.

"Unfortunately, I do," Jonathan said, and told her the story of his medical ordeal.

"What a weirdo." She raised her eyebrows. "And what you did was brave."

"Thank you," he said, blushing.

Half an hour later, after leaving the Chapel, they reached Trafalgar. "Well, this is my House," Jonathan said. "Let's not stay here for long. There's a lot more to see." He didn't want to run into Sleeth or any of his minions.

"Trafalgar looks impressive, with a column on each side of the front entry. So, this is where you live?" she observed.

"Depends what you mean by 'live'," he replied as they entered the House lobby. "It's more like 'exist'. Appearances can be deceiving."

"What time are you up in the morning?" she asked.

"The bell rings at 7:30. What about you?"

"I wake at six and go for a run. And my first class, biology or English, is at eight."

"Good for you." Jonathan grinned. "As for me, I'd rather sleep."

Olivia laughed and gave him a playful pat on the shoulder.

In the lobby, Jonathan walked over to the House notice board, but it was of no interest to Olivia. Before he realised, she'd opened the Houseroom door and marched right in.

He called after her, "Hey, wait for me!" but it took him a moment to recover and follow her.

Jonathan was briefly at loss for words. He saw Olivia in the middle of the room by the billiard table, casually looking around. The few juniors sitting in the Houseroom were unsure whether to stand or remain seated. They stared at Olivia with eyes agog, as if they'd never seen a girl before. She turned to Jonathan with a grin and asked, "Where's your locker? James told me that they inscribe the names of old boys on the doors."

"It's at the far end, top left." He pointed. "When I leave the school, they'll engrave my name on a door too, with gold letters. We should get going," he urged. "Like I said, there's lots to see."

"Sure." Olivia smiled radiantly. She turned and chirped, "Bye," and waved to the flummoxed boys.

They exited back to the lobby.

"Can I see the dorm where you sleep?" she asked.

"Sorry, it's off-limits to visitors."

"Parents too?"

"Well, yes, they're occasionally allowed to go there, but it's got to be cleared with the Housemaster."

Jonathan was steering Olivia towards the front door, but before they got there it burst open and in came Gabriel, returning from tennis. The snowy-haired figure jerked to a stop, dumbstruck upon seeing a beautiful girl in Jonathan's company.

Jonathan was still miffed at Gabriel for causing his disgrace in front of the corps, and would have walked right past him, but his good manners dictated an introduction.

"Uh, Gabriel, this is my friend, Olivia."

Gabriel, for his part, almost dropped his tennis racket in shock. He blushed, pulled himself together, and mumbled, "Pleased to meet you, Olivia."

"You too, Gabriel. Jonathan's showing me round the

school," she said with a twinkle in her eye. Turning to Jonathan, she asked, "What's next?"

"The lake, where there's a swimming pool," Jonathan replied, reaching for the door handle.

"Right, well, bye now," Gabriel said and sloped off to the changing room. *That was great timing*, Jonathan realised after all. *He can put that in his pipe and smoke it!*

Outside in the breezy forecourt, clouds filled the sky and gusts of wind tousled their hair. Olivia and Jonathan walked up a long winding path that turned into an avenue with tall chestnut trees on either side.

Dare I hold her hand? Jonathan wondered. At the end of the path, they came upon a forecourt, which fronted an impressive newly completed two-storey brick building partly enclosed by a temporary fence with a gate. Above the huge double door entrance were engraved the words "Performing Arts Building".

"They've just built this," Jonathan said. "Inside, there's a stage, an auditorium, and dressing rooms. Starting next month, they'll put on plays, hold concerts and recitals."

"What's the first performance?"

"*HMS Pinafore*… it's an operetta," he said authoritatively, hoping to impress her.

"Are you in it?"

"No, it's being put on by another House. The boys in Plessey build the sets and have all the acting parts."

"How do boys act in girls' roles?" Olivia asked. "There's lots of female roles in Gilbert and Sullivan."

"Well, the boys play the parts of girls – in dresses, wigs and makeup."

"The boys don't mind?" Olivia asked with a giggle.

"Not really." Jonathan shrugged. "Some of them kind of take to it."

There was uncertain moment as each considered the implication of what this meant. Finally, Jonathan said, "Do you like opera?"

Olivia broke into a smile. "I don't like it, I love it."

She walked up and tried the gate, but it was securely locked. Olivia made a pouty face in disappointment.

Jonathan looked both ways to ensure no one was in the vicinity. Then he said, "Olivia, we're not done yet. My friend David Gold is in Plessey. He worked on the *Pinafore* set and is helping to write the programme. David showed me round inside. Follow me."

He led her around to the side of the building and they came to a second gate that was unlocked. They passed through and went to the side of the building, where there was a brick placed between a door and the threshold. "Look," he said, "the workmen wedged this fire exit door open so they don't have to wait for someone to bring them a key on Monday morning. There are four fire exits, two in the front on either side, near the stage, and two, including this one, in the back near the unfinished seats."

They entered the building. Jonathan went over to a bank of light switches and flipped on a few lights. "Now you can see," he said, "the auditorium is newly carpeted and filled with seats, except for the area at the back. That'll be finished this week. The place holds about four hundred people." He pointed to the stage. "They've almost completed the set! That's the deck of the HMS *Pinafore*."

"Oh, I'd love to go up on the stage!" she pleaded, with her palms raised together in mock supplication. "Could we?"

"Alright," he said, eager to please, "but we shouldn't stay long. There are separate lights for the stage. I'd better turn off the auditorium lights first."

"Wow! Thanks, Jonathan." Her eyes lit up. "This is so great!"

Jonathan returned to the light panel and turned off the auditorium lights. The red exit lights above the doors provided just enough illumination as they made their way down to the stage, along the right wall and up the steps at the side of the stage. Jonathan went to another bank of lights and turned on one marked "1-C" that illuminated the centre stage under a focused beam. Olivia walked on and stopped under the spotlight.

"It's awesome." She bubbled with excitement. "Can I sing something from *HMS Pinafore*?"

"Please, go ahead." He smiled, impressed that she knew the operetta so well.

Olivia took off her berct, made like she was holding a basket of trinkets and sang aloud:

"I'm called little Buttercup, dear little Buttercup,
Though I could never tell why,
But still I'm called Buttercup, poor little Buttercup,
Sweet little Buttercup – I!"

Her resonant, pitch-perfect voice echoed through the empty auditorium. While he listened, Jonathan closed his eyes and wished time could stand still. Olivia finished her song, daintily curtsied to the empty seats, thanked the imaginary audience for their applause, and smiled, eyes glistening.

"That was super," Jonathan said, joining her at centre-stage. *This is an afternoon I'll dream about.* Jonathan's knowledge of opera was limited, although, when he could afford it, he loved to go to new musicals in London's West End during the holidays. But after hearing Olivia sing, he vowed to learn more about opera, and get to know some well-known arias.

They both jumped! There came the sound of a slow handclap from the shadows at the back of the auditorium. Jonathan was shaken by the sight of a hooded figure, who began walking down the centre aisle. To his horror, Jonathan recognised the bulky form of Miller, even though in the dark, he couldn't see his face.

Miller, cupped his hands on either side of his mouth and yelled, "Oy, Butterfly… I'm comin' for yer with me net!"

Miller let out a whooping wolf howl.

Olivia gasped and grabbed Jonathan's hand tightly. He felt his body tingle at her touch, despite the danger they were in.

"I know this place, stay with me." He led her by the hand back to the panel and turned off the spotlight, plunging the stage into darkness. Jonathan moved quickly but carefully behind the stage in the dark, holding Olivia's hand with one hand and feeling his way with the other.

"Quick, in here," he said and opened a door to what he recalled was one of two dressing rooms.

Jonathan knew that each room had locks. Once inside, he twisted the deadbolt into place, then turned on a light. Both were frightened, their hearts beating.

He turned to her. "Well, this is the school. What can I say?"

Olivia laughed despite herself. "What's going on, Jonathan?"

"Just a typical day at Blackleigh," he replied. "One senior or another looking to make another life miserable, any way he can. In this case, it's a jerk called Miller."

"Do we wait? Or make a run for it?"

As if on cue, they heard a far-off noise; that of Miller bumping into something, cursing, then silence.

"We'd best stay here until we know it's safe," Jonathan said. "Maybe we can wait Miller out and he'll tire of his game and go."

She furrowed her brow. "Do things like this happen to you often?"

"More than usual lately," Jonathan said contemplatively. "Something is brewing. I'm not sure what. But I have a bad feeling there's a plot going on. And I think I'm at the centre of it. Seems like every time I make a friend, something happens to them. My friend Peter was just expelled for something I'm sure he didn't do." Jonathan exhaled deeply. "I'm really sorry to involve you."

"No, Jonathan, this is my fault," Olivia exclaimed. "If I hadn't had to sing…"

"No, no, no." Jonathan stopped her. "This has nothing to do with you. I've had a target on my back since my first day here."

"Why you?"

It was time for Jonathan to tell her the whole truth, even though she might not like what she heard. He pointed to his face. "Well, this birthmark, for one thing."

"Come on, that's nothing. I…"

"Maybe it's nothing to you." He cut her off. "But to the blond, blue-eyed, perfect-looking boys, it's just as bad as being…" He broke off.

Seeing his pain, she looked worried. "Being what, Jonathan?"

"I'm Jewish," he confessed. "There. I've said it. I didn't tell you before because I was afraid of how you'd react, being Catholic and all."

Olivia looked amused, but not in a condescending way.

"What?"

"Paula's Jewish."

Jonathan was shocked. "Are you kidding me? You're Catholic and your best friend is Jewish?" He couldn't imagine such a thing.

Olivia explained, "In grade school, when Paula and I started hanging out together, her parents were against it. I think they were afraid that my Catholicism might rub off on her. But Paula and I don't care about race, colour, or religion. We only care about what's in a person's heart. And if they're a good person, that's enough for us."

"Wow, if only that attitude was everywhere."

Both jumped when someone tried to open the door. Apparently, Miller had found the backstage light and was able to move around the area.

"I know you're boff in there!" Miller deduced, finding the door locked. He smashed his fist against the hard surface. "Open up!"

"Go away, Miller," Jonathan replied.

"You wanna leave this buildin' in one piece?"

"I intend to, no matter what," Jonathan said.

"Let me put it anover way, wot about sweet little Butterfly there?"

"First thing, it's Butter*cup*, you oaf," Jonathan said calmly. "You may be a dumb brute who's taken too many punches to the head, but you're not stupid enough to hurt a girl."

"Who said anyfing about hurtin'? After I KO you, I'll get to know her in the biblical sense… if you get me meanin'."

There was a look of panic in Olivia's eyes. The nuns had warned her about boys like Miller, who, when it came to girls, only had one thing on their minds. And they'd stop at nothing to get their way.

He's going to rape me, Olivia fretted.

"Miller, you know there's a lake on the school grounds."

"Yeah. So?"

"How about you take a running jump into it?"

Olivia looked at Jonathan. "What are you doing?" she whispered, wide-eyed. "Don't provoke a tiger."

"Open that door or I'm breakin' it down," Miller threatened. "You don't wanna see me really angry."

Jonathan nodded to himself when he heard this and turned to Olivia. "I need you to trust me," he said softly. "See that wooden chair over there, in front of the make-up mirror? Go and bring it to me." He turned to the door and called out, "Miller, you want me? Come and get me."

There was a loud thud as Miller put a shoulder to the door.

Olivia jumped a foot.

Jonathan signalled for her to hurry.

She brought the chair over.

There was a momentary pause as Miller backed up to gain momentum, then charged again.

Jonathan and Olivia, and surely Miller too, could hear the cracking of the wood frame. There was another pause. This time, Jonathan placed the chair on its side about five feet from the door.

Another crash.

By now, Jonathan had the timing right. He reached out, opened the deadbolt, then stepped to the side next to Olivia. This time, when Miller crashed into the door, it broke open as if it were made of balsa wood. Miller's momentum sent him hurling into the room until his shins contacted the chair. With a scream of rage, he tripped and rolled over and over, before he smacked into the far wall; then he lay there on the floor, dazed and moaning.

Jonathan grabbed Olivia's hand. He flicked off the light, led her out of the room, and pulled the door shut behind him, leaving Miller in the pitch-black room.

Jonathan and Olivia headed for the backstage lights and he turned them off. The area was now in total darkness. They then made for the side exit.

Standing inside, a few feet from the fire door, frozen in indecision, was a short figure in a duffel coat with a hood. Jonathan didn't perceive the figure as a threat and led Olivia past him. In the momentary flash of light from the open door, Olivia glanced at the boy's clothes, although she couldn't see his face.

They kept on running for the safety of Trafalgar. When they reached the House forecourt, Jonathan was breathing heavily, bent over slightly, hands on his knees. Olivia was barely winded.

"Miller's not following," he gasped. "You-you did so well – and you're not even out of breath."

"I told you I'm a runner."

Jonathan straightened up. "Well, I'd say that's the end of our tour, even though the afternoon is only half over. We'll leave the lake for another time." He looked at his watch. "There's a bus leaving for Enderby in forty minutes. You should probably be on it."

Olivia didn't argue.

Twenty minutes later, with no one else waiting at the stop, Olivia said, "You need to report this."

"There's no reporting anyone at Blackleigh," he replied. "Even if I told one of our prefects, no one would back me. Miller and others will stop at nothing until I'm gone. That's how they've dealt with my other friends."

"Then how can you fight back?"

"I dunno yet, but I'll figure out something," Jonathan said. "In the meantime, I'll have to be on my guard and hope I can outsmart and outlast them until I do."

"I think you should get out of here. Go to another school."

"If I do that – they win."

"Jonathan, you can't make this about winning or losing." Olivia threw up her hands. "That small boy at the door? The one wearing the coat and hood."

"Yes?"

"I recognised him. He was sitting behind you at Janet's Café. I'll bet he listened to everything we said. He probably followed you to Enderby."

Jonathan was starting to get it. "Maybe that's how Miller was aware you'd be coming here."

He knew what he had to say next. It was one of the hardest decisions of his life, but he needed to tell her. "Olivia, we shouldn't see each other for now. I can't put you in danger too. It's just for now, not forever, but you know I'm right."

Olivia threw herself onto Jonathan, knocking him backwards a couple of steps. She hugged him with all her might, then kissed him long and hard. Jonathan thought he'd gone to heaven.

The bus pulled up to the stop. Olivia said, "This was quite an afternoon! Of course, I'll wait till you feel it's safe. Please look after yourself until then."

With that, she stepped up into the bus, turned and waved. It all happened so quickly. Moments later, the green bus pulled away, leaving Jonathan to wonder if he'd ever see her again.

16

PINAFORE

A week before the Christmas holidays, Jonathan eagerly awaited the Plessey House production of *HMS Pinafore*.

Everyone in Trafalgar was talking about the coming operetta. Jonathan planned to sit in the audience next to David Gold. Anthony Summers, David's special friend, was in the cast as Little Buttercup.

Before he went to the performance, Gabriel was on hand to give Jonathan a hard time. Gabriel, friendly with Tunk, was a year older than Jonathan. He knew more about opera and took pleasure in belittling Jonathan's limited knowledge, topping him whenever he could.

"Do you know anything about the plot?" Gabriel pressed. "The operetta is about a naval ship and a mix-up over the captain's identity."

"There's a song in it called 'Little Buttercup'," Jonathan pointed out, remembering Olivia's dulcet voice.

"Oh, that's a minor part of the score," Gabriel countered. "Do you like the chorus the sailors sing? The one that begins, 'Let's raise our glasses one and all'…?"

Jonathan's blank response was all Gabriel needed. "Are you telling me, Simon, that you don't know the words or even the melody of that refrain? I can't believe it. I mean it's *the* main chorus of the whole fucking thing," Gabriel spat. "You don't know shit!"

Before the performance, Jonathan and Jim met up with David Gold in the crowded lobby. Gold was immaculately dressed as usual.

"You two may be interested to know that Anthony Summers *is* the show," David piped up, "but it's hard to recognise him in all that make-up, a long dress, and a hairpiece."

"Then how will we know when he's on stage?" Jim asked innocently.

"You can't miss Little Buttercup," David assured them, "not with Anthony playing the part. Let's go in. We can't be late for the overture."

Jonathan again thought of Olivia and how much she loved opera. He settled into his seat and pretended she was with him. *Maybe if I think about her, she'll know.*

The crowded hall was filled with boys, parents, and relatives of the performers. Some masters had brought along their wives and children. Two rows behind Jonathan, Alec Morton was present along with his attractive wife and their teenage daughter. Dr Frank's wife was similar in appearance to her bulky husband, but her hair was styled in a grey bun, whereas his bald pate reflected a sweaty, unhealthy shine. *The Walrus and the Carpenter* came to Jonathan's mind.

Jim, in his seat, was on his guard since the episode with Peter Wynn and Jonathan's run-in with Miller.

From the first notes of the overture, Jonathan was swept away. The curtains parted, and his heart pulsed at the sight of the set, depicting the ship's deck and prominent main sail. At once, the scene came alive with a chorus from the gallant crew singing about the Captain, who "Never got sick at sea… well, hardly ever". Sailors swabbed down the deck, climbed ropes, hauled up supplies, and checked the lifeboats.

David nudged Jonathan. "Wait for it, I saw the dress rehearsal, and *the* moment's come."

And there was Buttercup on stage, selling her wares! Anthony Summers had been transformed into an attractive female. Anthony, in the role of Little Buttercup, sang her famous ditty. Jonathan pretended that Olivia was singing for him.

The complications in the plot were resolved. At the finale, the entire cast came onstage basking in the applause. They reprised many of the most popular melodies and each repeated chorus was greeted with thunderous cheers.

Jonathan acknowledged that Gabriel was right about the importance of the main melody, when the curtains closed. They opened again to a crescendo of drums, and the cast burst into one final chorus:

"Let's raise our glasses one and all
For the worthy captain of the *Pinafore*."

The audience stood and applauded.

In the lobby, after the curtain, David, in a jaunty mood, explained his contribution to the amazing production. "You may not know this, but I've had a talent for the theatre. Our two-page programme is this evening's crowning touch. Guess who put it together?"

"I can't imagine," Jonathan broke in.

"You're looking at him." David grinned with satisfaction. "See, my initials are on the bottom of the front page. The cover is a drawing of the *Pinafore* and it's signed 'DG'. That's me!" David puffed himself up. "I wish they'd made my initials bigger, though."

Jonathan was used to David's bragging by now. He'd read somewhere that a certain actor was "a legend in his own mind". *That fits David exactly*, he thought.

"Jim, do you know when Trafalgar will put on their play?" Jonathan asked eagerly. "We have to be in it." After seeing *HMS Pinafore*, he was bitten by the acting bug.

"Next term, it's our turn," Jim told him. "But we'd have to audition for parts – in the first week of school."

"Then let's try to be in it," Jonathan said, already feeling anticipation. He imagined himself being in a leading role. He'd seen Laurence Olivier in the film *Henry V* and Robert Newton in *Treasure Island*. A new world was opening to him.

In the crowded lobby, Nick Krill, in his duffle coat, standing with his back to Jonathan, covertly took note of their conversation.

The evening was one of Jonathan's happiest so far at Blackleigh; at that time, he had no idea of what was to come.

17

SPRING PREFECTS

At the start of the new term, Sleeth summoned the branded group to his study. Along with Tunk and Croat, he congratulated the two newly appointed prefects, Rodge Miller and Norman Snell. Sleeth looked with pride at the small gathering, all now prefects. With the two new promotions, he had achieved his goal of a power base that would be a juggernaut.

It was unusually cold for spring. Sleeth's radiator was turned up to the max. Two of the participants wore coloured waistcoats, with the bottom buttons undone – the latest fashion at school.

Sleeth, sporting his recent razor-cut shaven head, addressed his seated companions.

"Last term, we succeeded in expelling Peter Wynn. That leaves Simon and Bhasin to be eliminated. The Headmaster asked me to provide him with a report on discipline at Trafalgar. You need to be aware of my approach to Dr

Macleod and his constant interfering. I try to downplay the negative and provide as little information as possible. The man can't seem to understand that discipline here is traditionally the realm of our prefects, not the faculty.

"Among his written questions, the Head asked me about the deaths of two juniors from our House. In response, I ascribed those tragedies to both individuals, Stephens and Gracey, having pre-existing mental conditions before they came to Blackleigh.

"I also reported on Arthur Crown's expulsion last year. The fat loser was depressed after the death of his best friend, Gracey. He deliberately stole paltry items from other boys' lockers to get himself thrown out. I also made passing mention in my report to Peter Wynn's recent exodus."

Sleeth went on, "I assured Dr Macleod that we have only minor discipline issues in this well-managed House. I denied the existence of serious bullying, racial prejudice, or unhealthy relationships between some boys.

"I confirmed that we at Trafalgar live like an extended family in a nurturing, close, brotherly atmosphere, where opinions and suggestions are freely expressed. I concluded by stating that the juniors take pride in our school traditions."

"I like wot you said," Miller said, making sure he was the first to praise Sleeth. The others murmured their approval.

Sleeth continued, "I want to commend Tunk for his role in the apprehension and subsequent expulsion of Wynn. Also, I'm glad to report that Miller and Snell are also working on ideas to eliminate Simon and Bhasin.

We'll now increase the pressure on these outsiders. Is there any other business?"

"If I may," Miller said, "I heard from a 'likle bird' that our boy Simon fancies hiself as a thespian. He and Bhasin have signed up to audition for roles in our school play, when we present *Macbeth* wiv Hastings.

"This as an opportunity," Miller went on. "I've an idea to make their actin' unforgettable. If all goes to plan, this could be the last we hear from them... in what I expect to their farewell performance. How d'yer like that?"

"Thank you, Rodge." Sleeth beamed. "And what's your plan?"

"I'm still workin' out details. I'll tell you when it's all set up."

Sleeth looked up at Snell. "Norman, you're the assistant director of this play. Who's our director?"

Sleeth recalled that Snell had achieved his directorial position on the strength of having an uncle who appeared in a TV soap-opera series, *Hello Neighbor.* But Snell's thespian uncle made it a point to avoid his weird young nephew.

"The play was chosen by our Housemaster," Snell explained. "He's bringing in his friend, Mr Moore, the literary and drama master, to direct. That man knows what he's doing. He directed *Coriolanus* for the school drama club last year."

"Right," Sleeth affirmed, glancing at Miller. "I know *Macbeth*... having studied the tragedy when I passed A level English."

Miller broke in, "When Simon and Bhasin turn up for auditions, I need 'em to be given small but noticeable parts. I've read bits of the play. How 'bout makin' them the second and third witches? That'll work well with me plan."

"Consider it done." Snell nodded, stroking his receding hair. "The Indian, with his dark complexion, will make a good witch. My famous uncle always says that the trick in casting is to match the part with the strength, appearance, and voice of the actor."

"Good for yer uncle. But I could 'ave told you that." Miller rolled his eyes.

"Let's invite Snell's uncle, the great dramatic actor, to our performance," Tunk suggested with a smirk. It was hard to tell whether Tunk was serious or deliberately mocking his study mate. With Tunk's warped sense of humor he derived pleasure in extolling the talents of Snell's uncle on a far greater scale than was merited by a minor player in a soap opera.

"I don't know whether he'd be available," Snell snapped, clearly irritated by Tunk's cajoling.

"Quieten down, people," Sleeth said, impatient with the diversion. "Snell, as our assistant director, you need to post a notice on the bulletin board stating that auditions are next Saturday. We'll make use of one of the classrooms, as I hear that the Performing Arts Building isn't available that day."

"Who's got the lead?" Sleeth continued. "Macbeth is a soldier and a general, so you need an actor with military experience," Sleeth added, dropping a heavy hint.

"There's no one but you, Hugh, who so ideally fits the role," Snell said, sucking up.

"I second that," Miller chipped in.

"Good choice." Sleeth grinned. "What about Lady Macbeth?"

"I see either Rodge Miller or Tunk in the part," Snell proposed.

"I ain't playin' no Lady Macbeth." Rodge stood in protest. "Besides, I'm too big and muscular. That's a fuckin' stupid suggestion, Snell!"

"Then Tunk as Lady Macbeth it is," Snell concluded, turning to his study mate. "I know you see yourself as an actor, Tunk, and how much you admire my uncle's success. In this role, you must be ruthless… so much so that you become mentally unstable towards the end. Lady Macbeth requires great acting skill."

"Thank you for your confidence. Yes, I'll be your Lady M, though all her plotting and murderous ambition is so far from my true and calm nature," Tunk said, tongue-in-cheek. "But then, that's why it's called acting."

Sleeth stood to indicate the meeting was over. "I remind you all of your solemn oath. I want Simon and Bhasin out of here post haste. Let's get it done."

★ ★ ★

The classroom normally used for English Literature classes was crowded for the *Macbeth* auditions. Each hopeful actor hopeful came with a paperback edition of the play. The proceedings had yet to start and Jonathan was fortunate to find two empty seats for Jim and himself. With dismay, he saw that Gabriel took the remaining empty seat next to him.

"What are *you* doing here?" Gabriel scoffed. "I don't see you as an actor – unless we're doing *The Merchant of Venice*."

"I came for the same reason you did… to audition," Jonathan replied.

"Do you know anything about acting?"

"No, but I want to challenge myself. I'm in Mr Moore's Literature class and we're reading plays by Bernard Shaw, Chekhov, and Ibsen. *Macbeth* is my first Shakespeare play."

"You must be joking!" Gabriel exclaimed, with a shocked expression. "This is one of Shakespeare's great tragedies… and you've never even read it."

"So, what's it about?" Jonathan asked. "Since you're such a fountain of knowledge."

"Yes, I suppose I am," Gabriel agreed, missing the sarcasm. "Three witches prophesy that Macbeth, a great soldier, will become King of Scotland. He and his wife plot and kill Duncan, the King, and Macbeth ascends to the throne. The witches prophesy that he can't be killed by a man of woman born, or until the forest, near his castle, begins to move."

"What happens then?" Jonathan asked. "Does the forest move? I hope Macbeth gets what's coming to him."

"Find out for yourself – read the fucking play."

"Thanks for sharing that," Jonathan said. "And what part do you want?"

"I'm not after the lead… too many lines to learn, and I've other key commitments, such as my involvement in the School Debating Society," Gabriel answered haughtily. "But I'd probably get any part I wanted. I'd settle for King Duncan, who gets killed off early on. Maybe I'll also try for Banquo, the general who's murdered, but comes back briefly as a ghost. From then on, he obviously doesn't have any more lines to learn."

Gabriel paused. "Look. Mr Moore's arrived with Snell. Shh… we're about to start."

John Moore, the popular English Literature teacher, was gratified to see so many in attendance. In his mid-fifties, the handsome, lean, grey-haired master was popular at the school, where he was known for his high energy and dedication to work. Jonathan liked his literature class, where the man's love of language and intensity made the works come alive.

Moore, married for twenty years, met his wife at university. Their oldest son, Seth, was a new junior in Trafalgar. Among his responsibilities, Moore supervised the school drama department and the annual unified school play production. He occasionally helped direct House plays, as was the case in this instance.

"Before we hold this audition," Moore began, "I'd like to warn those interested that this play requires a time commitment to learn your roles. You need to be punctual for our rehearsals. One of your prefects, Norman Snell, will help with casting. He's my assistant director.

"I told my good friend Alec Morton, who asked me to direct this project, that I'm often away at conferences, so I'd need to rely on one of his prefects for casting advice. Norman Snell was his suggestion. Thank you, Snell, for your participation.

"Alec Morton and Walter Anderson, the Housemasters of Trafalgar and Hastings Houses, have also given their full support. There will be occasions when some of you will need to miss prep and attend rehearsals. If any of you have doubts about your ability to commit, please leave now as my demands on your time will be extensive."

Three boys stood up and departed; the rest remained seated.

The auditions began with boys reading from their seats. One by one each stood in place and read aloud a three-minute speech he'd selected from the play. Their acting was primarily graded by Snell, who occasionally consulted with Mr Moore.

Jonathan was surprised to see Harry Bates at the audition. Unfortunately, Bates forgot to bring his copy of the play, as specifically instructed, and no one volunteered to lend him one. Jonathan was about to wave Bates over, when Mr Moore intervened. "Bates, if you didn't bring your own copy, you can leave now. Forget it next time, and you're out." Bates dropped his shoulders, slowly turned, and shuffled out the door.

When his turn came, Gabriel confidently stood before his audience and read one of Malcolm's speeches, the future King. When he sat down again, he nudged Jonathan and said, "See how I project my voice? I know what I'm doing."

Numerous members of Hastings also took their turns. Some performed better than others.

Krill, a tousled fair-haired junior, effectively read out a short speech early in the play by a wounded sergeant returning from battle. Others confidently chose Macbeth or Lady Macbeth's soliloquies, unaware that these choice parts were already taken.

Jonathan knew that Jim also hadn't read the play, but when his turn came, his friend improvised well with Lady Macbeth's first speech, which included a reading of a letter from Macbeth.

Finally, Jonathan spoke the part of Duncan, the King. When he'd finished, Mr Moore gave him three short claps.

Gabriel's brief audition of a small speech by Banquo was met by silence. He was seething, having been shown up. Gabriel snapped, "Mr Moore must be hard of hearing… He certainly didn't listen to me."

Jonathan didn't answer but reasoned to himself that knowledge of a play was quite different from the ability to act in it.

As he was leaving the classroom, Jonathan heard Harry Bates ask Mr Moore, "Who is cast in the role of Exeunt? His name appears in so many scenes."

"Bates," Mr Moore sighed, "only *you* would ask that question. The word means 'exit'. That's a stage instruction; no one plays that part."

The results of the auditions were posted on the House notice board by Snell two days later. Jonathan, thinking that he'd landed the role of Duncan, was surprised to see Jim and he cast as the second and third witches. The role of first witch was given to Nick Krill from Hastings.

Most of the smaller non-speaking roles, such as soldiers or castle attendants, were assigned to members of Hastings. To the chagrin of several Hastings boys, the choice roles were taken by Trafalgar prefects, who hadn't even appeared at the audition. Sleeth was Macbeth; Tunk, Lady Macbeth; Miller, the future King. Croat was given the role of an assassin, without having any speaking lines.

Gabriel was cast as the porter at the gates of Hell, which Jonathan thought suited him just fine. He was assured by 'Whitey' that this was the very part he'd sought. Seth Moore, John Moore's quiet son, had the role of the wounded sergeant, who expired from his battle wounds soon after the action commenced.

Jonathan approached Croat, the only prefect with whom he had any kind of cordiality, and asked, "What makes the prefects so well-suited to each of their roles in this violent play?"

"Life experience," Croat replied.

18

CALLUM

Callum Davies, an only child, and a junior in his second term, came from Cardiff. His father ran a long-established men's clothing shop in the city centre, called Davies and Son, even though his son wasn't old enough to work there. Callum's mother often helped in the shop.

Early Sunday, the Welsh boy woke in his Hastings dorm, worried to the point of feeling nauseated. Callum was going out with his loving parents that afternoon but didn't want to worry them about what lay heavy on his mind. Yet the nagging feeling that he had to confront another boy scared him. If he did nothing, then he'd be a coward in his own eyes.

He was a studious boy with curly, light brown hair and thick eyeglasses. Boys teased him on account of his ungainly, oval-shaped body. Callum's plump, non-athletic appearance in a short-sleeved top and shorts, earned him the unfortunate nickname of "Peanut".

Callum hadn't lived away from home before. He was shy, introverted and a loner. Life at an all-boys boarding school was completely foreign to him. It was a wonder that he'd managed to survive his first term, but now he'd hit a roadblock.

The other boy involved was an enigma. When Callum looked at Krill, he saw an innocent-appearing boy with fair hair, freckles, and light blue eyes. And yet something he couldn't describe about Krill gave him the shivers. *Yes*, he acknowledged, *Krill may look like a choir boy, but he doesn't have a conscience.*

Callum somehow managed to summon up the courage to face his nemesis. The other boys in his dorm were making their beds as Callum went over to Krill, and said, "I need to speak to you alone after everyone's left."

Krill shot him a look of surprise. "What about? I've things to do and can't hang around yapping."

"I'll tell you when the dorm's clear," Callum insisted.

Krill didn't respond. He resumed his cold, offhand manner and finished making his bed.

Callum was trembling with emotion when he returned to his own bed. But he felt for certain that Krill would be curious and wait.

En masse, the other boys left. Fox, bringing up the rear, called back, "Are you coming to breakfast, Davies?"

"Y-yes," he stammered, "in a minute. I have to do something first."

The double doors of the dorm closed and Callum was left alone with Krill. Callum knew to proceed with caution.

"Well… I haven't got all day," Krill said. "What is it?"

The Welsh junior wasn't sure how to start. He inched closer to Krill but not so near that he couldn't run, if he had to.

"Krill, did you hear about that Trafalgar junior… Peter Wynn, expelled for stealing Pearl's and my wallets?" Callum paused, but Krill gave no response. "Anyway, Tunk returned my wallet that he found in Wynn's canvas bag."

"So," Krill said casually. "Why tell me? I didn't know Wynn."

Callum began to blink repeatedly, which was a habit he succumbed to when nervous. "I want to clear something up. You and I talked briefly in the shop that day. After you left me, I went for my groceries, but when I came to pay, I couldn't find my wallet."

"What are you saying?" Krill threw him an annoyed look.

"I'm not trying to suggest anything," Callum said defensively, "but soon after we spoke, it seems a coincidence that my wallet turned up in Wynn's bag." Callum knew he was on perilous ground.

Krill's response, when it came, was blunt and to the point. "Does it occur to someone with the brain of an ant like yourself, that Wynn could have stolen your wallet even before we talked?"

Callum wanted to say he was certain the South African boy never came anywhere near him, that Wynn's back was to him the whole time, but words failed. He was sure his wallet went missing right after Krill said a few words to him.

Krill moved closer. "I don't like your implication. In this school, anyone who snitches is in trouble. But someone who goes further and spreads false charges is finished." Krill's eyes went cold. "Never in all my born days has anybody accused me of stealing. My hands are clean."

"I'm not accusing you," Callum backpedaled. "I'm just saying that Wynn wasn't the thief. I-I just want to clear the air."

"Then piss off down some Welsh coal mine." Krill made a move towards Callum.

Here he comes!

Callum turned and bolted from the dorm as if the angel of death was chasing him. He didn't stop until he'd hurtled down the stairs to the floor below. There, he gagged for breath and threw up in a sink off the lobby.

★ ★ ★

That evening, Callum returned after the time spent with his parents. He was exhausted and ready for bed. Callum was relieved to be the first in the dorm and that Krill was still downstairs in the Houseroom. But all day their earlier confrontation was never far from his mind. Callum hadn't dared speak to his parents or anyone else about what he believed had happened.

He went to the wooden chest in the middle of the dorm and opened his allocated drawer to take out a fresh pair of pyjamas. The drawer was empty! Missing also were his shirts, underwear, clothes, and socks. He looked in his section of the wardrobes. *No trousers, jackets or shoes!* Even his clothes hangers were gone.

Already, he knew what to expect when he headed to his bed. He was right. Gone were his sheets, blankets and pillows.

In what might otherwise have been a moment of panic, Callum had extraordinary clarity. He knew who was responsible. This was Krill's warning of even worse to come, if he pursued the matter further.

Callum was determined to act as if nothing happened. The matron would provide him with sheets, blankets, and pillows. He had also set aside enough money at school for emergencies. He planned to cut his morning classes and go into Enderby to buy new clothes tomorrow. Any clothes he couldn't get locally, he'd arrange to be sent to him from his father's shop.

19

WYNN'S FATHER

The Headmaster pushed a file across his desk to Mark Evans. "Here are copies of the reports from our eight heads of Houses on how they exercise discipline."

"Were they helpful?" the Head Boy asked.

"Not in the least. Most are self-serving puffery. They seek to justify a separation between teaching as being the domain of the faculty and the handing out of discipline as solely the function of prefects."

"Yes, sir, that's the tradition at Blackleigh. It goes all the way back to the time since the founding of the school," Mark offered.

"I know, but this tradition results in problems," the Headmaster said, clasping the palms of his hands together. "For example, I now have to deal with calls from a South African parent."

"Trevor Wynn?" Mark guessed correctly.

"Yes, Wynn's son Peter was just expelled from

Trafalgar. His father claims it was a travesty of justice. Trevor is a respected old boy, or as we at the school call them, an *old Blackovian*. He left Trafalgar House in 1925. Trevor promised a 50,000-pound donation to our school this year. Obviously under the circumstances, it's not going to happen." Dr Macleod paused to let the implication register with Mark.

"I've yet to receive all the details of Peter Wynn's case. It's ridiculous for me to tell this man that I need to refer him to a prefect in Trafalgar to get answers."

"How was the matter left with Wynn's father?"

"I promised to look into the situation and call him back."

"Sir, my understanding is that, based on his findings, the decision to expel his son was recommended by Hugh Sleeth, Trafalgar's Head Prefect – and subsequently approved by Mr Morton, the Housemaster."

"I don't doubt Alec Morton's good faith in following the traditional practice," the Head responded. "My problem is that our *traditional* approach is severely flawed. There are no checks and balances. How can one boy have the power to decide another's fate? This is not justice. We must reexamine the way we handled this and other such situations. Now is a good time to start."

"What can I do, sir?" Mark asked.

"Work with me to rectify this. We need to review exactly what occurred in Peter Wynn's situation."

"How should I proceed?"

"See Hugh Sleeth, on an impromptu basis. Don't alert him that this is an investigation. You'll need to obtain the notes of his meeting with Wynn. Tell Sleeth you're merely following up on the material he sent me. Learn what you can and report back."

★ ★ ★

Later that afternoon, Mark located Sleeth in his study. Hugh Sleeth was about to have tea and still in his officer's uniform after supervising a corps activity.

"To what do I owe the honour of a visit from the Head Boy?" Sleeth asked. He was on his guard. This was an unexpected visit from Evans, and he cautioned himself to say little and provide as little information as possible. "Sit down, Mark. I'll rustle up a cup of tea for you. Do you take sugar?"

"One lump," Mark replied, sitting in a nearby chair. "I came by to thank you for the report on House discipline that you sent the Headmaster."

"Oh yes." Sleeth nodded. "I sent it right away, when I learned of Dr Macleod's request."

"I've seen your report. It's illuminative of the thorough way you handle serious issues," Mark said to loosen Sleeth up.

"Thank you. Frankly, Mark, we're usually too lenient in punishing wrongdoers. But we're making changes."

"Such as?" Mark pressed. He sipped his tea.

"It's an evolving process. I'll update you in my next report. How can I help now?" Sleeth said.

"I'm here to ask you about a recent situation, involving Peter Wynn, a South African boy in your

House, expelled for stealing." Mark paused to let that sink in. "Dr Macleod would like to know how this came about."

"Does he want a further written report? Or is he asking to see me in person?"

"Written to start," Mark replied. "If he's not satisfied, he'll ask you to come in."

Sleeth was not happy with the way this meeting was going; he tried to buy time. "I've a lot on my plate right now with my duties as Head of Trafalgar – additionally as an Officer in the Corps. But I'll see what I can do."

"Time is important," Mark pressed. "Why don't you go over the incident with me, and I'll pass on what you say to Dr Macleod? He's anxious to know details."

Sleeth would have preferred time to finesse the report in his favour, but Mark outranked him, so he had no choice but to explain.

"Right. I wasn't directly involved, but Tunk, one of our prefects, caught Wynn red-handed at the school shop. He nicked two wallets."

"Are you saying Tunk witnessed Peter stealing the wallets?"

"No, we were conducting spot-checks because Don Fry had noticed that over the last three months various items had disappeared from his shop. Interestingly, since Wynn left, I've not heard of any new thefts."

Sleeth looked at his watch. "Mark, I've a lot to do. I did follow our standard procedure with Wynn. It was 'Textbook', as they say. What are you driving at?"

"Well, I hope that you went through the appropriate channels before Wynn's expulsion," Evans said. "His father maintains that his son is innocent, and he could cause us major problems. The matter now involves the Headmaster. Mr Wynn had promised a substantial endowment to the school, and now, under the circumstances, he's withholding it."

Sleeth frowned. "I interviewed Peter Wynn. He had no satisfactory answers to the charges brought against him, just blatant denial – as any guilty person would do. I know a thing or two about interrogation from my father, a general in the army. I tried to help Wynn despite his obnoxious manner."

"How?"

Sleeth sighed, "Wynn claimed that someone else put the two wallets in his carrier bag. I asked him whom he suspected. He mentioned Rodge Miller – who's now a prefect. Otherwise, he said he had no idea who'd done it.

"Wynn couldn't even come up with the name of anyone with a grudge against him." Sleeth paused and corrected himself. "That is except for Miller. But then Wynn admitted that Miller wasn't even in the shop that day."

Sleeth blustered on with irritation, "Why can't Wynn accept his punishment like a man?"

"Well, Sleeth, he's not a man. Wynn is just a boy. Moreover, he's saddled with serious charges that will follow him wherever he goes. His father is pressing for more details."

Mark added, "Surely you have a record of your meeting with Wynn? I also need a report from Tunk on

Wynn's arrest to ensure he did everything by the book. I'll speak with Tunk and with any witness present. With the Headmaster and Peter Wynn's father involved, I have to be sure that Tunk's discovery of the wallets in Peter's possession was legitimate."

"Of course, we prefects keep records of everything," Sleeth replied. "Tell me, Evans, before you came to Blackleigh, did you go to a local school?"

"I don't see how that's relevant," Evans answered and stood. "It's common knowledge that my family still live in a council flat, and I came here on a scholarship. Why do you ask?"

"Just out of interest. It occurs to me that as your parents never paid for your education, you don't have the same interest in preserving our traditions and values, as those of us educated at a public school."

"I assure you that perhaps I have even more interest in preserving worthwhile traditions, and in disregarding those that impede the search for truth. I hope we can rely on you to provide comprehensive information on Wynn."

"Of course."

"Then I'll expect to hear from you soon." Evans abruptly stood and left the study.

Sleeth made a mental note to talk with Tunk, and, if necessary, have him provide reports, and make any appropriate changes or subtle additions needed to bulk up the limited file on Peter Wynn. In frustration he wondered, *How the hell was I to know that Wynn's father had connections to the school?*

20

TOIL AND TROUBLE

On Saturday morning, the Trafalgar Houseroom was reserved by Snell for the first read-through by the selected cast of *Macbeth*. Jonathan, the third witch, sat at one of four tables, his name-tag next to that of Jim, the second witch. Opposite him was Krill from Hastings, the first of the three witches. Jonathan noted that this taciturn, angelic-looking boy made no effort to be friendly. Krill avoided eye contact with his fellow witches, who soon forgot he was there.

The cast waited for Mr Moore and Snell to arrive. Jonathan used the time to observe. One long table was allocated to the actors in lead roles, which included Sleeth, Tunk, Miller, and Croat. The latter had a part as a nameless assassin but regarded himself as having a pivotal role in the play. Ben Winkler was an innocuous King Duncan, a role with an early expiration.

A small table at the front was reserved for the director and his assistant director.

At another table, Gabriel was enlightening boys from Hastings on his acting career. He casually glanced at Jonathan while pontificating aloud that his role in the tragedy was far more significant than that of a mere witch.

The other roles of consequence all belonged to seniors from Trafalgar. The minor roles were filled by boys from Hastings. These included the motley crowd, castle guards, and various unruly bands of tartan-clad Scottish soldiers.

"I've homework to finish. What are you doing after the reading?" Jim whispered.

"I had a letter yesterday from Peter Wynn. He wrote that he left his old bike here after he was expelled, and he's given it to me. I rode it briefly yesterday. The front brake isn't working, so I hope to get it fixed in Enderby. While I'm there, I'll also buy a bell that fits on the handlebars and a lock and chain at the bicycle shop in the High Street. Maybe I'll have lunch after at Janet's Café," Jonathan said. "Want to join me?"

"I wish I could, but French homework beckons. Be careful riding Peter's rusty, old clunker." Jim shook his head. "Peter's family is wealthy. Why didn't his dad buy him a new bike?"

"That's because Peter liked to be low-key. He didn't want to stand out in any way. He told me that his parents offered to buy him a new bike, but he refused. Anyway, in his letter, he warned me to be extra careful riding it, and to also watch out for anyone gunning for you and me."

Mr Moore and Snell came in. After a short burst of applause, the two sat at the small table reserved for them. Mr Moore rose to speak.

"I'm glad to see you all. Let me be clear, at our next meeting, we'll select backups for the main roles." He looked around the room and roared, "Where's Bates, my Banquo? Where the hell is that boy? Why is he *always* late?"

The Houseroom door burst open and a flustered Harry Bates, his black hair in disarray and wearing wire rim glasses, came in carrying his copy of the play. He managed to find an empty seat.

"There you are! You're meant to be a general, Bates, in line for the throne," boomed Mr Moore. "For God's sake, move *yuself.* I don't give a damn why you're late. Just be here on time."

Jim nudged Jonathan. "Bates didn't even read for a part. What's he doing here?"

Jonathan replied, "I heard Mr Morton insisted Bates be in the play, after Bates' parents made the request."

The cast began reading their assigned roles. After Jim read his opening line, "In lightning, thunder, or in rain," Mr Moore interrupted. "Bhasin, can you sound more like a Scottish witch on a rugged heath rather than an inhabitant of the Punjab?"

"I'll do my best, sir," Jim said. "In lightning, thunderrr, orr in rrrain?"

"See, you can do it!" Mr Moore nodded as he strutted up and down in a Napoleonic mood and exhorted his troops.

Jonathan read his lines without receiving comment. The reading continued until the end of the Second Act, when the actors were allowed a twenty-minute break.

After the interlude, Krill returned to his assigned place at the last moment and the reading resumed.

Jonathan had to admit to himself that both Sleeth and Tunk were ideal for their roles. Miller, the future king, had few words but was required to engage in a bloody fight to the death with Macbeth, involving detailed choreography. Jonathan wondered if Miller would deign to wear a kilt for the two performances.

With the rehearsal over, Jonathan left the House and strolled over to the bike sheds. The bicycles for Trafalgar boys were stored in a cellar-like basement, some ten feet below ground. Jonathan, exhilarated by the rehearsal, looked forward to an almost hour-long ride into Enderby and having lunch.

He reached the access to the basement and pulled back the wooden entry flaps on the ground, revealing wooden downward steps. Jonathan turned on a light switch and the interior steps were dimly lit by a naked hanging bulb. He walked carefully down the stairs to the grim-looking basement filled with bikes, each labelled with the owner's surname. They were stacked in separate racks, in alphabetical order. On first impression, the place looked like a grimy graveyard for dead and decaying bicycles.

The day before, when Jonathan rode Peter's old bike for the first time, was when he discovered that the front brakes were shot. Though there were three gears, it was also perpetually stuck in third. So he had to pump the pedals hard until he got some momentum going.

Jonathan had returned the rusty bike standing upright against a wall in a rack and marked with the letter "S". He'd tied a new label with his name to the handlebars and removed the old Wynn label.

Jonathan was determined to take his first long ride and build up his stamina for the upcoming corps camp. Ever since the corps competition, from which he'd been excluded, Jonathan was back in the squad, but Sleeth was riding him hard. Trafalgar had won the competition, and it irked Jonathan that he wasn't part of the victory.

Jonathan carried the bike up the stairs into daylight. He closed the wooden flaps, covering the entry, and wheeled the cycle over to the main road, which led to Enderby. For the first part of the ride the road was level, but then rose steeply uphill. For the last quarter mile, it headed downhill to a busy main road with a T-crossing at the bottom, where, upon turning left, the road snaked into the cobbled centre of the small town.

As he rode, Jonathan enjoyed the feeling of the wind in his face. The wheels whizzed around, and the bike picked up speed. Jonathan knew he could slow down by squeezing the one working rear brake slowly, although it made a terrible squeaking noise that irritated him.

Later, Jonathan had to pedal harder to reach the top of the hill. There, he stopped to catch his breath before starting the final downhill grade.

Off he went again. He was surprised how the bike rapidly picked up speed – much faster than he thought it would go. He squeezed the rear brake slowly, but except for the loud screech, it had no effect. Jonathan then squeezed good and hard. There was a distinct snap and the brake lever went limp. The bike sped faster and faster towards the blind intersection ahead.

Buildings on both sides blocked the view of cross traffic until it reached the middle of the intersection. In horror, he realised he was flying out of control, just as a blue Jaguar came into view, zipping across right in front of him. By mere inches he missed colliding with the car that sped on and hooted several times to shame Jonathan for his carelessness.

Oh God, he thought, *help me*!

Jonathan hurtled across the intersection. He hit the curb, on the other side, head-on and went flying over the handlebars.

This time, fortune was on his side. He had a soft landing, flat on his back, on wet moss. After, Jonathan stretched his arms and legs to make sure he had no broken bones. Satisfied he was fine, though he didn't doubt that there'd be bruises, he got up and returned to his bike.

The front wheel was bent so badly it was no longer round; rather almost U-shaped. He examined the back-brake cable wire even though he knew it had rusted through, which was why it had snapped. Jonathan almost turned away… until something that wasn't right caught his attention.

Yes, the cable was rusty, but at the point of the break it was shiny. On closer inspection, Jonathan could see that someone had used a file to saw halfway through the wire. And that someone had counted on Jonathan having to squeeze hard on the final downhill grade, which would be enough pressure to finish the job.

An elderly woman, walking her dog, stopped to ask if he was alright.

"Yes, thank God," Jonathan said, shaking out his sore hands.

"Then you should ride more carefully." She sniffed and walked on.

He was too muddy and roughed up to go into Janet's. Instead, he carried the bike over to the bus stop and left it beside the bike rack for someone else to take and fix it up, if they wanted to. He bade the bike a sad farewell, and thanked heaven for his safe deliverance.

A half hour later, he was on a bus leaving Enderby. Jonathan, the only passenger, sat numbed by his experience. *Some boy deliberately tampered with my bike. I could have been killed. Was that his intention?*

He ran through the names of possible saboteurs. The most likely suspects – Sleeth, Tunk, and Miller – were all prefects who wanted him gone from Blackleigh. But he couldn't imagine any of them stooping to such a diabolical act. *Or would they?*

His mind drifted to Gabriel. But despite Gabriel's persistent hostility, Jonathan regarded him as the all talk and no action type, and he didn't think he was that cold-blooded.

No matter who did it, this incident was proof that the stakes had risen. Someone would stop at nothing to eliminate him. First, there was a likely plot to expel Peter Wynn, and now Jonathan felt his life was on the line. And even if there was a conspiracy, Jonathan became even more determined to fight back and not let his enemies win. He had to make a stand, not only for himself, but for his friends who were gone, and for all those who would come after him. It was time for drastic action.

21

AN ALLY

After Monday morning classes, Jonathan walked over to Waterloo. He passed by the Administration Building, that housed the Headmaster's office, the dining halls, and the Assembly, and headed on to Waterloo House. An alternative route was for him to walk through a winding basement tunnel, accessed from a staircase at the rear of the Assembly.

In the Waterloo lobby, Jonathan asked a junior to help him find the Head Boy's study. The boy led him to Evans' door.

Jonathan knocked, and upon hearing Evans say, "Come in," Jonathan opened the door and entered the small room.

Evans, casually dressed in a T-shirt, shorts, and running shoes, was talking to Ridley, one of his prefects. They were about to leave for lunch.

"I'm Jonathan Simon, in my second year, from Trafalgar," he said hesitantly to Evans. "I need to see you, sir… it's a private matter."

Evans turned to Ridley. "Jack, I'll meet you later in the dining room."

Jonathan was relieved that Evans was willing to make time for him now, despite having other plans.

He glanced around the study, and saw a desk, two chairs, and an armchair. Above the desk Jonathan recognised a framed print of *The Hay Wain*, a landscape by Constable. Jonathan complimented himself that he knew the work. Only the previous week, his art class had studied some of the works by this great artist.

Against another wall was a large bookcase crammed with books on subjects such as the British Constitution and Economics. Jonathan also noticed a few silver cups and some framed black and white photographs of the school hockey and cricket teams. Evans was smiling in the centre of the first row of each team.

On the mantelpiece, a rugger ball signed by each player in the first fifteen team, occupied pride of place. There was also a framed photograph of Evans' parents and another that looked like a pretty younger sister.

"Take a chair, Simon," Evans said casually. "I'd offer you tea, but I have to get going soon."

"Yes, sir." Jonathan sat in his chair uncomfortably.

"You don't have to call me 'sir'," he said. "Evans is fine. Now, what's this about then?"

Jonathan took a deep breath and began, "It's like this, Evans. After much thought, I decided to come and see you because I'm being targeted."

"Go on," Evans encouraged him.

"There's a code of conduct here that no one snitches on

another, but things have gone too far for me to keep silent."

This was the break Evans had been hoping for. A young boy finally speaking up. Evans took a seat and listened to him carefully.

Jonathan went on, "At a boys' school, you expect juniors to be bullied, but I never expected what happens here. For some of us, surviving each term has become almost a matter of life and death."

"That's quite a statement," Evans spoke up, leaning forward. "Explain."

"Less than a year before I came to Blackleigh, Stephens, a junior in Trafalgar, committed suicide by jumping off the top of the bell tower in the old cemetery. My guess is that he was driven to it by bullies.

"Since I've been here, I've lost three close friends. Arthur Crown deliberately stole items from boys' lockers to get himself expelled. He was another boy abused from his first day here.

"Even worse, my best friend, Ian Gracey, was killed when he fell from the bell tower."

Evans broke in, "I've heard about Stevens, Crown, and Gracey."

"Well, the list goes on," Jonathan said. "A few weeks ago, my friend, Peter Wynn, was promptly expelled after he was accused of stealing two wallets. I know Peter very well. He'd never steal. Peter comes from a wealthy family – his father was also at school here. Peter had a good weekly allowance and was never short of money. Why would he need to steal a few measly pounds from two boys? I believe that somehow he was framed."

"I'm also aware of Wynn's situation, but not all the details," Evans said. "Tell me about you?"

"It's not just me. Jim Bhasin, whose family came to London from Calcutta, is also being threatened. I was dealing with it until two days ago, when someone tampered with a brake cable on my bike and I was almost killed."

Evans was aghast. "Why would anyone do such a thing?"

"It all started last year at the annual school charity fair. Jim and I reported a senior to the police. He was outright cheating at a coin-toss booth. The two innocent owners of the booth were wrongly arrested.

"We couldn't stay silent at the injustice. Tradition is one thing, but why be loyal to liars and cheaters? After that incident, we were ostracised for being snitches by most of the school."

"I didn't know about this," Evans said.

"That's not all. Last term, I invited a girl to visit me. I was showing her the new Performing Arts Building when another senior cornered us in a dressing room. He threatened to harm us, and without going into details, I'll just say we were lucky to escape.

"There's so much more I could say. I haven't mentioned the sadistic dorm initiations and other forms of excessive discipline in the corps. Frankly, I don't know how much longer Jim and I can hold out. The odds are stacked against us."

"I saw Hugh Sleeth the other day," Evans said. "He presented an entirely different picture of senior-junior relations in your House."

Jonathan replied cryptically, "I'm not surprised," then shook his head. After a moment, he said, "Look, I want what's best for the school, and I hope to stay. Nobody likes a snitch, but for the sake of many besides myself, I'm speaking up." Jonathan frowned. "But if anyone learns I came to see you, I'll be finished."

"If what you say is true, you're brave to come and see me. I've noticed you've been careful not to name names of the offenders," Evans noted with empathy, "but that's alright. It's enough that you tell me these terrible things are occurring.

"You said that someone tampered with your bicycle. That's a mile beyond bullying. I need you to tell me who did it."

Jonathan admitted that in the case of the bike, he honestly didn't know who the culprit was. And all the suspects he could think of seemed unlikely. Then he decided to withhold his theory that there might be a conspiracy, since he had no proof, and it was all a guessing game at this point.

Evans deliberated for a moment. Then he said, "I'm thinking of asking you to do something for me, but…"

"But what? Please tell me."

"Here's the thing: it will put you in even more danger. And I wouldn't ask this of you, but you do have direct access at Trafalgar, which I don't. So, would you be willing to be my, uh, eyes and ears?"

"You mean your spy."

"Well, if you put it that way… yes," Evans said.

They looked at one another; Jonathan nodded.

Evans went on, "Be very careful! But do what you can to dig up real proof of one or more of the seniors behind this. And then I can present this to the Headmaster. I assure you he will act and put a stop to this – permanently. Let me share a confidence with you."

"Of course," Jonathan agreed.

"You may be going through hell, but you're doing a great service. I'm already carrying out an investigation for the Headmaster regarding extreme discipline and bullying. We'll get to the bottom of this. I don't doubt you, but I need proof."

"Then I'm glad I came to see you. I swore an oath to Gracey and Crown that I'd never give up. I can't let them down."

22

SNELL'S SCORPION

Mr John Moore, who was directing *Macbeth*, also taught Jonathan's English Literature class. The master was passionate about passing on to his students his love of plays, classic novels, and poetry. He had a cherubic appearance and was clean shaven with a receding hairline. Moore was accessible to the boys and encouraged their efforts, yet would go ballistic if anyone showed a lack of commitment.

Filled with confidence after his meeting with the Head Boy, Jonathan went to see Mr Moore in his office. He intended to raise an issue arising in the text of the play. He knocked at the half open door and waited for the master to say, "Come in."

As he entered the master's office, Jonathan avoided a tall bookcase, stacked from floor to ceiling with books and magazines, neatly arrayed in rows. The cabinet occupied a precarious position, dividing the room into two halves.

The master sat at his desk, a window behind him, and an empty chair to the side for a student. Behind this extra chair was one side of the floor-to-ceiling shelving, on an uneven floor. The edifice precariously wobbled at the slightest touch and Jonathan dreaded that he might accidentally lean back in the chair, while talking to Mr Moore and nudge the shelves.

It looked like as if a slight jostle would cause an avalanche of years of accumulated fiction, literary criticism, plays, and poetry. Jonathan sat down carefully. The unsteady bookcase reminded him of his cautious relationship with the master. He wanted to remain on good terms, and not do anything to cause a rift.

"What can I do for you, Simon?" Mr Moore greeted him.

"Sir, I came to see you about one of my lines," Jonathan explained. "Late in the play, the witches throw the ingredients of their spell into a cauldron as they chant. Could 'liver of blaspheming Jew' be excluded? Being Jewish myself, I'm sensitive about this."

"I see your issue, but there's a problem," Moore replied. "If we cut 'liver of *Jew*' out, the next rhyming line, 'Tongue of goat and strips of *ewe*,' is impacted. Then who knows what else we'd have to exclude? We could omit so much verse that there'd be nothing left of the witch's spell, and no ingredients bubbling in the pot."

Jonathan saw the logic of Mr Moore's position. One card omitted in a pyramid of playing cards could result in the entire edifice collapsing, like the shelves in the master's study.

"Think about this," Mr Moore added. "You make a believable third witch, leave it at that. I don't want to cut your few lines more than necessary. As far as I'm concerned, your rehearsals are going well. Remember, the three witches cast their spells and prophesy Macbeth's future, but they are not responsible for his evil. The choices he makes to realise his ambition and pursue personal power are his own, step by step, murder by murder."

"Thank you, sir, I'll remember that. I should leave now to catch the bus into Enderby. The bike shop sells secondhand bikes, and I want to see if there's one that I can afford."

Mr Moore gave it but a moment's thought and said, "Well, if you can wait until three o'clock, I'm going go on to Enderby myself for a dental appointment. I could give you a ride there, but you'll have to come back on your own. I'll be leaving in a blue Ford from the car park on the other side of the Administration Building."

"That would be great, sir. Thanks so much. If I buy a bike, I'll ride it back; otherwise I'll take the bus."

As Jonathan stood up, his chair nudged the bookcase and it began to rock. He reached out with both hands to steady the wobbly structure. Jonathan heaved a sigh of relief when it came to rest. He wanted nothing to impact his positive relationship with Mr Moore.

★ ★ ★

Snell was sitting at his desk, pinning a butterfly to a board, when he heard a double knock at his study door. Sleeth walked in without waiting for an invite and settled his formidable frame in an extra chair by Snell's desk.

Snell ignored him, assuming it was his study mate, Tunk, whom Sleeth wanted to see.

"I've come to see *you*, Moth," Sleeth said to get Snell's attention. "Since we swore our oath, I'm getting results from Miller and Tunk, but a fucking zero from you. What's happening?" Sleeth leaned forward aggressively, awaiting an answer.

Snell looked up from his project. "I've been thinking about that, and I've a plan. But it's a matter of timing."

"Be more specific," Sleeth demanded.

"My plan involves Simon, Mr Moore, and his son Seth – a junior in our House. It'll take patience and finesse. When I'm done, I expect Simon to be so embarrassed, he'll be happy to leave."

"I'm intrigued, tell me more."

"I relate my plan to trapping specimens in my killing jar," Snell explained. "Even though they may fly hither and thither in panic, they don't survive. The same will be true of this boy."

"I don't follow," Sleeth said, frustrated. "We can't put Simon in a jar! Enough of this bug talk!"

"Trust me," Snell replied. "But my scheme is not one for a Head of House to know about before the fact. That way you won't have to *act* surprised. You'll be removed from any blame."

Sleeth considered Snell's evasive answer. *"Moth" is a strange and devious creature. I lose nothing by leaving him to his own creepy devices.*

"Moth, I've already made you a prefect. Is there anything else you want by way of a reward, to boost your determination to succeed? By 'succeed', I mean force Simon to actually leave the school… nothing less than that."

Snell didn't have to give it a moment's thought. His tongue unpleasantly swiped along his bristly lower lip, and he said, "As it happens, there is something. For as long as I can remember, I've always wanted to procure a scorpion for a live insect collection."

He indicated a fish tank on a shelf behind him, swarming with all kinds of creepy crawlers. "Now that I have a home for one, a small monetary contribution towards his goal would be beneficial. I can buy an Emperor Scorpion for about ten pounds."

"Right then, if that's what you want, I'll take the risk and contribute five pounds towards the cost. I'll also help you get one. Packages for all the departments are delivered to the armoury. You'll have to forge a requisition from the biology master. I'll intercept the package when it arrives and deliver it to you. How about that?"

"For me, an arachnid would be a great addition."

"When will I learn if your plan worked?"

"You'll know when Simon announces that he's leaving," Snell said with a crooked smile.

Sleeth took out his wallet and dropped five pounds on Snell's desk.

"You deliver Simon – I'll deliver the scorpion," Sleeth said, and promptly left the study.

★ ★ ★

Snell, as cold-hearted as he was eerie, had not exaggerated when he assured Sleeth of a plan to bring down Simon. As assistant director, he had noticed the boy's eagerness in rehearsals to impress Mr Moore, and acknowledged Simon was becoming more confident as the days went by. This had prompted Snell to act to effect Simon's undoing.

A confluence of events and timing had fused for his plan to work, even before Sleeth saw Snell. It had come in the unexpected form of Tim Bell, the junior responsible for cleaning his and Tunk's study. Tim, an avid photographer, almost always carried a Brownie camera strapped around his neck, and frequently snapped pictures of boys going about their activities in and around the House. They called Tom Bell "Snap" for short, and no longer paid him any attention. His uncle owned a chain of camera shops, one of which was in Enderby High Street, where Tom had his voluminous rolls of film developed.

Tom had often heard Tunk and Snell, in their study, discuss their animosity towards Jonathan Simon. To gain favour, Tom had approached the two of them with a photograph he'd recently taken, which he knew would be of interest.

"Bell, my boy, what have you there?" Tunk asked. Bell had placed a photo on the counter, where the two prefects were standing.

"It's a picture I took a few days ago."

"I trust you're not wasting our time," Tunk said. The two prefects studied the photo and Tunk broke into a smile. "Hmm… What's this? Well, I do believe it's Mr Moore getting into his car with… yes… Simon on the passenger side. Hey, what a lovely couple! A master and a boy together in a car. Snap, thank you. Contrary to my first impressions, I see a promising future for you."

Bell was dismissed, and Snell immediately hatched his plan. He shared it with Tunk, after having sworn him to secrecy.

Tunk had noticed during play rehearsals at Hastings that Simon and Seth Moore had become friends. After rehearsals, they often walked to Trafalgar together. Tunk frequently went with Gabriel.

On this day, Tunk timed it so that he and Gabriel left just ahead of Simon and Seth Moore on their way back to the House. Halfway there, at what he thought was the right moment, Tunk took out a photo and showed it to Gabriel. He, in turn, grabbed it. "Holy shit, Simon," Gabriel exclaimed. He turned around and shouted to Simon, "This is a picture of you!"

Jonathan and Seth caught up with Gabriel. Jonathan grabbed it, and he and Seth looked at it together.

Gabriel, delighted with the evolving situation, let loose. "Don't you see yourself, Simon? To me, this looks like the secret is out. Simon is Mr Moore's little crush boy. Don't you just love a romantic picture?"

Gabriel snatched the photo out of Jonathan's hand and waved it in Seth's face. "Did you know, Seth, that

Simon is one of your father's little favourites? When are you two getting together again, Simon?"

Hobbs, a silent assassin in the play, and in Jonathan's English class, joined in, "I'll bet Moore's got the hots for you. That's the only reason you do well in our English Lit class. Are we talking romance in the classroom?"

"Now we know!" Gabriel quipped. "Simon is Mr Moore's adorable little crush boy. When are you two getting together again? Do you know about Simon and your father Seth? Take a good look."

Jonathan blushed with embarrassment. He was stunned and speechless.

But the damage was done. Jonathan saw Seth Moore turn around with a glazed, shattered look on his face. "How could you?" Seth exclaimed. "I thought you were my friend. Were you using me to get close to my father?"

Jonathan felt a shudder run through his body, as if he were plummeting down an endless, tight spiral, round and round, and out of control. He tried to defend himself. "Seth, no, it's not how it looks."

But it was too late. Seth stomped off, and said over his shoulder, "Don't ever talk to me again, Simon."

Jonathan reached the House and found Jim outside at the back.

"My God," Jonathan exclaimed, when he was sure they were alone. "I'll bet Seth tells his father."

"If you ask me," Jim replied, "you've done nothing. It's what they keep trying to do to you that counts. This is just another frame-up. You told me at the time how you got a lift into Enderby. They destroyed Peter Wynn and you're next. But they won't get anywhere."

"Don't be so sure, Jim. How will Mr Moore react to me in his poetry class three days from now?" Jonathan said. "Will Seth tell his dad about the photo? Maybe Mr Moore won't want me in the play.

"Mr Moore could be in a world of trouble too, if word somehow reaches the Headmaster. And what about Tunk? Will he show the photo to other boys? Then there's Gabriel with his big mouth. Maybe he'll go around telling everyone that Mr Moore and I are in a relationship.

"Look, we both know that the masters are not supposed to give boys rides in their cars," Jonathan added. "It's an unwritten law that happened four or five years ago when a maths teacher and a boy from Hastings were caught by a group of boys on a House run, parked on a country road and making out in a car. I, and apparently Mr Moore as well, didn't think of this."

For the first time, Jonathan asked, "Maybe it's best if I do leave the school?"

"But that's exactly what they want," Jim replied. "They got Peter, and you're next."

"Well, one thing's for sure, Tunk is behind this. And if that's the case, somehow, I'll have to see this through. I can't let him win."

"If there's a way I can help, just let me know," Jim said.

Later that day, Jonathan had a note pinned to his study door, to see Tunk immediately in his study.

Fearing the worst, but determined to weather the storm, Jonathan knocked at the study door. Upon hearing Tunk say, "Come," from inside, he entered the creepy domain.

"Ah, Simon, good of you to come," Tunk said, seated in an armchair, with a smile on his face. "Don't bother to sit, I'll make this quick. As a lover of the theatrical arts, you know that I have the lead part of Lady Macbeth in our production. For this reason, I am loathe to deal with your scandalous situation, until our two night's performances are concluded. I know that it's too late to replace you. So, for the sake of my love for this tragedy, you can wait for a resolution until the play is over.

"Then you will announce to all that you are leaving the school. Otherwise, I will have to post the picture on the notice board for all to see. I'm sure you receive my meaning. That will be all."

Jonathan left Tunk's office in dismay and went straight to see Evans. After Jonathan had explained the situation, the Head Boy told him that he would be in the play and assured him that he'd take care of the photo.

"I'll see Tim Bell, or Snap as he's called," Evans told Jonathan. "I will simply tell him that if he wants to take another photo at Blackleigh, he'll have to do as I say."

"Which is to do what?" Jonathan asked.

"Trust me," is all that Evans would answer.

23

MACBETH

A thrill of expectation pervaded the atmosphere on the first of the two evening performances of the Trafalgar-Hastings play. The production was staged in the new Performing Arts Building before a packed audience, which included the Headmaster, the Housemasters of Trafalgar and Hastings, members of the faculty, parents of the cast, and boys.

The opening scene resembled a ragged heath, suitably bleak, somewhere in Scotland. The lighting, in varying shades of green, was resolved.

Backstage, the ensemble maintained a hierarchy. Mr Moore strutted around issuing orders to everyone but avoided eye contact with Jonathan. He, in turn, along with Jim, spoke briefly with Krill. Those in the lead roles, Sleeth, Tunk, and Miller, maintained their regal distances from lesser thespians with minor roles in the cast.

As Jonathan waited, he was enthralled to see that since the dress rehearsal the stage manager had installed a projector behind a plaster-painted grassy mound. The beam cast an image of slow-moving dark clouds against a gloomy background.

Consistent with the Scottish theme, the play also featured ragged soldiers, mud-smeared with bloody faces, who would let loose with muffled oaths and battle cries. Most had false beards, scars, and were attired in tartan kilts, berets, and knee-high coloured socks. Some even wore leather sporrans with tassels. They all brandished swords and daggers. In addition, two castle guards were assigned to climb up and down the steps of Macbeth's castle and occasionally blow pre-recorded bagpipes.

In the interior scenes, Scottish flags and banners were arranged to drape the castle walls. The elaborate banquet scene, which occurred later in the play, was planned to commence with sword dancing. The banquet to follow was to be interrupted by the silent entrance of Bates, as Banquo's ghost. Mr Moore hoped he'd materialise on time, having removed his eyeglasses.

Jonathan sat still in a dressing room as streaks of hideous green and black makeup were applied to his face. He also wore a dishevelled wig of shoulder-length grey hair, a long black cloak, and a cone-shaped black hat. He glanced at himself in the mirror and was taken aback to see the face of a demented, toothless apparition. He turned to Gabriel, in the next chair, being made up as the porter at Macbeth's castle. "What do you think?" Jonathan asked.

"God, you look scary!" Gabriel said. "Did they give you that red bruise on your cheek and long nose on purpose?"

"No... no, they didn't," Jonathan replied. He reflected that Gabriel was becoming even meaner and more spiteful.

Snell summoned the three witches to their designated places near centre stage. When all three were huddled together, Jonathan was taken aback to see Krill, young and handsome, transformed into something haggard and wizened.

The performance was about to begin. Jonathan, Jim, and Krill, the three witches, crouched around a black cauldron, which regularly belched out puffs of smoke.

Across the stage, dim patches of green light revealed a series of hillocks on the bleak Scottish moor. Dark clouds scudded briskly across the backcloth. The presence of foul weather was enhanced by occasional flashes of lightning effected by stagehands, and ominous rumbles of thunder, achieved by Harry Crown, an able musician, crashing cymbals and pounding a kettle drum.

Jonathan carefully avoided standing on a large plastic tube, feeding into the bottom of the huge pot, the source of smoke rising from the witch's cauldron. Beyond the closed curtain, he heard the packed house settling in their seats with occasional coughing. A hush descended on the large hall. All was ready. With the sound of drums, the curtain opened on the barren heath.

The three witches appeared, huddled together out of a storm. Krill, the first witch, crouching down, spoke first, "When shall we three meet again."

Jonathan experienced a palpable sense of excitement as the action surged forward. Jim uttered his opening lines, and Jonathan quickly followed, "That will be ere the set of sun..." followed by a bloodcurdling screech.

How Jonathan wished his part was ten times larger! He eagerly awaited his next moment of glory, limited to the single word, "Anon!" The third witch's part had few superfluous words.

At the end of the short first scene, Jonathan knew there'd be a fiery explosion followed by a belching cloud of smoke. These special effects enabled the three witches to dramatically vanish offstage in a smoky mist. Jonathan was unaware of how big of an explosion to expect. The bang was included in the dress rehearsal, but the witches were warned that it would be louder on the nights of the two performances. The blast would come after they recited together the final two lines of the first scene.

The words "filthy air" were the stage manager's cue to set off the explosion. In rehearsal the small explosion, followed by a big puff of smoke, was the witches cue to back away from the cauldron and exit the stage.

Tonight, Krill moved back a couple of seconds ahead of the explosion. Jim simply followed Krill's lead and moved back too. Jonathan just happened to see the movement out of the corner of his eye and instinctively jumped back.

"Fair is foul and foul is fair:
Hover through the fog and..."

The witches concluded the line with "filthy air". The expected bang detonated more like a thunderclap… BOOOOM! The crescendo was so loud that Jonathan's ears were numb with shock.

Jonathan stumbled back, covered in black dust. Krill was already well out of harm's way, while Jim had disappeared in a film of thick, inky smoke, now swirling over half the stage. This thunderous, filthy blast had defied all expectation. Had any of the three been nearer to the cauldron at the time, who knows what injuries would be sustained.

As it was, the Scottish moor was transformed into a scene of devastation. Jonathan saw the other two witches had managed to disappear by exiting at the side curtain, and before anyone realised anything was seriously amiss, he followed.

The audience too had been jolted by the explosion.

As the smoke cleared and the audience settled, Macbeth and Banquo made their entrance with the ironic and appropriate words, "So fair and foul a day I have not seen."

Later in the play, Jonathan sat on a chair, behind the side curtains. He thanked God for the miracle of yet another near miss. Someone gave Jonathan a harsh shove in the back. Jonathan turned around. Sleeth, as the new King, stood behind him, in his purple attire, a gold crown on his head, and the gold chain of his office around his thick neck.

Sleeth scornfully shook his head as if Jonathan's participation in the play was as worthless as the actor playing the part. "You almost wrecked the play in the first scene by your clumsy exit."

"It's *my* play too," Jonathan protested. "I had nothing to do with that explosion."

"You can't do anything right!" Sleeth snapped.

Jonathan remembered Mr Morton's words, and added, "As a witch, I can prophesy *your* future, although I can't change it. 'All hail Macbeth'… Thou who won't be king for long." Jonathan wondered how he got up the nerve to say that.

He watched as Sleeth's face grew rigid with fury. But time was on Jonathan's side; the moment had come for Macbeth's stage entrance at his banquet.

"I won't forget that," Sleeth hissed and was gone.

After Macbeth's entrance, the sword dancers performed before the banquet, and all waited for the subsequent entry of Harry Bates as the ghost of the murdered Banquo. As Jonathan listened to the action, he heard a heated exchange offstage between Mr Moore and the unfortunate Bates.

"I can't remember my lines," Harry yelped, "and I'm on any minute."

"For Chrissakes, pull yourself together," Mr Moore ordered. "You've been murdered, and now you're a bloody ghost. You've got *no* lines to remember. Just appear in a trance at the banquet table… Heavens! Act as you do normally! And for God's sake, don't say anything onstage. I'll tell you when to walk on."

"What'll I do?" Bates moaned.

"Someone's strumming a harp," Mr Moore hissed. "That's your entrance. Go boy, NOW! Be a silent ghost!

And don't try to eat anything at the banquet. Ghosts don't eat."

Bates hurried off as Mr Moore rested his head in the palms of his hands.

Jonathan saw an opportunity. Mr Moore wasn't acknowledging or talking to him either in class or at rehearsals. He had nothing to lose and risked approaching Mr Moore. "Sir, I need to speak to you."

"What do *you* want?" Mr Moore said, feeling shame and revulsion, knowing that the photo existed, and Gabriel was spreading rumours.

"Please listen… just for a minute. Some people are telling lies about you and me. I don't know who they are, but I do know this: I'm being targeted."

"What are you spouting on about? We're in the middle of a play."

"That big explosion in the cauldron… it was no accident. Also, my bike was tampered with after a rehearsal." Jonathan took a deep breath and raced on, "And the talk about us and that photo are a frame-up."

Mr Moore was taken aback. "Who would spread such preposterous rumours? And why?"

"Some seniors are trying to pressure me to leave Blackleigh. They're out to get Jim Bhasin too. Two of my closest friends have been wrongly expelled, and another, Ian Gracey, is dead."

Mr Moore looked at Jonathan in disbelief. "I heard the excessive cauldron blast. I'll talk to the stage manager later. I can't begin to think about this now. These are serious charges you're making."

"Sir, thank you, for listening."

Jonathan returned to the side curtain, feeling a huge weight off his mind. He then made his final appearance as a witch without mishap.

After the final curtain, Mr Moore thanked the cast then quickly left the building. On his drive home, he didn't know what to make of Simon's allegations. He needed time to think this through. After all, he'd brought this on himself. He should have known better than to give the boy a ride in his car. The term would be over after the second night's performance; he'd make his decision then take the appropriate action after the short school holiday.

★ ★ ★

On the second and final night of the play, while Tunk and Snell were acting out their roles, Tim Bell let himself into their study. He went through Tunk's desk drawers until he found the photo. Tom removed a brown bottle and paintbrush from his pocket, unscrewed the lid and dipped the brush into the bottle. He swiped a liquid across the photo. Tom shook the photo to speed up the drying process, then he looked at the result.

Sure enough, the faces of Mr Moore and Jonathan Simon had been blurred unrecognisable. Tim returned the photo to Tunk's hiding place in exactly the position that he found it. Then he quietly left.

He was also ready with answers, should Tunk or Snell question him. By putting acid wash on the photo, he could claim that the photo with a Brownie camera wasn't exactly top of the line and that the photo had faded. His uncle had also thrown out the negative.

Later, on the last evening, Miller waited for Nick Krill at their usual spot.

"I got somefin' for you, Nick," Miller said, handing Nick an envelope.

Nick opened it and gasped. "Wow, a fiver! What's this for?"

"C'mon, you earned it."

"Thanks, Rodge." Nick pocketed the note. "It's good to be appreciated."

"You rid us of Wynn. I 'ave to admit the way you handled 'im was brilliant."

"But there's still Simon," Nick replied. "So far he's led a charmed life. During a rehearsal for *Macbeth*, I nipped out and filed a cable on his bike. Should have been a nasty accident, but he came through. I had hoped that another scare during the play would put it in his mind it's best not to return after the holiday break."

"You also almost had both Simon *and* Bhasin with that explosion in Scene One," Miller said.

"Just before the performance, I added a handful of gunpowder to boost the explosion," Nick explained. "I wanted to send them the message: leave Blackleigh – or else!"

"Good thinkin', Nick, now listen up, this is important," Miller said. "After the 'olidays, it'll be Sleeth and Tunk's last term. Sleeth's got a plan."

"I'm all ears, Rodge."

"One week during next term is set aside for the annual corps camp. The boys in the corps are goin to an abandoned army barracks somewhere out on the Yorkshire moors. It's a place wivout hot water, and most cadets will sleep in tents.

"During the camp, Sleeth and Tunk will take care of Simon. But Bhasin isn't in the corps," Miller stressed. While we're away, I want you to deal wiv Bhasin."

Nick chewed his gum thoughtfully. "Sounds good to me," he said. "I'll get him blamed for something which will lead to his exit."

"Now you're talkin', Nick."

"I fancy something with a twist of the unexpected," Krill said. He spat out his gum. "In fact, I already have an idea. And this one's a real beaut."

★ ★ ★

When Jonathan didn't announce that he was leaving the school, Tunk went to get the photo and tack it on the House notice board. "What the hell!" he exclaimed when he saw the faded photo, which was too blurred to identify Mr Moore and Jonathan.

With no photo to back up the rumours Gabriel was spreading, they would die out over the holiday break and were soon forgotten. Just Gabriel spreading gossip as usual.

24

CALLUM'S PLIGHT

Over the Easter holiday, Callum Davies experienced a brief respite. But on his first day back at school, he received some troubling news.

After breakfast, he found an envelope taped to the door of his Hastings locker: "Callum Davies, please see me in my study in Waterloo, three o'clock this afternoon. Mark Evans, Head Boy."

The note didn't mention the subject of the meeting, but the summons sent Callum's heart pounding.

That afternoon, Callum sat and fidgeted nervously in Evans' study, while Evans, at his desk, finished writing a note. He sealed it in an envelope. While Callum waited, he took off his thick eyeglasses, huffed on the lenses, and cleaned them repeatedly with his handkerchief.

Callum contemplated what he feared most: if Evans' questioning had anything to do with Nick Krill, there was the possibility of a viscous reprisal if he said anything to incriminate his fellow junior. He waited on edge, not knowing for sure why Evans wanted to see him.

"Give this note to Mrs MacNally over at the Headmaster's office," Evans said, waving an envelope at Gooding, a junior waiting by the door.

"Yes, Evans." The dark-haired junior came over, took the note, and left.

Evans turned his attention to the Welsh boy from Hastings. "Thank you for coming, Davies."

Like I had a choice, Callum thought.

"I called you in to talk about that unfortunate incident last term, in the school shop."

Callum tried to control his unease but blinked repeatedly as he spoke. "I though the matter was settled once Wynn was expelled."

"Not quite," the Head Boy said evenly. "There may have been a rush to judgement considering some new information that's turned up. Your wallet was one of the items that Wynn was accused of having stolen, correct?"

"Y-yes," Callum answered, aware of his left leg shaking uncontrollably. He tried to cast a positive light on the matter. "But my wallet was returned with nothing missing."

"The problem is that what appears on the surface may not be the case," Evans elaborated. "We've a witness who recently came forward who spoke of Wynn's character. The witness claims he has good reason to believe that Wynn is honest and wouldn't steal anything. I'm charged with determining whether his expulsion was a miscarriage of justice. A further concern is Peter

Wynn's father is an old Blackovian, who is demanding a more thorough investigation into his son's dismissal. What can you tell me?"

"My wal… wallet was stolen and found in Wynn's bag with another wallet." Callum decided to keep his answers vague, based on what was at stake if Krill ever found out about this meeting. "How could anyone other than Wynn have stolen the two wallets?"

"Yes, that's how it looks, but I have my doubts," Evans said. "On the Thursday in question… first, are you sure you had your wallet with you when you came into the shop?"

"Yes, I remember checking."

"Did you see Wynn?"

"The shop was crowded. I saw Tunk and Croat. I didn't see or even know Wynn."

"When did you notice that your wallet was missing?" Evans asked.

"Not till I got back to the dorm."

"What about purchases? Didn't you go to buy some groceries and needed money from your wallet?"

"I didn't try to make any purchases; the place was too busy," Callum lied.

"Anyone talk to you?" Evans probed.

"No one." Callum was unable to stop blushing.

"Think carefully, Now, besides Wynn, who could have stolen your wallet? Did anyone else have the opportunity?"

Callum paused, not knowing how to answer. *Damn that thieving Krill!* he thought. *How can I tell Evans that my wallet disappeared after Krill talked to me? Then I couldn't pay for my purchases because I found my wallet missing.*

"Your answer is of vital importance," Evans insisted. "If you have the slightest belief that someone else took your wallet, other than Wynn, it's your duty to tell me who that person was."

"At Blackleigh, we don't snitch," Callum answered.

Evans raised his voice, having tired of playing nice. "All I'm hearing are evasive replies."

Callum remained speechless, wracked with indecision. He knew that Evans was only doing his job, but the repercussions of his telling the truth were too awful to contemplate. *I need to buy time. Once I point to Krill, there's no turning back.*

"E-Evans," Callum managed to say. "I hope Wynn wasn't wrongly expelled. But I need time to think."

By now Evans had figured out what was going on. "Who are you afraid of? WHO?" Evans barked – then realised he was using the wrong tactic, and said calmly, "If you tell me who you suspect, I can protect you."

Callum didn't believe this for a second. He knew that Krill would have his revenge at any cost.

"I – I'm confused… if you give me the weekend, I may be able to come up with someone."

Evans gave this some thought, then conceded. "Alright, you have the weekend. But I want you here, same time, on Monday afternoon. Then I expect you to name names. Furthermore, I'm going to have Mrs MacNally call your parents and invite them to attend the meeting. You can go now, Davies."

When Callum closed the door to Evans' study, he could feel the sweat pooling under his armpits, and was thankful for his brief reprieve. He took two steps, then froze in his tracks. The look on his face was as if he'd seen a murder being committed. Maybe it was his own.

Standing at the end of the long corridor, casually leaning against the wall, arms folded, was Nick Krill. Nick pushed off the wall and turned to face Callum. Krill slashed his fingers across his throat and walked away.

★ ★ ★

On the following Monday morning, Evans arrived for his usual appointment with the Headmaster. He found Mrs MacNally in a sombre mood.

"What's up?" Evans asked.

"He'll tell you." She gestured with her head. "The doctor asked me to show you in as soon as you arrive."

The Headmaster stood and shook Evans' hand without saying a word, and they both sat down.

The doctor looked overburdened. "I received your note telling me that you saw Callum Davies on Friday after lunch."

"Yes, sir, I think we're getting somewhere. I've a follow-up with Davies and his parents this afternoon."

"I'm afraid that meeting won't happen, Mark. I received a call from Paul Donaldson, Callum's Housemaster, this morning." The Head clasped his hands together. "I'm deeply sorry to tell you this, but Callum Davies is dead."

"What!" Evans jumped out of his chair.

Dr Macleod shook his head in disbelief. "According to the police, on Saturday morning, Callum Davies ran across the High Street in Enderby and was struck by a lorry. The driver, Jim Phelps, told the investigating officers that he was driving within the speed limit, but the boy dashed out into the street, well before the upcoming pedestrian crossing. The driver was tested and found free of any alcohol in his system.

"Of course, Mr Phelps is griefstricken… Said he had no time to stop.

"Paul Donaldson performed a thorough search of Davies' locker, bed, and dresser draws. He didn't find any note Callum left behind. This gives rise to the question of why Callum took such a risk? So, unless something else comes to light, the police are treating this as an accident."

"This is hard news to fathom, sir," Evans said, slowly sinking back in his chair.

After Mark pulled himself together again, he filled Dr Macleod in on his meeting with Davies.

"What was your impression of him?" Dr Macleod enquired.

"The boy was terrified, sir," Evans replied. "I think he feared that if he revealed the name of who he thought was the real culprit, he'd be putting himself in grave danger. Maybe we'll never know for sure if his death was an accident or deliberate. But something doesn't feel right."

Evans paused to reflect, then added, "I feel terrible.

Callum asked for time to decide if he could risk giving up the name of the person he feared. And I agreed to wait until today to see him again. But I don't know what else I could have done."

"You did all you could," the Headmaster reassured him. "Now our task is to find out if someone had indeed threatened him – and if so, who?"

Evans replied, "I agree. In the meantime, I'll ask Sleeth again to give me more detailed information about the events leading up to Wynn's expulsion. Sleeth assured me, somewhat reluctantly, that I'd hear from him shortly."

"To move this along," Dr Macleod said, "I'll send a confidential instruction to the Housemasters. Going forward, I will have the final say in all cases involving expulsion. I'll also personally interview the individuals involved."

Evans hesitated, then said, "What I'm about to tell you, sir, was revealed to me in confidence."

"Please continue."

"Jonathan Simon, a second-year boy at Trafalgar, recently came to see me. Given the ironclad 'no-snitching code', he was brave to do so. He's convinced that certain seniors in Trafalgar will stop at nothing to force him to leave Blackleigh before the end of this school year."

"My God," Dr Macleod exclaimed. "Does Simon have any proof of his allegation?"

"Ah… that's the thing. Nothing in concrete so far. But I have reason to believe he's telling the truth."

"How did you leave it with Simon?"

"He and I are working together to get to the truth of this," Evans replied.

Dr Macleod steepled his fingers in thought, then said, "The annual corps camp is scheduled in two weeks. I'd like us to make substantial progress before then. You already have enough on your plate. I'll arrange for you to take time off to continue your investigation rather than attend the camp."

"Good idea, sir."

★ ★ ★

When Mark Evans returned to his study, there was a note taped to his door. Mr Moore, the English Literature master, had left him a message. He returned the call.

"Mr Moore… Mark Evans here… you phoned."

"Yes, sorry to bother you, Evans, but an incident occurred while I was directing the Trafalgar-Hastings play at the end of last term. It may amount to nothing, but you should know about it. It concerns Jonathan Simon, one of the actors in my production."

"Please go on," Mark replied, feeling a sense of excitement as he hung on to Mr Moore's every word. "I know Simon."

"My son, Seth, is a junior in Trafalgar. He happened to overhear a sensitive conversation between Simon and some others in the cast of *Macbeth*. They outright accused Simon of being in… How shall I put it? …A sexual relationship with me. These scandalous accusations are totally untrue, I can assure you."

Mr Moore swallowed hard, then continued with his confession. "I'm afraid I made a grave indiscretion on one occasion. I did Simon a small favour and gave him a ride into Enderby, as I also had a dental appointment there that afternoon. Someone took a photo of the two of us in my car."

Moore went on, "Simon protested to me vehemently during the *Macbeth* performance that someone – he didn't say who – was out to get him and spreading these false rumours. He also told me he was nearly killed when someone tampered with his bike.

"The boy further claimed that the inordinate blast during *Macbeth* was not an accident. And I have reason to believe he was right – that someone meddled with the explosives, intending to cause harm or send a clear message to Simon: leave school… or else!"

"I greatly appreciate you coming forward with this information – even at your own peril," Mark replied. "I'm telling you in confidence, that I've spoken with Simon. I also believe him that… if you'll excuse me, 'Something is rotten in the state of Blackleigh'.

"Again, Mr Moore, please keep this between us, while the Headmaster and I review this and other serious issues."

"My God," Moore said. "Thank you for telling me. The sooner you get to the bottom of this the better. If there's any way I can be of assistance, let me know."

"I appreciate your offer," Mark said. "Thank you again for your call."

Mark put down the phone. He reflected that whatever was happening at the school, enough was enough. The problem was where to start searching in a maze of lies and cover-ups.

He started to see what Jonathan had refrained from saying: that there was too much going on for one person to be orchestrating it all. Mark was deeply concerned that there might be a conspiracy. And if he was right, he wondered how many boys were involved?

25

REUNION

Jonathan was going downstairs to the Houseroom, when the matron called from her open door, "You have a message, Simon. Here it is."

He came back up the stairs and Mrs Ambrose handed him a note.

His heart skipped a beat. Olivia had phoned.

It seemed so long since they'd spoken; he couldn't wait to hear her voice. His next free time to call would be at the mid-morning break.

Jonathan's French class dragged on interminably, but finally the buzzer sounded.

Ten minutes later, his hands were shaking as he dialled Olivia's number at the payphone in the Assembly lobby. He breathed in to relax and let the air out slowly.

She came straight to the phone. "Hello?"

"Olivia, it's me, Jonathan."

"Oh, Jonathan… I've been so worried, and I've missed you. Is it safe yet?"

Jonathan let out a sigh. "As much as I want to see you, it's probably not a good idea."

"You weren't going to let them win," she pleaded. "There must be something we can do."

Jonathan considered this, then said, "I'd have to be sure I'm not followed this time."

"What are you thinking?"

A plan began to form. "Next weekend, if it's good for you – be there ahead of me, say twelve-thirty. Sit on the bench in front of Janet's Café. The bus will be full of boys going into Enderby. But if I ride there on the bike I just bought, I can look back from time to time, and check if anyone is following me. If I see anyone suspicious, I'll just go to the Enderby bike shop, buy something for the bike, and ride back to school. But, if I walk into the café for lunch at one, that'll mean the coast is clear."

"You're good," Olivia said, amazed. "Let's do it."

The rest of the week passed ever so slowly. When Saturday came, Jonathan cycled into Enderby, frequently checking behind him. Satisfied that no one tailed him, Jonathan parked his bike in the rack near the bus stop. He looked over at the bench across the street and in front of Janet's Café. There she was in a dark blue sweater, sitting by herself, as lovely as in a dream, and pretending not to see him.

Jonathan headed over to the café, while Olivia remained stoically on the bench. As he passed her by,

Jonathan, as if preoccupied, didn't look directly at her but winked at the last second, then disappeared into the café.

Olivia stayed right where she was for another two minutes. Then she glanced at her watch in frustration, as if her date or friend had stood her up. After another thirty seconds, she stood up in a huff, and entered the café, as if to say, *No problem then, I'll have lunch alone.*

Inside, she looked around but saw no sign of Jonathan, although there were some free set tables. Olivia was thinking that she didn't know what to make of this, when their favourite waitress walked up to her. "I put him in the backroom," she said. "We use it for the overflow crowd – even though it's closed right now – so you'll have it all to yourselves. Come on."

The waitress showed Olivia to the backroom entrance and left. Olivia flipped her hair, saw Jonathan at a table, and skipped over to him.

He looked up; she'd come. Olivia was standing beside his table smiling; she looked down at him. He took in her long, flowing blonde hair, light blue eyes, and the aroma of her perfume. She wore pink lipstick and had painted her nails. He couldn't believe that someone so radiant and effervescent was his girlfriend.

He stood, and Olivia surprised him by taking his face in the palms of her hands and kissing him. They then took their seats, briefly at loss for words. Both started to say something at the same time, stopped, and burst out laughing.

"You go first," he said.

"We made it." She grinned. "Jonathan Simon, what a coincidence seeing you here!"

He marvelled how his life, difficult as it was, offered unexpected wonders with a silver lining. Olivia made such a difference! Despite the pain and tension at school, knowing she was there, yielded so much. Now he'd reached the horizon, he saw a wider vista ahead. And beyond that, a further view of the promised land.

"I… I've missed you," he said. "But we didn't have much choice."

"I know… missed you too. Just tell me what's happening?"

"I could do with a less exciting life," he admitted. Jonathan filled her in on the spring term. "Besides seeing the performance of *HMS Pinafore*, and being in a House play myself, I just met with Mark Evans, the Head Boy. He's turned out to be a real ally. He believes me and wants to make things right but needs proof."

"I'll give them proof," she said. "After that guy threatened us in the Arts Building, I even carry an extra chair with me."

The waitress came. They ordered sandwiches and a jug of lemonade.

Jonathan went on, "A junior from Hastings was hit by a lorry on a Sunday – in Enderby. To put it bluntly, the police ruled it an accident. But boys who knew him think it was a suicide."

"My God," Olivia gasped. "Things keep going from bad to worse. I feel so, so sorry for that poor boy and his parents."

"Still, enough of my travails, tell me about you?"

"Well, I was home for a week. I'd like to audition at a music school."

"What instrument do you play?"

"Piano..." She paused and then went on, "Also, when I last spoke on the phone with James, we discussed the loss of my uncle – his father. It made me realise that I didn't want to be to be estranged from my dad. I talked it over with my mother and I called him in New York. I'm so glad that I did."

"I'm pleased for you too. Before I forget, next week is the corps camp, for cadets from all the Houses," he said. "They're holding it in some godforsaken place on the Yorkshire moors... The senior I have to watch out for the most is in charge."

"You know I'll be with you, in spirit and supporting you every step of the way," she said. "What about your friend... the one with you when we first met?"

Jonathan laughed. "David should be at the camp, but knowing him he'll probably come up with some impossible-to-diagnose medical condition. Somehow, he always finds a way out."

She took his hand in hers. "You'll make it," she said confidently. "Somehow, I just know. You were so brave when we were trapped in the Performing Arts Building. If you could handle that, you can handle anything."

"I hope you're right."

"Call me when you return. I've been working on a plan to help you fight back," Olivia said enigmatically.

"In the meantime, remember what you told me about your two friends and your oath: to pay those bullies back and more."

204

26

NICK'S SECRET

Nick Krill sat slumped at a desk, in the back row of his history class. He'd been doodling in his notebook and was looking over his sketches. Most of them were of bizarre faces and ghoulish apparitions resembling Jim Bhasin, his next victim.

Krill had no need to take notes. He had an ongoing arrangement with Pearl in Wellington, whom he regarded as a brain and the best student in the class. Pearl always provided him with copies of his latest class notes. It had been easy to scare the boy shitless into sharing.

Meanwhile, Mr Bathurst, the knowledgeable history master, droned on – to those paying attention – with the machinations surrounding the marriages of Henry VIII.

Nick reflected on the current talk in Hastings. The main topic was Callum Davies, who most boys believed had purposely stepped in front of that lorry. Nick was relieved that Callum hadn't left an incriminating note behind. The boy, gone forever, would no doubt be laid to rest in some Welsh green valley. There'd be no need for further threats to remind him to hold his tongue about the Wynn incident.

As Krill saw it, he'd done the school a favour by putting pressure on Callum. The plodding loner was hopeless at sports and would be of no value to the corps. It was just unfortunate that Peanut knew too much.

While Mr Bathurst switched the topic to the fate of Anne Boleyn, Nick thought about how his parents, James and Rita Krill, were pleased to pack him off to boarding school for five years. His parents spent little time with Nick and left him mostly to his own devices.

His thrifty father, a director at the National Provincial Bank, kept Nick on an unnecessarily tight budget. And his simpering mother was forever preoccupied with running a struggling dress shop in Hampstead High Street. Rita was always whining about problems related to shipments, the shop's two inefficient salesgirls, and her own hopeless bookkeeping.

Whenever his parents went away on one of their holidays abroad, they rarely considered taking him along. Although they could well afford the expense, his father was reluctant to spend money on an extra hotel room or purchase another flight ticket for their young son.

James rarely offered Nick advice, other than to use his time at school wisely and cultivate his talents, whatever that meant.

Nick never thought he had a talent for anything, other than having to make it on his own. Certainly, his lusterless academic performance at his prep school in north-west London gave off few positive signs for the future.

He reflected on his pluses and minuses. No matter what he attempted, he liked to rise to the top. No rules ever held him back. Playing football was great, especially when he could goal-hang and receive acclaim for scoring goals. He was also effective in his short, brutal fights with other boys in the schoolyard, as a swift kick to the groin always put a peremptory end to it. But engendering fear among others and making yet another 'spastic' blub-off to the matron never gave him satisfaction. He craved more… if he were a wolf, he'd run at the head of the pack.

Only by good fortune, Nick discovered early that he possessed an innate skill in which he excelled. At the beginning, Nick thought of his gift just as a game. Then he realised it had practical applications.

The origin of his breakthrough occurred when his parents brought home Spark, a boxer, from the pound. The dog, sensing Nick's disinterest, took an intense dislike to him. Spark would bark and bare his teeth whenever Nick came near. The turning point came when Spark bit Nick's hand, leaving teeth marks.

While his parents were away in Corfu, they once again left him home with Spark and Theresa, the Spanish live-in maid. Nick added rat poison to Spark's food bowl. He later buried Spark in an unmarked grave, at the far corner of their back garden, where his parents never ventured. Before they returned from their holiday, he'd silenced Theresa from reporting on Spark's fate. Nick warned her that if she so much as hinted as to what really happened, his parents would be furious to learn that her boyfriend had slept overnight at their home.

"The dog ran away," Nick lied. "And no, I don't want another dog."

Nick learned from this experience that he felt no pangs of conscience about Spark's demise and no fear of discovery. If anything, he was turned on by the thrill of honing his talent in more profitable ways. He had no scruples about edgy activities.

He recalled how he began taking pound notes from his father's wallet and his mother's handbag. But that thrill soon wore off. The game was too easy and presented little challenge. His parents rarely counted their money, concealing it in places they wrongly believed safe. *And my father's a banker!*

Bored with the ease and monotony of such petty crimes, and wanting new adventures, Nick widened his horizon. He moved on to taking the Tube and hanging around department stores in London's West End. His tactics were simple. Get off at Oxford Circus and find an elderly female victim weighed down with shopping.

Nick learned how to distract these women. After they had left the shop, he'd "accidentally" stumble into them. The collision would cause them to drop one or more bags and spill the contents. Innocent-looking Nick would apologise profusely while helping the women reload their shopping bags.

The women were always too distracted by his dazzling light-blue eyes to notice him reaching into their handbag, lifting their wallet, and slipping it into his deep coat pocket. Because they'd already left a shop and paid for their purchases, they wouldn't discover their wallet was missing until the next day or so when they went to buy something else. They could have lost it anywhere. So, tying theft to the kind, polite, cherubic boy was unlikely.

Nick would wear his lucky uniform, a hooded duffel coat with a new addition of black woolen gloves, and prowl the crowded streets, as daylight turned to darkness. He never stole from anyone in a large department store, to avoid the risk of being confronted by a security guard. No one was going to trap him.

But over time the thrill wore off, and Nick found himself craving more elaborate adventures. One time, he managed to doctor the accounts receivable ledger and ferret away some of the funds from his prep school charity for War Widows.

Nick saw nothing wrong with his actions. Rather, he considered them as necessary practise in refining his heaven-sent talent. The greater the danger enhanced his thrill. His goal evolved into pulling invisible strings to bring a selected victim crashing down.

One evening proved to be a profitable game-changer; his parents surprised him by taking him out for dinner. They were joined in a Haymarket restaurant by the flashy Sam Miller, his bejewelled wife Sonia, and their son, Rodge.

Mr Miller, a scrap metal entrepreneur, talked big, laughed often, and frequently stretched his mouth to reveal a gold-toothed grin, which gave him the appearance of a smiling shark. Sam Miller was a top client of Nick's father's bank. Sam frequently used the expression, "I like it!" in response to any idea proposed by James Krill.

Rodge, his burly son, was three years older than Nick. While their parents were preoccupied and chatting about their favourite holiday destinations, Rodge recognised by talking to the smart-as-a-whip, twelve-year-old boy, a younger version of himself – relentless, with few scruples – and with a cunning that surpassed his own.

Rodge was boarding at Blackleigh School and encouraged Nick to think about the same destination. They hit it off. Both laughed at each other's warped sense of humour, and for once in his life, Nick felt safe in confiding in another.

"I like wot I hear," Rodge commented. "Nufin' wrong wiv takin'."

With his own lofty ambitions, Rodge suggested that with Nick's skill, together they could turn Blackleigh into a money-making machine. "I tell you no lies, Nick, your admishun to the school, notwivstandin' the Common Entrance Exam, is a sure thing. Me faver is on the school Board of Governors. He'll write you a smashin' letter of recomodashon."

The older boy proposed that they'd work together on challenging projects. Rodge would give Nick the name of a troublemaker, or some obstacle in his way to the top, and Nick would devise a way to remove the problem.

For his efforts, Rodge, flush with cash, promised to reward his young protégé. This for Nick represented an ideal situation. He was often short of money; he also admired Rodge Miller and sought his approval.

Their friendship based on mutual benefit evolved. After Nick came to Blackleigh, Wynn's departure was their first success. But even when Nick's efforts failed to result in a victim's expulsion, Rodge still complimented him. The bomb blast intended to injure Simon and Bhasin during *Macbeth* was, Rodge told him, "bloody creative".

Nick yawned and sat up at his desk, done with his daydreaming. In a few minutes the history hour would be over. On the following Monday, those in the corps would leave for nearly a week. The annual faraway camp was a blessing in disguise. Most of the prefects would be going along, and out of the way.

In a few days, he'd ceremonially put on his duffel coat, raise the hood, and don black gloves for his next mission. He would head over to Trafalgar after midnight. The Indian boy could never imagine what lay in store for him. Nick prided himself as always improving on his previous capers. And sealing Bhasin's fate would be his masterstroke.

27

HEATHRICK

Jonathan sat in the back of a noisy army transport. He and other Trafalgar cadets were heading over winding, pock-marked roads to the Heathrick Camp for the six-day annual corps retreat. The pouring rain only compounded his feeling of entering a long dark tunnel. He held on to his memory of his last meeting with Olivia to boost his spirits.

The cadets were dressed in army denims, berets, gaiters, and boots. The only sounds came from those talking above the grinding noise of the coach whenever the driver changed gears. A frequent clatter of corps boots issued from the centre aisle, as cadets went to and from the putrid toilet facility at the rear.

Jonathan worried that Officer Sleeth, and his Sergeants Tunk and Miller, were plotting something, and he abhorred being at the mercy of those who hated him.

Now, an hour from camp, Jonathan listened to Gabriel sounding off to a few cadets in seats nearby. "This isn't civilisation – we're going to an abandoned army camp. They don't have fuckin' anything. Don't you know you'll likely have to use your hands to wipe. The food will be unmitigated shit. Also, we sleep on hard, wet ground. Don't expect comfy mattresses.

"See, the idea is to learn how to survive in the wild, as if you were stranded in enemy territory," Gabriel elaborated. "I heard from last year's boys that they drop you off in the middle of nowhere, and you have to find your way back to the base at night. Better watch out for swamps and marshes. There are a few boys I wouldn't miss, though, if they were lost." Gabriel threw a glance at Jonathan.

It was already dark when the passengers arrived at their destination. Jonathan stepped down from the bus, carrying his kitbag, and flashed his torch. He saw lines of khaki canvas tents in a freezing, wind-blasted field. One row of tents was allocated to each separate House. He'd been told that every tent slept up to three cadets.

Jonathan walked over to the designated Trafalgar section and peered into an empty tent. He saw Harry Crown, holding a torch, passing by and called to him, "Let's share this."

"No thanks, I'm looking for a place with a telly and a fridge?" Harry said, then burst out laughing. "Don't worry, Jonathan, if yours doesn't, I'll share with you anyway."

Harry, always cheerful, and now a senior, was the elder brother of Jonathan's friend Arthur, who'd voluntarily left Blackleigh near the end of the last school year. They crawled inside to find, contrary to Gabriel's prediction, three tattered and soiled mattresses, albeit without blankets or pillows.

Jonathan and Harry left the tent to check out the washing facilities. These comprised a group of square enamel sinks, over which hung decaying pipes with spouts on the end, and rusty cold-water taps that released a smelly brown liquid. There were no showers. Hot water, as Gabriel forecast, was not to be had.

"It's not quite like home." Harry chuckled.

"It's not like anything," Jonathan added.

A piercing whistle sounded, followed by a grating voice over a loudspeaker. "Trafalgar cadets, this is Officer Sleeth. Army chow is in the mess tent; it's marked with a yellow flag. You have fifteen minutes to eat before you make way for Plessey cadets. No latecomers served."

On their way to the mess, Jonathan and Harry passed a row of ten decrepit-looking temporary toilets. Jonathan winced at the stench; he didn't want to contemplate what awaited inside and suppressed his urge to pee.

They entered the mess, a large tent lit by Coleman lanterns, and joined a queue of cadets waiting to receive cutlery. Each were handed a small stained rectangular metal box with a fold-down metal handle, containing a plastic knife, fork, and a spoon.

"What's this?" Harry asked Corporal Croat, who was supervising the distribution.

"These," Croat replied, holding them up, "are your eating utensils. Keep them in your kitbags. The tin box serves as a plate. Tonight, there's a choice of fried bread and Spam or baked beans. Help yourselves.

"Tomorrow, reveille is at five-thirty. After you stir your stumps, breakfast is at six." Croat added, "Officer Sleeth will address you in the open field at seven o'clock prompt."

"Thanks," Harry said to Croat with sarcasm. "Point me to the buffet?"

"It's at the rear of this tent in round metal pots on the long table," Croat replied. "I can't promise you home cooking."

★ ★ ★

Back in the tent, Jonathan removed his boots and closed his eyes. He rested his head on his kit bag, absent a pillow, but barely slept.

The next morning at reveille, he got up, already feeling exhausted. Jonathan dressed, washed, and hurriedly endured the latrine ordeal. He then moved like an automaton to the mess and breakfast, where he and Harry nibbled on burnt sausage and greasy fried bread.

Minutes before seven o'clock, Jonathan stood next to Harry in a windy open field. They waited at attention as Jonathan surveyed the surroundings. He saw that between the tents were a group of large Nissan huts. Each hut had a dormer window on either side of an entrance door. These facilities were reserved for officers, sergeants and corporals. Beyond the camp, all was a green, uninhabited, and rocky terrain.

At the stroke of seven, the nearest Nissan hut door opened and Officer Cadet Sleeth emerged. He looked well-rested, shaved, a baton under his arm, his corps boots reflecting like mirrors. Sleeth was accompanied by his two sergeants, Tunk and Miller, under his leadership. They conducted a brief inspection of the cadets lined up and under their command. Although Sleeth appeared to be in a hurry, he deliberately paused in front of Jonathan.

"I'll need *you* for sentry night duty at 0230 hours," he snapped. "You will be at your night post for an hour. Then you'll be relieved by… Crown here."

Jonathan could hardly believe his ears. He responded with outrage, quite forgetting Sleeth's rank and seniority. "Sentry duty? Sir, we're on the Yorkshire moors, with no one else around for miles. Who's going to attack us? Apart from the cadets in other houses, anyone else would be crazy to be here."

Sleeth responded with fury. "Silence. That's an order. You will collect a rifle from the mess this evening and stand guard. If you hear any noise, shout, 'Advance one and be recognised,' at the first sign of an intruder. That's it! Another word and you'll be on duty all night."

Sleeth stalked off, his sergeants in his wake. He mounted a grassy mound, looked down at his unit and spoke with a sneer on his reddish, pock-marked face.

"Men, this week is a test of endurance, like nothing you've experienced. During the first four days, you'll train as if you're in the British Army. The exercises are designed to build up stamina.

"There are about two hundred cadets at this camp and thirty of you are from Trafalgar. We will be co-operating with cadets from Plessey. The rest of our combined cadet force have their own missions and will operate from different locations on the moors. You will be unlikely to run into those from other Houses, apart from Plessey. At any one time, we will have a maximum of fifty or so cadets in our group on the moors.

"In the final two days, you'll be divided into small teams and left at various locations. Your team's mission is to find your way back by hiking to designated check points, and then on to our base. Do you receive my meaning? Any questions?"

In the same breath, and before anyone could raise a hand, Sleeth went on, "Each small team will be equipped with a map, on which your checkpoints will be clearly designated, and a compass to help you find your way. This final test will involve arduous trekking over harsh terrain and marshes. Food provided will be in your backpacks. You'll sleep in the small tents we provide. I will personally handle slackers. There will be serious consequences for anyone who fails to obey orders."

At this point, Sleeth cast a glance in Jonathan's direction. Tunk and Miller, standing together, wore suppressed grins. Tunk then performed his new habit of placing one hand over the other and, with evil delight, cracked his finger joints.

Jonathan paled at the thought of what lay ahead. Everything else in the camp could be endured, but the ominous final mission was a precarious challenge. *What'll I do if my enemies try to gang up on me, in the wilderness – where there are no witnesses?*

Every inconvenience in the camp diminished in his mind compared with his anxiety of being stranded on the isolated moors. Certainly, Sleeth, Tunk, and Miller wouldn't let such an opportunity pass them by.

28

AFTER MIDNIGHT

Late Monday night, Nick Krill climbed out of bed, placed two pillows under his blanket so it'd appear he was sound asleep, and gathered the warm clothes he'd prepared earlier. He crept out of his Hastings dorm, dressed in the adjacent washroom, and put away his pyjamas in a chest of drawers in the corridor.

Krill put on his duffel coat over his clothes, raised the hood, tied his gym shoelaces extra tight so he could run, wore black gloves, and carried a torch.

He left Hastings and headed along a path towards Trafalgar. Even though he'd dressed warmly, it was freezing cold, and he found himself shivering. Harsh, biting wind pounded against his face. *This is my last job for now*, he mused. He vowed that if Rodge Miller rose to became Head of Trafalgar, he'd plan anew, but after tonight he'd lie low.

This was the rare opportunity he sought with so

many boys away at the camp. He wouldn't disappoint Rodge.

Nick had previously landed his minor role in *Macbeth* thanks to Rodge Miller and Snell being in cahoots. The rehearsals were often held at Trafalgar. He'd taken the opportunity while there to check out their Houseroom. Nick had even casually walked into the Housemaster's study and looked around while Mr Morton was at a meeting in the Headmaster's office.

In the darkness, Nick trudged on past the Administration Building and a series of classrooms.

After twenty minutes, Nick reached Trafalgar. He wiped his runny nose and heaved a sigh of relief that no lights were on. Nick pushed open the main door and crept inside the lobby. Satisfied no one was around, he slipped into the Houseroom. He deliberately left one of the Houseroom swing doors open, as well as the side door to the outside, in case he had to make a quick escape. Nick then flashed his torch and settled the beam on his victim's locker.

In the crammed-full locker he scanned two rows of textbooks. He then shone his beam on the back of the locker door and was satisfied to see several pinned photos of Jim Bhasin with his proud mother and father.

Next was the risky part. Nick turned off his torch and approached the Housemaster's rooms on tiptoe, opened the entry door, and went into a small lobby. The door on the left, he recalled, led to Morton's wood-panelled study. The door on the right accessed Morton's living quarters. Nick entered the study and attuned his hearing, ready to flee if he heard a stirring followed by footsteps next door.

He turned his torch back on and slowly swept the room. It was tidy and uncluttered with two small bookcases and two armchairs facing Morton's large desk.

One by one, Nick opened each of the Housemaster's desk drawers. In the top left-hand drawer, he hit the jackpot: a white-faced, gold-rimmed Rolex Oyster Perpetual watch with a brown leather strap. Nick turned the watch over and noticed what might have been an engraving that in his haste he read. He pocketed the Rolex and closed the desk drawer, leaving it open all but a crack to draw Mr Morton's attention to it.

He turned off his torch and slipped out of the study. In the Houseroom, he hid the watch behind some books on the top shelf of Bhasin's locker.

Nick's plan was to wait a couple of days, then return around midnight and slip an anonymous note under the Housemaster's door, directing him to Bhasin's locker for the stolen item.

He quickly closed Bhasin's locker and was congratulating himself on his ingenious plan when he heard a gasp; then a young boy's voice called out, "Who's there?"

Most boys in Nick's position, right now, would panic and do something stupid. Not Nick. His mind instantly became focused, and in a split second, he knew exactly what to do. Nick's torch had two settings: low on one end, high on the other. Nick selected the high beam, spun around, and pointed it directly in the boy's eyes, which, given the pitch-dark room, temporarily blinded him.

As the boy automatically went to shield his eyes, Nick made a mad dash for the side door, blew through it, and kept on running, without looking back. He returned to Hasting as fast as he could.

Hastings was in darkness, but Nick wasn't ready for bed. He went outside and stood in the grassy square, where he and Miller often met, and sat down. He lit up a cigarette, inhaled deeply and breathed out the smoke. *Maybe I'm getting too old for this kind of thing?* The thirteen-year-old laughed to himself.

His mind raced through his achievements. Wynn was expelled, Callum gone forever, and soon Bhasin would be at the end of his line. He thought about Alan Pearl. The day he'd set up Wynn in the shop, he'd briefly spoken to Pearl, as a distraction, right before he stole the boy's wallet. Maybe "spoken" was the wrong word. He'd threatened Pearl and wanted to know why Alan was late in giving him his history notes.

And finally, try as he might, Nick couldn't imagine how anyone could pin any reason why he'd go after Wynn. He'd never known or even met Wynn.

Still, Nick asked himself the nagging question: *Are there any loose ends I'm not seeing?*

★ ★ ★

At eight o'clock on the following morning, a notice typed by Mr Morton on his letterhead stationery was tacked to the bulletin board in the House lobby: "It appears that I have misplaced my Rolex, a gift from a group of seniors in 1953. The person finding and returning this item will have my deep gratitude, along with an appropriate reward. Alec Morton, Housemaster."

Although Mr Morton was incensed over the obvious theft, he was more concerned about getting the keepsake back than punishing the thief, and thought that this tactic would work best.

Shortly after breakfast, there was a knock at the Housemaster's door.

"Come in," Mr Morton called out.

Christopher Jenkins, a mousy boy with dark hair, and a cowlick that wouldn't stay down, entered. "It's about your watch, sir."

Mr Morton perked up. "Where did you find it?"

In his wildest imagination, Mr Morton couldn't imagine that this boy could be a thief.

"I didn't find it, sir," Jenkins contradicted him. "But last night I saw something suspicious. Maybe it was stolen, Mr Morton?"

"Tell me, Christopher, what you believe happened."

"After midnight, I couldn't sleep, so I came down to the Houseroom to fetch a book."

"About what time?" Morton asked, as he focused intently on the boy.

"Around two o'clock, sir. The Houseroom door was open, and I thought I heard a locker door close. I stopped at the entry, when suddenly a short figure, in a duffel coat with the hood up, flashed his torch in my eyes, ran across the room, and went out by the side door. It was too dark for me to see who he was. I'm sorry, I shouldn't have come down so late."

Morton paused, then said, "Thank you, Jenkins. You shouldn't have been there, but we'll let it pass."

Alec Morton was hopeful, but knew he had to proceed with caution. He said kindly, "I'm aware of the no-snitching code, but if you could give me a hint – a clue as to who I should look to…"

Jenkins shoulders slumped. "I wish I could, sir, but he blinded me with his torch. The only thing for sure is that he was on the short side, probably a junior. Sorry, but that's all I have."

Mr Morton hid his disappointment. "Christopher, this is very useful. I am indebted to you."

Soon after, Mr Morton posted another notice: "I regret that word has come to me, that my watch was likely stolen from my office. I have reason to believe that the culprit then hid the watch in his locker. So, I must ask that before you leave for your classes, all of you stand by your lockers and open the doors for an inspection. Alec Morton, Housemaster."

With so many boys away, the Houseroom was only half full. Mr Morton came into the room punctually and wasted no time in beginning his search in the lockers.

Jim, unconcerned with the development, stood ready, as one at a time, the Housemaster checked the contents of each locker and moved along to the next boy waiting for the search.

Jim's was the last locker to be inspected. Jim readily

opened the door and waited as Mr Morton checked the lower shelves, then worked up, examining shelf by shelf.

To Jim's complete shock, the Housemaster let out a deep sigh and withdrew his hand from Jim's top shelf. Mr Morton held out the lost watch.

"Bhasin," Morton snapped, "I've found what I'm looking for. How could you?" The Housemaster pocketed the item.

Jim was stunned and protested, "Sir, I never took the watch."

Boys in the Houseroom crowded around. Those who knew Jim were almost as stunned as he was. A few began calling him names. One boy gave him a shove.

"That's enough," Mr Morton ordered. "Bhasin, it's appropriate that we discuss this in private."

A few minutes later, Jim sat in the Housemaster's study, totally confused by the fast-moving events.

Mr Morton said, "We have a witness. Jenkins interrupted the culprit, at about two in the morning, with the crime in progress. He heard a locker close; it was dark, but he was able to make out a boy. He was the same size as you, in a duffle coat, with the hood up, and he ran out of the side door of the Houseroom. And now the stolen watch has been found in your locker."

Jim gasped, trying to make sense of his dire situation and the tangible evidence mounted against him. "Sir, I don't know how your watch turned up in my locker. I've never seen that watch before now. The boy in a duffle coat wasn't me."

"Well, the evidence points to you."

"No! No!" Jim cried out in tears. "I didn't steal anything."

"Then explain yourself, boy."

"I-I can't," Jim sobbed. "All I know is that it wasn't me."

Morton went on. "There's a new school policy. Your fate will not be decided by me. The Head of House will make a recommendation, as always, but in grave matters, such as this, the Headmaster will make the final decision. You'll see him next Monday when he returns from a conference.

"For your own protection, I don't want you mixing with the other boys. There are a couple of spare rooms in the back of the san, that I believe are currently unoccupied. I'm going to arrange that you stay in one of them until the situation is resolved by the Headmaster. The matron will bring you any personal affects you may need."

Mr Morton shook his head. "I don't know what the world is coming to. First Wynn is caught stealing, and now you of all people."

29

JONATHAN'S ORDEAL

With each passing day, Jonathan's apprehension increased. The last two days of camp came all too soon. At dawn on Thursday morning, he and Harry Crown joined a group of anxious cadets heading in an army lorry to various drop-off points on the moors.

The participants wore denims, boots, gaiters, berets, and gloves. Each carried a backpack with a khaki drinking flask, a torch, a compass, and a metal food container. For food, like the others, Jonathan had two apples, biscuits, and a wedge of cheese.

The groups could choose their own teams. Jonathan had anticipated that with Harry he'd be in a group of four, but no one else joined them. When Jonathan and Harry's turn came, the lorry stopped to let them jump off the open back of the vehicle. With barely a glance, the army driver revved the engine and took off to the next drop-off spot.

Jonathan watched ruefully as the transport with the rest of the cadets drove up a hill and disappeared on the other side. They were left at the foot of a wind-whipped field. Jonathan gazed at the bleak surroundings. An early-morning mist hung in the air. The only sounds breaking the silence were bird calls.

"Croat gave me this map. Our first checkpoint is about five miles away, near a marsh," Harry said. "To reach it, we've lots of climbing over rocks and hills. We're heading to the same destination as cadets from Plessey."

"I wouldn't trust even the compass Croat gave us," Jonathan replied. "It's strange, but I've hardly seen Sleeth, Tunk, or Miller since we've been here."

They moved out and crossed an old stone medieval bridge, over a shallow stream. Ahead was a steep, cloud-covered hill. They began the climb over craggy rocks, taking care not to trip and fall.

An hour later, they reached a plateau at the top of the hill, where the mist had cleared. It was then that Jonathan came upon one of the most beautiful, wild, and striking landscapes he'd ever seen.

A field, covered with a mass of ferns, rippled in the wind. A narrow path ran through it. At the far end, the land sloped away to a wide valley, filled with undulating green hills tinged with yellow.

As they moved on and closer, Jonathan could see the land was partly covered in ferns and stone walls. Streams and small waterfalls abounded.

They hiked on, and the landscape became a blend of open scrub, heather, and rocky areas. In places, the grass grew so high that it tangled with foliage and bracken. In other areas, pools of shimmering water from the previous night's rain flashed and dazzled in the early sunlight. Absent were roads, villages, cottages, electric pylons, or any sign of other cadets.

The walls had endured through time. Huge boulders had been placed in formation, one above the other. The past was ever present. They came across ancient Roman steps, tunnels, and pathways. Some remains of walls were six feet high, others were low enough for Jonathan and Harry to jump over… ribbons of chalky grey stretched way up into the emerald green hills.

"The Romans built some of these walls over two thousand years ago, when they invaded England," Jonathan marvelled. "There was even an earlier story about Romulus and Remus jumping over the first walls of Rome."

"Unless we find the first checkpoint, we'll be here for another two thousand years," Harry quipped. "Best we keep moving."

By afternoon, they'd spent hours hiking and edging their way down rocky slopes. An occasional reward was to come upon a running stream. Hearing a rushing sound, both ran to the edge and flung themselves down. Flat on the ground, Jonathan immersed his hands and face in icy water and relieved his parched throat by swallowing fresh gulps. The water wasn't deep, otherwise he'd have been tempted to dive into the crystal-clear depths.

As the two cadets rested on the banks, Jonathan, soaked to the bone, saw sheep grazing nearby. Everywhere he looked was a story, an epic poem. Something about this landscape made him want to write and capture some fraction of its magnificence. He felt like he was on a quest to find something great. As he watched water gush by, he mused that despite all the craziness at school, there were still perfect moments of bliss such as this.

Refreshed and renewed, the two of them headed in the direction of the checkpoint, halfway to their destination for the night.

They approached marshland. Directly ahead came the sounds of beating wings. In the next instant, two wild geese flew up from their nesting place. They squawked and dipped across the path ahead. In these moments, Jonathan thought they'd disturbed the silence of the ages. Moments later, all was still; the birds had settled elsewhere.

An hour later, with a glorious sense of achievement, Jonathan and Harry swept down to the base of a hill, where directly ahead were two single tents. One had a black flag with yellow stripes mounted on the top, designating checkpoint #1.

Jonathan staggered into the tent to find Snell, in his capacity as a corps sergeant, sitting at a table, a butterfly net close at hand. Snell glanced up upon their arrival but was distracted by having caught an insect specimen. He didn't acknowledge them by name until the desperate flutter of yellow wings stilled in his killing jar. The clouded yellow's fate was sealed.

Moments later, Harry dragged himself into Snell's tent and dropped to the ground. He yanked off his boots and gaiters. "God Snell, my feet hurt," Harry complained.

"You can't rest here, Cadet Crown," Snell snapped. "I'll mark you down as having reached this checkpoint. Use the other tent – and take your stinking boots with you. By the way, it's *Sergeant* Snell to you. When you speak, refer to me by rank."

Harry mumbled something under his breath as he struggled to his feet, then headed to the other tent in his socks, leaving his smelly boots behind to spite Snell. Jonathan stayed and approached Snell.

"How far to the base campsite, Sergeant Snell?" Jonathan asked.

"Four miles," Snell replied. "It's a hike through muddy marshland. But I'm not here to give you directions, Cadet Simon, look at your map!"

When Jonathan joined Harry in the second tent, the older boy was already asleep. Jonathan, tired and hungry, used the rest time to eat his last apple, and take a swig of water from his flask.

Twenty minutes later, Harry, wakened by Jonathan, yawned and unsteadily rose to his feet. He and Jonathan stepped outside. They saw four cadets from Plessey moving out.

Harry and Jonathan entered the tent. Harry looked to the left and right but didn't see his boots. "Where the hell are my boots and gaiters, Snell?" Harry asked.

"Don't ask me," Snell curtly replied. "I'm not your fucking valet. Over thirty boys have been in and out of here. Someone must have swiped them – God knows why?" Snell pointed to the flap of the other tent. "Wait there for transport. I'll have to mark down your mission as incomplete.

"As for you, Cadet Simon, there are only a few routes to the base campsite for the night. I'll designate you as taking the one through the marshes." Snell handed Jonathan a small map. "Continue on and don't forget to report to Officer Sleeth."

"But I can't go there by myself at night; it's too dangerous," Jonathan protested.

"Well, Crown can't continue without his boots. Simon, it looks like you're the last one – I can't pair you with any other group. So, you're on your own.

"Dismiss," was all Sergeant Snell had to say.

Outside Jonathan turned to Harry. "Let me have the compass."

Harry didn't want to give it to him and tried to protest. "You don't know what's out there, Jonathan."

"True, but I can't let them fail me." Jonathan grabbed the compass out of Harry's hand and pocketed it. "No choice… Gotta go, Harry… See you later."

After making sure Jonathan had left, and Harry had returned to the second tent, Snell checked and confirmed the schedule. A corps transport would arrive for him – plus one extra bootless cadet.

He went over to the second tent, and peeked in at Harry, already back to sleep inside. The coast was clear. Snell went back to his own tent, gingerly removed Harry Crown's filthy boots, which he'd concealed in a box under his table, and hurled them as far as he could into a distant field. Sleeth, he knew, wanted Simon alone on the moors.

★ ★ ★

As the sky darkened over the marshes, Jonathan tried to blank out fear. He trekked on, aware that somewhere along the trail, a ruthless enemy might be waiting.

It started to rain. Jonathan made his way on the designated route towards the campsite. By torchlight he cast an occasional glance at the map. He fretted how often the thick line indicating his pathway became dotted to indicate its disappearance underwater.

The surface of the water was black, putrid, and ice-cold as he waded cautiously across soggy cover. The marshes could be a trap. Sloshing across what looked like shallow water, he often found his footing give way beneath his boots. The next moment he'd be up to his waist in sludgy mud.

He stopped under a tree and waited and waited… until the pounding rain began to stop.

Despite the difficulty, Jonathan was determined to reach the campsite before dawn. In soggy denims and squelching boots, he cursed the fates that ordained he endure this predicament.

Out of the blackness, a large, indistinguishable shape was charging at him in a blaze of speed and light. Jonathan froze and tensed, expecting Sleeth, Tunk, or Miller to barrel into him in the next split second.

Jonathan heard a bleat, and a sheep whizzed past him, then vanished into the night. He closed his eyes, got a hold on himself, and laughed nervously at his fright. *I must have spooked it.*

Jonathan slogged on. He checked the map and the time on his watch – *I've an hour to go.*

Fifty-five minutes later, wet and shivering with cold, when he could hardly lurch forward another step, he was comforted to see the welcome sight of a carpet of lights and hear distant voices.

He'd reached the base camp in a wind-swept, moss-covered valley, surrounded by trees. Supplies were being packed, which included boxes of apples, tins of beans, and canvas tents. He couldn't believe that Sleeth hadn't ambushed him on the moors.

Jonathan knew he had arrived at the camp with only a minute or so left. A cadet shined a beam of light in his face and Jonathan shielded his eyes. He heard the voice of Sergeant Miller: "Cadet Simon? That you?"

"Yes, shut the light off, will you?" Jonathan said wearily. "What do you want?"

"Follow me," Miller growled. He turned around sharply and marched towards the largest tent.

Jonathan followed, dragging his feet all the way.

Per Sleeth's order, Miller had been stationed for quite some time, waiting for Simon to arrive. He knew something was up but wasn't privy to it. Miller was anxious to hear what Sleeth had in mind for Jonathan.

He held the door flap open, and as Jonathan went in,

Rodge gave Simon a swift kick in the behind to speed him along.

Sleeth looked up and said, "Thanks, Sergeant Miller. I'll take it from here. That will be all."

Miller was miffed as he'd been dismissed, but in the corps an order was an order. You didn't argue. So, without questioning his superior, Miller left.

Coleman lanterns lit the large tent. The two occupants were expecting him. Officer Sleeth, dressed in denims, belt buckles glimmering and boots shining, sat grim-faced on a fold-up chair. Sergeant Tunk, with a shifty look, also in denims, pointed Jonathan to a third chair.

Sleeth eyed Jonathan, suppressing a smile. Sleeth had planned to have Miller lie in wait behind a hedgerow, jump Jonathan from behind, then rub his face in sheep dung. Then Miller was to run off before Jonathan could identify his attacker. But with a new development involving Jim Bhasin, Sleeth now had an even better plan.

"Sit," Tunk said pleasantly. "We've been waiting for you, dear boy. How about some tea?"

"Yes," Jonathan replied, taken aback. He was wary of Tunk's nonchalant attitude and expected to be roughed up at any moment.

"I forget," Tunk went on casually. "Milk? Sugar?"

"Yes, both," Jonathan replied.

Tunk passed him a hot mug of tea, which Jonathan eagerly cupped in his hands to warm his fingers. He closed his eyes and sipped.

"I heard," Tunk said, "that Harry Crown abandoned

you. Too bad. Soon you'll have no friends left." Tunk added, "I'm afraid we've had some rather troubling news. Your pal, Bhasin, is in deep shit."

"What are you talking about?" Jonathan felt confused and wondered what the two had planned.

"Let me update you," Tunk said, smirking. He now adopted his signature pose with the points of his fingers touching, prayer-like. "It's like a game of chess, isn't it? Only on your side of the board, oh, dear me! …You have no pieces left."

Tunk looked up and glanced at Sleeth. "But, then again, Officer Sleeth, I always regarded Cadet Simon as a disposable pawn."

Sleeth looked on in silence. Just relishing the moment.

Tunk continued, "We call the Housemaster from an isolated telephone box each day and report in. It's hard to believe what he's told us."

Jonathan tried to gather his thoughts. "What? …Just tell me."

Sleeth beckoned to Tunk. "Sergeant, give me a few minutes with him alone."

Tunk wasn't happy about being dismissed, just when this was about to get good. But like Miller, he obeyed the order and left the tent. Jonathan knew that the moment he dreaded had come.

Sleeth began, "Since you arrived at Blackleigh you've been nothing but a thorn in my side. Now it's time to pay the piper."

"What do you mean?"

"Your friend, Bhasin, that insolent Indian, is about to be expelled in disgrace."

The news hit Jonathan like a thunderclap. "I don't believe you… What trumped-up crime is he accused of?"

"The Housemaster confronted Bhasin after he stole a Rolex watch from his study desk, and was later found in Bhasin's locker." Sleeth said. "Bhasin will see Dr Macleod on Monday. The Headmaster, not Morton, will make the final decision on Bhasin's future. As Head of House, I'm still duty bound to write a letter with my recommendation for Bhasin to take with him to the Head – as I did with Wynn. As of now, my letter will recommend immediate expulsion."

"Where's Jim now?" Jonathan asked.

"Isolated in the san, awaiting the Headmaster's return. A theft from a Housemaster's study is indicative of Bhasin's unstable state of mind. As of yesterday, he can no longer participate in school activities."

Jonathan was boiling inside, but his expression gave nothing away. He refused to give Sleeth that satisfaction.

Sleeth continued, "There's only one way Bhasin can be saved, and I hold the key."

"I'm listening." Jonathan was beginning to see where this was going.

"At the end of this term, you will tell Mr Morton and Mark Evans that *you've* decided not to return to Blackleigh. When they ask why, you'll just say, 'For personal reasons,' and leave it at that."

Jonathan was disgusted by the extent of Sleeth's ruthless conniving, but was determined to learn more without revealing his reaction to Sleeth's trap. "Go on," he said quietly.

"There's more," Sleeth went on. "You will swear an oath to me promising never to say anything negative about me or our relationship."

"I see. What reason would you give for letting Bhasin off the hook?" Jonathan asked.

"Leave that to me. The bottom line is that either you or your sidekick will leave Blackleigh. Of course, I'd prefer it be you."

"So, you want to hush up all the sick and perverted things you've done to those weaker than yourself, like rough sex with boys," Jonathan replied in anger.

Sleeth's eyes glinted, "I don't give a fuck *what* you think. I only care what you decide. Do you agree?"

Jonathan's mind was racing. After a moment, Sleeth prompted him, "Simon? Do you agree?"

"I need to know you'll keep your word," Jonathan said. "I'd like our agreement to be in writing. I want to see a letter from you recommending leniency and that Jim be allowed to stay. And that you'll separately guarantee he'll be free from harassment after I've gone."

Sleeth gave this some thought. "For that, I'd want you one hundred per cent committed to take Jim's place and leave. Naturally, Bhasin will, of course, be subject to an appropriate punishment for his crime."

"So," Jonathan repeated the agreement back to Sleeth, "you'll write a letter to the Headmaster recommending leniency rather than expulsion for Jim. I'll write one for you, acknowledging I'm willing to go in place of Jim.

Since neither of us trusts the other, let's exchange these letters at the same time."

"Yes, the exchange of letters will be in my study, after breakfast on Monday morning," Sleeth said.

"I'll agree to that if you will too," Jonathan said. "When the corps returns to Blackleigh on Saturday, I'll need to talk to Jim – to convince him that I want to switch places."

"Whatever happens, one of you goes."

Sleeth stood and barked, "That will be all, Cadet Simon. Dismiss."

30

ALAN PEARL

Mark Evans studied the junior sitting opposite in his study. As Head Boy, Mark had reached the top of the ladder at the school; meanwhile, the trembling boy was perched on the lowest rung in Waterloo. Prior to their meeting, Mark pinned a note outside on his study door that he wanted no interruptions.

He found Alan Pearl, small, with brown hair and wearing glasses, to be intelligent and amiable. Mark realised the junior would be nervous, so he tried his best to make him feel comfortable.

"Alan," he said, deliberately calling the boy by his first name, "I want to ask you about that time your wallet was stolen. I looked over my notes and I've unanswered questions."

"I understand," Pearl replied. "Am I in trouble?"

"No, you're not. I'm sure you've heard that that Callum Davies had a fatal accident in Enderby."

Alan quietly said, "Yes… but I didn't know him."

Mark went on, "Well, you can understand why we need to review what happened, especially as you're the other boy whose wallet was stolen."

"What do you need to know?" Pearl asked.

"I looked through my earlier notes of the meeting you had with your Housemaster right after the Wynn incident. You said you didn't know when your wallet was stolen."

"That's right. I went to buy a few things, but it turned out that I couldn't pay for them. I thought I'd left my wallet back at the House. I've no idea how it ended up in Wynn's carrier bag."

"There must be a link between you and Davies, as both of you had your wallets stolen. So, think back… Did anyone talk with you, or brush close by, before you went to the cash register to pay?"

"Well… it's kind of embarrassing," Pearl replied. "A person did say a few words to me… about something he wanted."

"And that was…?" Mark followed up.

"I don't know if it's relevant."

"Go on, Alan."

"Well, he tapped me on the shoulder, and reminded me that I still hadn't given him my class notes for Mr Bathurst's History class, from three days ago."

"Why give another boy your notes? Doesn't he take them on his own?"

"I suppose so, but he told me that my notes are the best in the class. He doesn't like to take notes himself."

"But why help him?"

"It's something we agreed between us; I promised not to tell anyone. I can't see how this has anything to do with Wynn being expelled."

Evans put his hands together in a supplicating pose. "Alan, this is for me to work out, but I need your help. Small details can lead to big discoveries."

Alan became frustrated. "Yes, but you want *his* name. One rule they keep reminding me about here is that there's no snitching."

"As Head Boy I'm in charge of discipline. I've been instructed by the Headmaster, Dr Macleod himself, to get the truth about the Wynn matter. The consequences of your failing to give me this name could mean that Wynn was wrongfully expelled for a crime he didn't commit. Put yourself in Wynn's place. Would you want someone to withhold information that could prove you innocent in the name of honouring an old-fashioned school code?"

Alan gave this some thought. "Well, Evans, since you put it that way… but what does someone wanting my class notes have anything to do with the stolen wallets?"

"Let me ask you this: did this boy threaten you in any way?"

Alan blushed. "Well, he could make my life hell if I didn't cooperate."

"And you believed him?"

"Absolutely! I've heard the story: he and John Berge in his House had a disagreement. That night there was a dead rat in Berge's bed. In my case, he said he'd start by putting a dead rat in my bed and boasted that he'd already done the same thing to John Berge."

"Berge is in Hastings, so we're talking about a boy from there, who's also in your history class. *Who* is he?" Evans pressed. So much depended on Pearl's answer.

"Do I have to say?" Alan mumbled in a low voice.

"Do the right thing, Alan," Evans coaxed. "Yes!"

Alan paused and reflected. "His name is Nick… Nick Krill."

Evans let out a deep sigh. "Finally, we're getting somewhere. So far, I haven't had occasion to meet Krill. Tell me about him."

"Other than wanting my notes, Krill hardly speaks to me. He's got an innocent look… kind of like a fair-haired choir boy. You'd think butter wouldn't melt in his mouth. I look at him and think, 'How could this boy ever do anything wrong?' But believe me, he's trouble."

"Now I remember him. Didn't Krill have a role in the Trafalgar-Hastings House play?" Evans asked.

"Yes, in *Macbeth*," Alan replied. "He was the first witch. And Krill certainly cast a curse on me, even before he was in the play."

Mark closed his eyes briefly. He tried to piece together the jigsaw puzzle. The shock of what he now realised almost made him feel nauseous. But he had a connection between unrelated random events and a possible new suspect in the enigmatic Nick Krill from Hastings.

Davies was a Hastings first-term junior in the same dorm as Krill.

Evans then recalled the explosion before the witches' exit in the play. Krill was the first to back away from the cauldron. The uncontrolled blast could have injured both Simon and Bhasin. *Was Krill responsible for that too?*

Mark returned to the link to Alan Peal. Alan's wallet was found in Wynn's bag after Krill stopped to say a few words to him. Could Krill have taken both Pearl's wallet and Davies' at about the same time, one after the other?

In the silence, Pearl plucked up his courage and asked, "What are you thinking?"

"I want you to carry on normally," Evans replied. "Keep giving Krill your history notes. We can't alert him that he's under investigation. I'll take care of the rest. If you have any inkling of a problem, see me immediately. Alan, you're doing a great service for the school."

"Am I?" Alan said doubtfully.

"Yes," Mark said, smiling at the young boy. "Sometimes a little honesty is all it takes."

The phone rang on Evans desk. Alan knew that a private phone was a privilege extended to the Head Boy.

Evans picked up. "Hello… how are you?…Hold on a second, I'll be right with you.

"Alan, that's all for now. Thank you."

Alan left.

Mark resumed his call. "Good to hear your voice again… It's all arranged… We'll put you up at The Golden Harp in Enderby. Call me when you arrive, and we'll keep in touch."

31

JIM

Jonathan returned from the camp on Saturday evening. He knew he'd have to dig deeper than ever before to save Jim. If the decision came down to a choice between him or Jim leaving, he determined to bow out and let Jim stay. Jonathan also agonised as to whether Sleeth would keep his word.

He had to talk to Jim. The san was closed on the weekend, except for emergencies, with just a skeleton staff.

As he was leaving the House, Jonathan heard his name called. Harry Crown ran out to join him in the forecourt.

"It's great to see you," Harry said. "What a relief! You made it alone across the marshes."

"Thanks, but how about you with no boots? How did you get back?"

"That's a different story." Harry burst out laughing. "I never found my boots, and an army lorry drove me back to the main camp. After that experience, I came up with a great idea for next term.”

“Tell me.”

“I’ll transfer from the corps to the school’s small Air Force unit, where I’ll be free of Sleeth and those corps scum… and you know what?”

“Go on.”

“The Air Force doesn’t wear boots; rather black shoes! I’ll just brush my walking shoes, which I do anyway – takes me about five minutes, instead of two hours to spit and polish corps boots.”

“Will they teach you to fly?”

“Not a chance. The school Air Force is mostly theory. The one glider they have stays in the hanger. I doubt it could get off the ground, anyway.”

Jonathan debated whether to share his plight with Harry. In the end he decided best not. “Some people have all the luck.” Jonathan grinned.

“And so they should.” Harry winked.

Jonathan smiled and waved goodbye. Talking to Harry always made him feel better.

He reached the san and saw through a front window that the two duty-nurses were sitting together in the lighted front office. He immediately went around to the back of the building, and entered through a rear door that he knew was kept open for deliveries and medical supplies.

Inside, he walked along a short dark passage which opened out into a long, wide corridor extending to his left and to his right. There was a spare room at each end of the corridor. He turned right and crept along until he came to a closed door at the end. Jim would either be in this room, or the room at the other end of the building. Jonathan knocked softly and whispered, "Jim, it's me, Jonathan."

To Jonathan's relief, he heard Jim say, "I'm here."

Jonathan walked into a small room, to see Jim dressed, but lying on a bed reading George Orwell's *1984*. When he saw Jonathan, he cast the book aside.

"Thank God, you've come," Jim exclaimed, with tears in his eyes. "I'm so pleased you're back here, safe from Heathrick. I thought I'd never see you again. I'm sure you know what's happened. Here I am like a prisoner…"

"Yeah, I heard the story," Jonathan said and sat down on the bed.

"Thanks for not asking whether I'm guilty, Jonathan."

"C'mon, I know you'd never steal anything. The question is, who did? I know the 'why' already. It's part of the plot to send us packing."

"Whoever set me up did a great job. I can't answer the charges," Jim fretted. "What am I going to do?"

"There's a solution, but it comes at a high price."

"I dread to hear," Jim said.

"On the last night of camp, Sleeth made me an offer."

"What?"

"It's quite simple," Jonathan replied. "He wants me gone more than you. If I agree to leave Blackleigh, he'd recommend leniency for you."

"Oh NO! You can't agree to that. No way. Jonathan. I want no part of his offer. I hope that you're not even thinking of accepting it."

"I've already thought this through. If I take Sleeth's offer and leave, the deal will also be that there's no harassment of you. Sleeth must promise in writing that you'd be protected. Only then would I voluntarily leave."

Jim protested, "I'd rather live with the dishonour of being booted out of Blackleigh than live with the guilt of having you take my place."

"Look, Jim, I've already lost most of my friends. Ian Gracey and Arthur Crown last year, and this year Peter Wynn and now you. What would be the point of staying?" A weak argument, he knew, but Jonathan hoped Jim would bite. Saving his friend was Jonathan's foremost goal.

"C'mon, Jonathan, there must be something we can do!" Jim pleaded. "Think of something."

The challenge sent Jonathan's mind whirling. After a moment, his eyes lit up. "Well, I have one thought. We'd have to play our last card."

"What's that? Now you're talking."

"I do have an ally – Evans, the Head Boy. We see him together and explain our predicament. I've already told him, in general, what's going on."

"You know Evans?" Jim said, with surprise.

"Yes."

"Makes sense then… I'd go with you, but I can't leave this damn place. If anyone sees me out and about, I'm finished."

"At this point, you're already finished. What do you lose?" Jonathan pointed out. "It's dark and neither Dr Frank nor his nurse are around. The two nurses on duty are in the front office. Let's go to Waterloo and find Evans. Wear your duffle coat with the hood up. I'll go first. You follow a little behind, so it doesn't look like we're together. Then we'll take the basement tunnel."

Jim pondered briefly. Then, with a gleam of hope in his eyes, he said, "Well, it's better than hanging around here."

★ ★ ★

After checking that the corridor was clear, Jonathan and Jim left the san separately, through the rear door, and headed for Waterloo. Jim trailed about thirty yards behind Jonathan. They made their way along a path behind the classrooms. Although they passed a few boys on the way, they each reached and climbed the steps of the Administration Building without incident.

Both hurried through the deserted Assembly Hall and entered the small lobby at the far side. Seconds later, Jonathan, with Jim, hurried down the narrow metal steps with a decorated balustrade and handrail, and entered a long, poorly lit tunnel. Jonathan saw the Waterloo entrance at the far end and headed in that direction.

Just before the entry, there was an alcove in the wall.

"Wait here, Jim. I'll try to find Evans, and then I'll come for you."

Jonathan went on into the Waterloo lobby. He'd been there before and made his way towards Evans' study, hoping to find him there, even though it was late. On the way, he ran into Rimmer, a tall, brown-haired boy in Jonathan's French class, whom Jonathan often helped with his homework.

"Rimmer, do you happen to know where I can find Evans?" Jonathan asked.

"Yeah, he's in the Houseroom."

"Do me a favour. Could you ask him to meet me at his study?"

"Sure, Simon." Rimmer left to get Evans, while Jonathan went back to bring Jim.

"This is a surprise," Evans said when he saw the two standing outside his study door. "Come in… Jonathan, you and your friend take a seat."

They sat. Jonathan introduced Jim.

"As you probably know, I'm not meant to be here," Jim said. "I've been confined to the san."

"Then it's just as well I didn't see you," Evans quipped. "I know your situation, Jim. I was informed by Mr Morton."

Jim, now at ease, said, "I'm due to see the Headmaster Monday afternoon, when he'll probably expel me. Much depends on the letter I'll take with me from Sleeth with his recommendation."

"Then tell me your story, Jim."

Evans listened carefully, while Jim walked him through the series of events that led him to pleading his case here and now. Jim concluded, "Sitting in the san has given me plenty of time to think. Let's be logical about all of this. Why would I steal a watch I could never wear? Every boy in Trafalgar would recognise it. Mr Morton always wore it for special occasions."

"You could pawn it," Evans said, playing the devil's advocate.

"I thought you might say that," Jim said with a twinkle in his eye. "The watch is inscribed to Mr Alec Morton. A pawnbroker would pick up the phone and call him."

Evans nodded. "Two good points, Jim."

"Could Jenkins be involved?" Evans tossed out. "After all, Mr Morton told me that Jenkins reported that in the darkness he saw a figure run across the Houseroom and out through the side door."

"I believe Jenkins is innocent," Jim replied. "I know him. He's a first-term junior, and not the type who'd lie. I saw the look on his face when Mr Morton pulled his watch from my locker. Jenkins was in complete shock. He was brave to have reported all this to Mr Morton in the first place, and risked punishment when he admitted that he came down the stairs so late, when he should have been in bed."

"But there's an unusual element," Jonathan broke in. "Sleeth made me an offer at the camp. He said that he'd support Jim staying, if I agree in writing to leave Blackleigh at the end of this term and promise never to say anything negative about him and the despicable things he's done, while he's been here."

"Such as?" Evans prompted.

"There's the no snitching rule and 'I promised not to tell'." Jonathan threw his hands up in the air as if checkmated.

"Sleeth and I will formally exchange letters confirming our agreement on Monday morning."

"So much for justice," Jim huffed. "It bends in the wind."

"Is that so?" Mark commented thoughtfully. "Well, you boys just gave me an idea."

Both boys leaned forward in anticipation.

"For a start, Jonathan, tell Sleeth that you agree to his terms, and you're ready to leave Blackleigh." Evans paused before continuing. "Then in return, ask Sleeth to write a letter with his recommendation of leniency for Jim and giving his reasons. Jim, you'll take that letter to your Monday meeting with the Headmaster. Also, you'll remain in the san. It's the safest place for you right now.

"Jonathan, as soon as you exchange letters with Sleeth with your promise to leave Blackleigh and the conditions, I want a copy of those letters in my office Monday morning. I'll do the rest."

32

FACE-OFF

Alan Pearl left the chapel after the Sunday morning service. He was relieved only a few days remained in the term. But he was far from worry-free, after his meeting with Evans. Alan hoped he'd done right by revealing the name of his nemesis.

He returned to Waterloo, decided to go for a swim, and collected his towel and swimming trunks. This, he figured, would be a good time, when the makeshift pool would be deserted.

It was nearly a half-hour walk to the pool area of the lake, marked off by wooden planks adjacent to a changing hut.

With every step, Alan hurried, and wondered if he was being followed. As he increased his walking pace, he became ever more certain of footsteps somewhere behind him, matching his gait. With his heart pumping, Alan defiantly turned around, expecting to see Krill.

But… no one, just the open range of the golf course, absent players. *Is the pressure getting to me?*

Alan continued, aware that at some point after his meeting with Evans, Krill would confront him anyway for his latest class notes, as there was a history exam ahead.

By the pool area, Alan changed in the small hut and left his clothes on a bench. Outside, in swimming trunks, he walked along the path that led to the pool.

At the water's edge, Alan gingerly lowered himself into the pool. *God, the water's cold!* But swimming often helped clear his mind, even though his endurance was limited to two or three laps.

Alan cringed as the water level rose above his waist, and he plopped down further up to his neck. Then he put his head down under the water to wet his hair. Alan took a deep breath and swam the forty yards' length of the pool, pausing to catch his breath after he reached the far end.

His teeth were chattering. Alan wasn't sure whether he was shaking from the cold water or fear. But the image of Krill, with his cherubic face and innocent light blue eyes, had assumed the appearance of an angel of death in Alan's mind.

The awful question haunted Alan… *What might Krill do should he learn I snitched?*

The sun moved behind a cloud. Alan let his mind wander. At present, Krill wanted class notes; next term it could be much more. When Krill next confronted him, would he be able to act normally, like Evans had instructed him? Or would he overreact in some way and tip Krill off that something was up? Alan believed that with Krill's intuition, he could sense the thoughts of others.

Alan turned and with determination began his second lap.

He reached his starting point at the shallow end, held on to a raised wood plank at the right side of the pool with one hand, and with his free hand he wiped his watery eyes. His sight cleared and Alan gasped in shock.

Beside him, Krill sat on a towel, at the edge of the pool, his tanned feet dangling casually in the water. Krill was wearing a short-sleeved shirt and shorts. He greeted Alan with a smile.

"Pearl," Krill said as if to an old friend, "I came to see you."

"K-Krill, I can't talk n-now," Pearl stammered. "I'm cold, let me get out of the water." Alan thought, *Don't say anything to upset him.*

Krill frowned and his next reaction was to unleash a savage kick in Alan's face that connected with a harsh sound at the side of his jaw.

Alan clutched his chin and whimpered, "Why … Why do that?"

"To remind you to hold your tongue," Krill said pleasantly.

"Please, let me get out of the water."

"Have you snitched?"

"No… No," Alan replied.

"Right, let's find out for sure… First, hand me your swimming trunks."

Alan dared not argue. He took off his trunks in the water and handed them to Krill.

"Now, climb out," Krill said quietly.

Alan did so. He stood naked and freezing at the side of the pool, a hand over his genitals.

Krill, clutching the shorts, turned to face Alan. "That's better." He smiled. "While you were swimming, I hid your towel and clothes. You've nothing to wear until our little talk is over. Your glasses are on the bench in the changing hut. Go in there and wait for me."

Alan, shivering, did as he was told. In the hut, he found his glasses, put them on, and sat, dripping wet, on a bench. He crossed his legs and wrapped his arms around himself while he waited for the unpredictable Krill.

The door of the changing hut opened, and Krill walked in. He went over to Alan, cowering naked in the corner, and stood over him. Krill felt a thrill, a surge of inner power, having rendered this pathetic boy so helpless. Yet his facial expression gave nothing away.

"Pearl," he said, "for the last time, did you blab?" Krill raised his right hand and balled it into a fist.

"Hold off." Pearl raised his hand, surprised by his own courageous response. "If I talked, you'd already know." Alan was unsure what to say next, but he recalled Evans' advice to carry on normally with Krill as if nothing had happened. The words came tumbling out of his mouth. "After you threatened me in the shop, I found my wallet missing. If I'd accused you, something would have happened by now. But no one has questioned you, have they? That's because I never reported you."

Alan, feeling even braver, added, "Hit me again and that's the last you'll see of my history notes. Our exam is in three days. Leave me alone. I mean it."

Nick Krill was taken aback to hear a boy standing up to him – something he had rarely experienced. He reflected, *Pearl has a point.* Until now, no one had spoken to him about Wynn. Maybe his treatment of Pearl was overreacting. Besides, he desperately needed Alan's notes for the exam.

Nick relaxed and said, "Alright, I believe you."

Alan let out a sigh of relief.

"I'll give you back your clothes, but I want those notes tomorrow by midday."

Alan nodded. "I promise."

Krill opened one of the six swimming lockers, reached in, then tossed Pearl's clothes and towel in a heap on the wet floor.

Krill walked out, leaving the hut door open behind him.

Alan, now alone, thanked heaven for his deliverance. In a strange way, fate had intervened. If Krill hadn't been lying in wait, Alan would never have known how brave he could be.

33

JIM'S LETTER

On Monday afternoon, Jim arrived on time for his appointment and sat waiting in the Headmaster's foyer. He had an unopened letter with him, sealed in an envelope, and addressed to the Headmaster. Mrs Macnally told him that Dr Macleod would see him shortly.

Jim reviewed in his mind what had happened that morning. Jonathan told him that he'd met with Sleeth and insisted on reading Sleeth's leniency letter first. Once satisfied that it was legitimate, Jonathan had handed Sleeth his resignation letter. Sleeth allowed Jonathan to leave his study, after Sleeth was satisfied with Jonathan's letter.

Before he left, Jonathan had asked for an envelope to make it official, and Sleeth handed him one with his name stamped on the top left-hand corner. Jonathan had put the letter inside and sealed it shut. Jonathan then came to the san and handed Sleeth's letter to Jim.

Jim was now seeing the Headmaster per the new school protocol where the Head had the final say about his fate. Jim knew he had to act as if he didn't know the contents of Sleeth's letter in front of Dr Macleod.

His thoughts were interrupted by the house phone ringing on Mrs MacNally's desk; she told Jim that the Headmaster was ready to see him.

Jim entered the expansive study. He was taken aback to see Dr Macleod with Mark Evans, next to each other at a round table on the side of the room. Dr Macleod pointed to an empty chair opposite them and Jim sat.

"Jim Bhasin," the Headmaster opened. "You should have a letter with you for my attention."

Jim was jittery. Evans nodded a greeting and said, "Just relax, Jim."

The Headmaster continued, "We understand you're going through a hard time, but it's a small part in the larger picture we're investigating. I'm sorry that due to my absence you've had to wait in the san."

"Thank you, sir."

"Let me see the letter from Sleeth." The doctor held out his hand. Jim passed the envelope over to him. The doctor opened the envelope, and he and Mark read the contents together. Neither showed any emotion.

"I'll cover some key points," the doctor said.

"First, it is apparent that Sleeth never interviewed you about this matter. His recommendation is based from a conversation he had with Mr Alec Morton."

Jim who, of course, already knew the contents of the letter and was playing along that he was hearing it for the first time, appreciated that the doctor had identified Sleeth's lack of involvement.

The doctor went on, as he looked at the letter, "James Bhasin is accused of stealing a Rolex watch from Mr Morton's study. A witness, Christopher Jenkins… stolen property… discovered in Bhasin's locker. Bhasin denies the accusations."

The doctor paused and looked at Evans. "Here's where it gets interesting – Hugh continues, 'I believe we should avoid a rush to judgement. In my opinion leniency with a punishment rather than immediate expulsion is the wisest course of action. It will be necessary to impose the punishment next term, to impose a serious punishment and to make an example of Bhasin. Blackleigh will understand that, while theft and dishonesty cannot be tolerated, we're not entirely heartless.'"

Jim had rolled his eyes and acted surprised when he heard that Sleeth didn't recommend immediate expulsion. Then he shook his head and acted upset over the idea that he should be severely punished for his crime.

"We'll discuss this," the doctor said, "before making a rational decision how to proceed. I'd like your response, Bhasin, to the charges against you."

"Mr Morton's watch did turn up in my locker; but I didn't steal it."

"So, what's your explanation?" the Headmaster asked.

Before Jim could answer, Evans held up a hand to answer him, then spoke on Jim's behalf. "Without going into details, sir, I've already had a discussion with Jim on the subject. He made a solid point: why steal a watch with the owner's name engraved on it? That will come back to bite you. While I've no idea who masterminded this, I'm convinced Jim was framed.

"Sleeth is recommending leniency for Jim because he made a separate agreement with Jonathan Simon that Jonathan would agree to leave Blackleigh instead of him."

Jim saw Mark Evans directly glance at the Headmaster, then Mark said, "Jonathan Simon brought his letter to me before delivering it to Sleeth, and I made a copy, which is in my study desk drawer."

"Understood," the Headmaster replied. "Also, have you made any progress on the Peter Wynn case?"

"Sleeth is still stonewalling me. He hasn't provided me with additional information on the dismissal of Peter Wynn. But I'm following up later this afternoon. In the meantime, I'd like to suggest we briefly delay a decision on how we handle Jim's situation while we continue to investigate the matter and try to learn who else might be involved. We absolutely must find out who stole the watch from Mr Morton's study, so Jim's innocence is clearly established."

"I agree, Mark." The doctor nodded. He turned to Jim. "Sleeth should think we're seriously considering his recommendation. So, for the time being, Jim, I must ask you to stay in the san. But rest easy, Evans will come and check on you each evening."

Jim was greatly relieved. Things had turned out beyond his wildest hopes. He could hardly believe the outcome of the meeting.

"Our task here is like lifting a huge boulder," Dr Macleod went on. "Beneath is an ugly, black mass of deceit and injustice festering at our school for years. I intend to root out this evil.

"I'm sure you recall, Jim, a line in *Macbeth*. 'So far… we have scotched the snake not killed it.'"

Jim was excused and he left.

The Head said to Evans, "He's a fine young man. I'll do all I can for him."

Evans replied, "I have two meetings scheduled for this afternoon, and I'd like to use your office, for effect, rather than my own study. This formal setting should make the first individual uneasy. I want him to believe that at any time you might walk in. Then I've another meeting set for an hour later. Mrs Beal from Hastings will handle the logistics. Will that be an inconvenience, sir?"

"Not at all. Who are you meeting first?"

"Nicholas Krill," Evans replied.

34

KRILL'S MEETING

At five o'clock on Monday afternoon, Mrs MacNally looked up as the double doors to the Headmaster's offices swung open. She was taken aback to see a good-looking junior, fair-haired, with light-blue eyes, swagger in.

"How can I help you?" she asked.

"Maybe there's a mistake," Krill replied, "but Evans left a note for me to come here. This is inconvenient."

"Well, take a seat. He'll be with you shortly. What's your name and House?"

"Nicholas Krill… I'm in Hastings." He chose to stand rather than sit. "Will this take long?" he asked.

The House phone rang on Mrs MacNally's desk. She picked up, listened, then nodded to Krill. "You won't have to wait. He can see you now."

Krill entered Dr Macleod's office, expecting to see the Headmaster. He was surprised to find the Head Boy sitting at a table on the near side of the room.

Nick's plan was to offer up as little as possible, gather information, and try to learn what Evans' approach would be. Up until now, he'd only seen the Head Boy from afar, and Nick was intrigued by the senior, who was selected to occupy such a position of power in the school.

"Nick Krill from Hastings," he said. "You wanted to see me, Evans."

"Yes, Krill, thank you for coming in." There was an awkward silence as Evans waited for Krill to speak. But the boy just stood there looking as pure as the driven snow.

"We're holding a series of meetings," Evans finally spoke, "so I'm borrowing Dr Macleod's office."

"Will he attend?" Krill asked.

"The doctor may come by. Please sit down." Evans pointed to one of the empty chairs at the table.

"I'm already late." Krill made a show of looking at his watch. "I have someone waiting."

"Then I'll try not to keep you long," Evans answered politely. "Please sit. Who's waiting, if I may ask?"

"Every week at this time I call my father. He's on the board of the National Provincial Bank," Nick announced. "If I wait too long, he might get worried." Nick never called his dad ever. But this provided an opportunity for him to have a reason to leave the study if things started to go downhill for him. He planned to say to Evans, "My father will be really worried by now. I seriously need to call him." Then get up and go.

"Then I'll get to the point," Evans said. "I'm seeing you about Callum Davies, the Welsh boy who was killed in Enderby. We know that he pretty much kept to himself, but we're interviewing boys who may have known him, hopefully to shed some light on what happened."

Nick's expression showed some concern. "I thought the police ruled his death an accident."

"Yes, they did," Evans acknowledged, "but I'm trying to learn more about Davies' state of mind at the time. You and Davies were in the same dorm at Hastings."

"Yes, but I didn't really know him well," Krill replied. "Like you said, he was a loner."

Evans felt that it was time to raise the stakes and gauge Krill's reaction. "We have reason to believe that someone was intimidating boys in your dorm."

"Intimidating how?"

"Threatening to put a dead rat in boys' beds," Evans pressed. "I hear it actually happened to Berge in your House. What do you know about that?"

"Evans, you know how boys are here. They love rumours," he replied noncommittedly.

Evans considered the boy sitting opposite. Krill… Smart, confident, gives the impression of sincerity and innocence… his responses sound believable.

He decided to be more direct with his questions. "We spoke to Don Fry and asked for a list of boys in his shop at the time Callum Davies' and Alan Pearl's wallets were found in Peter Wynn's bag. Not only were you on the list, but he remembered seeing you talking to Davies."

"How can you expect me to recall so far back? Where's all this going?"

Evans went on, "Callum came to see me a few days before he died. He was afraid… told me that someone had threatened him. He wouldn't give me the name. Since you're both in the same dorm, Perhaps you know who it was?

"Even if I did, there's a school code… And this has nothing to do with me."

"I'm aware of the code," Evans said with some frustration, "otherwise this investigation would be over by now, and the guilty punished.

"After Wynn's father demanded a thorough report," Evans said. "I spoke with Davies and Pearl to see what they could tell me. Neither could say he was a hundred per cent certain that Wynn stole the wallets. I had the distinct feeling that it wasn't because of the no-snitching code. Rather that they were both being intimidated by someone. Perhaps it was the same someone who put rats in boys' beds? So, help me here, Nicholas. For the sake of argument, let's say that it wasn't Wynn who stole the wallets…"

"But it was Wynn. Everyone knows that," Nick broke in.

Nick shot a glance at his watch and then the door.

Evans readied to reveal the surprise he had for Krill. Don Fry had also told Mark that he recalled seeing Nick talking to Pearl in the shop.

Evans took a long pause. "Let's talk about Alan Pearl. You and him are not in the same House, correct?"

Based on their conversation at the pool, Nick trusted Pearl had kept his mouth shut… So, he decided to deny any knowledge of him. Because if he didn't take Pearl's wallet, Evans would have to look for another boy. "Alan Pearl?" Nick said with a blank face. "Don't know him, even though he's in one of my classes."

"Excuse me a minute. I have to make two calls." Evans got up and went to the phone on Dr Macleod's desk, then buzzed Mrs Macnally. "Send him in."

He then dialled another in-house number. "Hello, it's Evans, Mrs B… Go ahead with the arrangements we discussed. Yes, check everything. Call me back in the Headmaster's office." Evans returned to the table.

"I'm done with this fishing expedition," Krill retorted dismissively.

There was a knock at the door. Alan Pearl tentatively walked in. "Hello, Nick," he said pleasantly.

Krill registered shock to see him, but quickly recovered. "Good one, Evans," he said.

Alan ignored Krill. The tension in the study became almost tangible.

"Krill is helping me with some enquiries, Pearl. I asked you here as I have questions for you both. Take an extra chair at this table."

Alan didn't want to sit next to Krill. He picked up a chair, lifted it, and put it on Evans's other side.

"Pearl, there's a great deal at stake here," Evans said. "Think back to when your wallet was stolen."

Evans had Pearl state that Krill briefly stopped him in the shop that Thursday to remind him that he wanted his class notes. Alan realised that right after Krill had badgered him, he had found his wallet missing.

While Evans and Pearl spoke, Krill looked around the room and whistled through his teeth, as if the conversation had nothing to do with him.

"Krill, pay attention," Evans ordered. "Here are my questions for you. Did you steal both Pearl's and Davies' wallets and drop them in Peter Wynn's canvas bag?" Evans pressed on, "And was your goal to throw suspicion on Peter Wynn for stealing and have him expelled?"

Krill remained silent.

Evans turned to Pearl. "Since the theft, have you two spoken about the stolen wallets?"

Alan glanced over to see Krill staring fixedly ahead.

"Well, we've had difficult conversations." Alan paused, before becoming bolder. "Only yesterday, Krill trapped me in the swimming pool and warned me to keep my mouth shut about the Wynn situation."

"This proves nothing," Krill retorted. "It's still his word against mine. Pearl's a naughty boy for spreading a pack of lies."

"I've heard enough, Krill," Evans snapped. "You'll see the Headmaster at ten tomorrow morning. In the meantime, you probably heard me on the phone when I spoke to Mrs Beal, your House matron. She will bring over any personal effects you may need."

"Why call her?" Krill demanded. "She has nothing to do with this."

Evans continued, "You will be spending your time in the san, until the Headmaster can meet you tomorrow morning. Meals will be served there. You may not attend classes or participate in any sporting events. You are also forbidden to talk with anyone apart from the nurses at the san.

"In the meantime, to ensure that you go directly there, Brian Devine, your Hastings Head of House, is waiting in the lobby outside. He will personally check you into the san. Further, the staff at the san have been told that you cannot leave the facility until your meeting with the Headmaster tomorrow morning."

"You haven't heard the last from me," Krill said calmly. "You don't know who you're dealing with." He turned to Alan. "And as for you… I thought we were friends." Krill left the study without another word.

When he was sure Krill was gone, Alan said, "I wouldn't want to face him again. After I learned that my wallet was found in Wynn's bag, I was as stunned as he must have been."

"And why was that?" Evans prompted.

"Because," Pearl continued, "the whole time I was in the shop, Peter Wynn and I were never within ten feet of one another."

"How can you say this for sure?"

"Wynn was over by the clock shelf, setting off alarms, and irritating nearly everyone in the shop. I didn't want to go near him."

Evans said, "It was very courageous of you to volunteer to come and testify against Krill."

"Thank you," Alan replied. "Believe me, I gave this a lot of thought. In the end I realised that sometimes, no matter whatever the consequences, you just have to do what's right."

And with that, Alan about to leave, said at the door, "I don't know what I'd have done without your help. It's taken a weight off my mind." He closed the door quietly behind him.

Half an hour later, Mrs Beale called Evans back and said, "I found something interesting I think you should see."

"What did you find? …Then say nothing… Wrap it in paper and have Gooding bring it over to me at the Headmaster's office. It's important that we don't reveal this until we're ready."

Evans put the phone down. He slammed the top of the desk with his open palm and exclaimed, "YES!"

35

A GOLD BRACELET

Nick Krill spent the night in the san. At ten o'clock on the following morning, he was escorted by Devine, then Mrs MacNally led him into Dr Macleod's office. Krill stood and waited for the doctor to offer him a chair. Meanwhile, Dr Macleod was preoccupied at his desk, studying the contents of an opened package. The brown paper wrapping hid the contents from Nick's view.

Finally, the Head looked up at Nick, and without a word pointed to a chair, facing him on the other side of his desk.

As Nick sat, he thought, *I'll admit nothing to the old coot.*

Finally, Dr Macleod spoke. "Nicholas Krill, I'm sure you know why you're here."

"No idea, sir," Nick said calmly, "but I saw Evans yesterday. He badgered me with false accusations. I couldn't believe my ears."

"I've spoken with Mark Evans," the Head replied. "Your House matron was collecting possessions from your Hastings locker to send over to the san for you and found this small package."

Krill waited as Dr Macleod proceeded to uncover the wrapping to reveal a small diary.

"I believe this is yours, Krill… Here's your name on the inside cover. You've made brief diary entries since the beginning of the school year. On certain dates you've written names. Among them are James Bhasin, Jonathan Simon – mentioned numerous times – then there's Peter Wynn, Callum Davies, and Alan Pearl. The name Olivia also appears.

"I find it interesting that some dates relate to days when crimes occurred involving these boys. Most recently when the corps were attending camp, you wrote 'Bhasin… Trafalgar', followed by a star, which I assume represents a success. This was on the same night a Rolex watch was stolen, and subsequently found in Bhasin's locker."

"I've nothing to say," Krill replied, stunned by the development.

"My reasonable conclusion is that you are responsible for numerous crimes, where others have been wrongly blamed. On the day that Jonathan Simon's bike was tampered with, but he wasn't badly hurt, there's an exclamation mark beside his name. The night of the cauldron explosion in the play, the same thing. However, next to Peter Wynn's name on the day he was expelled there is a star. And you put an exclamation mark after

Jim Bhasin the night of the watch theft, which indicates a near miss. That was crossed out and replaced by a star on the day he was sent to the san. How do you explain this?"

Nick gave no response.

Dr Macleod continued, "But here's what I find most interesting. I see no motive. There's nothing for you, a junior, to personally gain by targeting these particular boys. On the other hand, there are some seniors, who, without revealing how I know, have an agenda to remove from Blackleigh, certain juniors they deem as 'undesirables'. I'm going out on a limb to suggest that one of these seniors put you up to all this."

Nick maintained a poker face.

Dr Macleod could see that he was wasting his time. "I need you to think about this. That's why the san is a suitable place for you. It's a place where you can think things over and stay until the end of term. In the meantime, I want you to think about your future and who you'll be loyal to at your own peril. Because someone is going to pay. If the name of your co-conspirator should happen to come to you, we'll talk again, and I will factor your cooperation into my final decision of how I shall deal with you, Nicholas Krill, and what I will write in my letter to your parents."

Nick remained silent, and with no change of expression when Brian Devine walked in, took him by the arm, and led him to the san.

★ ★ ★

Around ten in the evening Rodge Miller snuck into the san. He went up to one of the backroom doors, put his ear to it, and heard nothing. He then went down the corridor, put his ear to the second door, and heard Nick whistling the tune, "Singing the Blues". Rodge knocked twice, so as not to startle Nick, then entered. To Miller's surprise, Nick's countenance was anything but bluesy.

Miller said, "When you failed to show at our usual meeting place, I did some investigatin'. I learned from boys in yer dorm that you were bein quarantyned in the san. Why are you here?"

"I face almost certain expulsion," Nick replied.

"What!" Rodge exclaimed.

"I went too easy on Pearl and he ratted on me." Nick continued with unintended irony, "What has become of integrity in this place?"

"Did Bhasin's name come up when you saw the Headmaster?"

"Not specifically. The doctor was too busy asking whose orders I followed. Of course, I haven't told him. Bhasin is also in the san, and pretty much keeps to himself."

"I don't know wot to say, Nick." Miller paused, overwhelmed by the frustrating turn of events. "I feel bad for you. We're a team… We work so well togever. Still, I need to ask a delicut question: can they pin 'anyfing' on me?"

"I don't see how," Krill said, as he shrugged his shoulders. "Not unless I were to finger you."

"Wiv yer silence you've done right," Rodge commented, looking relieved. "What happens now?"

"Because of our long-term relationship, my silence will cost you only five quid a fortnight, for as long as you're at Blackleigh. You can send it to me in the post at whatever school I land in next."

"Wow, that's a hell of a lot for me to pay for keepin' *your* trap shut," Rodge complained.

"Not really, Rodge. You get to stay on here; I take the full blame. So, that's why I also expect something else besides this twice-monthly stipend, for my trouble."

"Am I hearin' right?" Rodge asked, glaring at Nick. "What now?"

"How about that gold bracelet you're wearing? I've always fancied it. Luckily, you haven't put your initials on it yet. Probably cost me, I mean you, a fiver to have it engraved – with *my* initials, of course."

Rodge stared back at his young protégé, stunned by Nick's outlandish proposals. He weighed his options, then said, "If you were anyone else, I'd knock your block off."

"But you won't, will you?" Nick said, smiling. "C'mon, you've got what you want, and you're off scot-free."

Rodge considered the situation. "Blimey, you've some nerve! Even so, after all we've been through... I 'spose you've earned it."

Rodge added with a shrug, "One way or another we'll have a great future." He took off his gold bracelet and gave it to Nick. "Here – don't forget to keep yer mouth shut."

"Thanks, Rodge, I'm glad you see it my way. Don't forget the extra fiver for the engraving. And I've an extra bonus for you too – free advice."

Rodge took out five pound notes from his wallet which he handed to Nick, who promptly pocketed them. "What's yer advice?"

"Here's what I know," Nick said. "One or more seniors are going down. Simon is going to triumph. Which side do you want to be on? The winning or the losing?"

"Winnin', of course," Miller replied.

"Then you'd better get ahead of the game – ahead of the others."

"How?" Miller looked completely stumped.

"Get yourself in Simon's corner," Nick said resolutely.

"But," Miller protested, "after all I've done to him, how do I get Simon to believe me?"

"Simple," Nick said. "Evans doesn't believe Bhasin took the watch. Side with Bhasin and Simon will become a believer.

"Making up with Simon will be a hard about-face for you, but it's the only way out of this mess."

Miller paused while he thought over Nick's advice. "Makes sense," Rodge agreed. "I thought there'd come a day when I'd have to shaft Sleeth. But wiv your input and my great loyalty to the school, I'll drop him pronto. What will I do wivout you?"

"To tell you the truth, Rodge, I'm tired of this place. It was fun while it lasted."

"Nick, even though we're good, you may 'ave a problem explainin' your departure to yer parents. How you gonna handle them?"

"They aren't a problem… piece o' cake! They are not going to find out that I was expelled. Letters from the school often get lost at the house. That's what'll happen to the nasty one being sent at the end of this week from the Headmaster.

"So, what'll you say?"

"That I'd prefer to be at a school in London because Blackleigh isn't challenging enough. They won't follow up; they never do. In fact, I'll tell them that Blackleigh gave me this gold bracelet, with my initials on it, as an academic award for history. They'll love that! But, Rodge, what about your parents, when they notice your bracelet is missing?"

"I'll say someone stole it," Rodge replied. "You can't trust anyone these days. That way, Dad will buy me anover one wiv me initials. And if they ever see you wearin' your bracelet, they'll know it's not mine, as yours' will have NK engraved on the back."

"Sounds good. So now we're settled. I'll rest up at the san for now and get ready for my next adventure. See you over the holidays. Don't do anything I wouldn't do."

"Believe me, Nick, that gives me plenty of leeway. That's why we get along so well."

Nick sat back on his bed and stared with pride at his bracelet. As Miller left the room, he glanced back and saw a boy who didn't have a care in the world.

36

MILLER'S MOVE

Jonathan hurriedly dialled Olivia's number from the lobby phone in the Administration Building.

"Hello, it's me. I survived the camp," he greeted her.

"Great," she chirped. "I've been thinking of you. I'm so glad you're in one piece."

"I'll bring you up to date. I'd love to see you," he said.

"Alright, how about we meet at the usual place in Enderby… tomorrow, Thursday?"

"Ace," he said with relief, his heart thumping. "It's the end of term. No one's going to be following me."

"I've a surprise," she told him.

"Tell me!"

"But, Jonathan, then it wouldn't be a surprise," Olivia said coyly.

"Alright, I'll wait."

"See you soon," she said and gave the receiver a little kiss.

Jonathan put down the phone feeling energised. As he crossed the assembly, he saw Miller coming his way, from the opposite direction.

Jonathan was taken aback when Miller signalled by pointing a finger at him. *What the hell does he want now?*

"Just the person I'm lookin' for," Miller said cordially. "You and I should talk. Join me on a bench outside… under them trees."

Jonathan found Miller's amiable approach so unexpected that he wasn't sure that he'd heard him. But he followed Miller outside and down the steps, wondering what he was up to this time.

Miller sat at one end of a bench on the grass, on the south side of the Administration building. Jonathan joined him, at the other end of the bench, leaving plenty of space between them. Jonathan never knew quite what to expect from Miller, so he waited for him to speak.

Miller took in a lungful of air, blew it out, then turned towards Jonathan. "It's like this," Miller began. "I bin thinkin'… you and I started on the wrong foot. I've come to see that I picked the wrong side," Miller pretended to confess. "At first, bein' with Sleeth made the most sense, given Sleeth's position as Head Prefect. Sleeth promised to promote me as prefect in the House and make me a sergeant in the corps. But there was a price. I had to do what he told me. But Sleeth took things too far this term, and we stopped seeing eye to eye."

"How am I supposed to believe you?" Jonathan challenged him.

"You were at the camp and also there in his tent – remember how Sleeth dismissed me?"

Miller then brought up the incident at the Performing Arts Building. "That wasn't my idea," Miller claimed. "Sleeth put me up to it. He also paid some boy to follow you into Enderby – I've no idea who – then sent me to mess with you and Butterfly."

"Buttercup," Jonathan corrected him.

"I'd like to fink that, between us, it's water under the bridge. Anyway, sorry for gettin' carried away. Please give me apologies to the girl."

Jonathan didn't know whether to believe him or not.

"And, I've been thinkin' about your pal Bhasin's situashun," Rodge went on. "To tell you the truff, I always had me serious doubts as to his guilt."

Jonathan was rendered speechless. Miller's doubts were news to him.

Miller expostulated, while motioning with his heavy arms. "I know, Simon, what others would say. 'Rodge boy, wise up, there's clear evidence of Bhasin stealing from Mr Morton.'

"But I say… Rodge, you're the prefect in charge of Bhasin's dorm… Do you remember seeing 'im leave his bed that night when things went missin', even to pee? My answer is no! So how could he pull off a bloody burglary from the Housemaster's study? Besides, Bhasin isn't the type and I never believed it was him. Who did it then? Beats me. I'll bet Sleeth had a hand in this, too," he lied.

Jonathan was astonished by Miller's complete turnaround. He knew that Sleeth had pleaded for Jim's leniency with a harsh punishment, next term, and most thought Jim guilty.

Jonathan said, "If you're convinced Jim is innocent, you need to send a note about this to the Headmaster before it's too late."

"You took the words out of me mouth. I wrote a short note today and dropped it off with Mrs Macnally. Comin' from there, who do I run into but my next stop: you!"

"That's great!" Jonathan said. "Well, I take you at your word. You've really surprised me."

"I'll tell you, from now on, you got Rodge Miller in yer corner – coz I had a revelashun. Know wot I mean?"

"You mean a revelation?"

"Right, that's what I said."

Miler gave Jonathan a light, friendly shoulder jab, hopped to his feet, and strutted away.

37

TURMOIL

Wednesday evening after supper, Sleeth and Tunk conferred in Sleeth's study. Sleeth paced the room with frustration, while Tunk sat back calmly in an single armchair, the palms of his hands and fingers together.

"I've yet to send Evans that additional Wynn report we worked on," Sleeth said. "I held off until we needed to provide it. But I don't know what the fuck's happening." Sleeth smashed his huge fist into his open palm. "I exchanged letters of our agreement with Simon. Bhasin delivered his letter to the Headmaster. Since then I've heard nothing. I expected a response from Evans, and I don't trust silences."

"What exactly, my dear fellow, do you need to know?" Tunk asked. "In exchange for Bhasin, Simon has agreed to leave the school. You couldn't get rid of Simon and Bhasin, but let's face it, Simon is the one you most want out."

"Here's my worry," Sleeth countered, his bullet-head wet with perspiration. "I sent Croat to see Mrs MacNally today at the Head's office to learn the latest news about Bhasin. She told Croat that because the matter doesn't involve him, she's not at liberty to say. Why is such a simple task taking so long?"

"Then, Hugh, what, pray tell, do you propose to do?" Tunk asked, losing patience.

"Mr Morton informed me that Bhasin is being held in the san, in one of two small patient recovery rooms. The place has a minimum staff at night. I say, we pay a visit to Bhasin and learn exactly what's going on. We could reach his room through the back entrance, and no one would know."

"Then what?" Tunk shook his head. *What's all this "we" business?* Tunk thought, but kept a straight face, reflecting on the untenable position Sleeth placed him in. If anything went wrong as a result of a rash move, Sleeth wouldn't think twice about sacrificing him. This was a turning point in their relationship. Tunk could see a red stoplight flashing in his mind.

He tried to get through to Sleeth one more time. "Look, Hugh, you've already snared Simon. Even if we get to Bhasin and try and find out what's happening, there's no guarantee he'll talk, or tell us the truth."

"Believe me, Tunk, I have ways to make him talk… and truthfully."

"I suppose you're asking me to go with you," Tunk concluded. "If you insist, I will, but it's dangerous. We should each wear a duffle coat with the hood up to hide our faces… and we'll need torches. When do you want to go?"

"Now," Sleeth replied. "No time like the present."

"You're the boss," Tunk reluctantly agreed.

Upon reaching the san, only one room in the front far right of the facility had a light on. Sleeth and Tunk slipped round to the back of the property and entered through an unlocked door. Once inside, they tiptoed by torchlight to the wide corridor.

"Someone needs to be on the lookout," Sleeth said, "in case a nurse comes back here. I'll keep my eyes peeled. Lean on Bhasin hard – get him to talk. You know how to do it. This doesn't take two of us."

Tunk didn't know what Sleeth was up to, but… in for a penny, in for a pound.

"The two rooms kept free are at opposite ends," Sleeth explained. "You go to the room at the far left. Signal me with your torch when you find Bhasin. I'll wait here. The two patient rooms are at opposite ends," Sleeth whispered. "Try the room at the far right first, but leave the door open, if Bhasin is inside. I'll wait here."

"Shouldn't we go together?" Tunk insisted.

"I'm Head of House, don't question me," was the abrupt response.

Sleeth's plan was that if he heard a nurse coming, he'd warn Tunk and both would run together. But only if Sleeth felt that there was time. If not, Sleeth would bolt, leaving Tunk on his own. No way could Sleeth explain to Evans or the Housemaster what he was doing in the san, and he had enough faith in Tunk that he'd trained him well… *And Tunk has too much pride to snitch on me, even if he knew I'd deserted him.*

Tunk followed Sleeth's instructions, but not without resentment. *Why,* he wondered, *do I always play second fiddle to Sleeth's hair-brained schemes?*

Tunk crept along the corridor.

At the far end he paused at the door, turned off his torch, slowly turned the handle, and stepped into the small room. Tunk stood motionless, letting his eyes get accustomed to the dark. He then made out a shape in the bed – a mound under a blanket.

I'll give Bhasin the shock of his life, Tunk thought gleefully. With that, he turned on the ceiling light. "Greetings, Bhasin! It's talky time!" he exclaimed.

The shape in the bed moved. The sleeper woke, threw back his blankets, and, to Tunk's astonishment, it wasn't Bhasin who sat up.

"Who the fuck are you?" the occupant exclaimed, rubbing his eyes.

The two stared at each other in confusion. Tunk realised he'd made a dreadful mistake.

"Y-you're Krill… first witch in *Macbeth*," Tunk stammered, as he recognised the boy. Tunk swiftly recovered his composure and added, "If memory serves, your performance as a witch was truly memorable."

"I know you too," Krill said, ignoring the compliment. "And if it isn't Lady Macbeth!" Krill countered. "Now Tunk, compliments aside, what the fuck are you doing in my room?"

"Sorry to barge in on you. I was looking for Bhasin," Tunk replied, as calmly as he could.

"No, he's in the spare room, at the other end of the corridor," Nick replied. Krill tossed a thumb in that direction.

Tunk played his hand. "I've a score to settle with the Indian."

Nick almost jumped on Tunk's comment, and said, "So do I." But he kept his mouth shut because he'd already worked out a way to handle this. His thinking was: if the Headmaster wanted anything known such as who the suspected thief was, he'd have already made an announcement by now. But Dr MacLeod hadn't, and wouldn't make any kind of announcement. The reason: there was more to lose by letting any of this go public. It would cast a negative light on the school. Who was to tell how many parents would withdraw their boys from Blackleigh next term with the theft of watches and wallets going on, and their boys coming home to tell them about it?

Nick would inform Dr MacLeod that if he found that his name had been tainted, he'd inform the press what a hot bed of evil, deceit, and larceny existed at Blackleigh – with boys tampering with bikes and cauldrons loaded with enough gunpowder to blow a head off. And so on. Nick concluded, *I'm not telling Tunk anything.*

Nick yawned, climbed out of bed, went to the adjoining toilet, took a long pee, and washed his hands in the sink. When he returned, he said to Tunk, "I need my beauty sleep." Nick faked a yawn. "Turn off the light on your way out and good luck with Bhasin."

His thoughts were disrupted by a noise outside Krill's door. Tunk heard footsteps in the corridor and assumed that Sleeth was headed his way. He flicked off the light and went to intercept him and to tell Sleeth that he was in the wrong room.

Tunk stepped out on the floor and froze when he saw Evans walking towards the room at the opposite end of the corridor. There was no sign of Sleeth.

Tunk backed back inside Krill's room. "What the hell! It's Evans."

Krill piped up from his bed, "Ooops, I should have warned you. Evans comes each night to check on Bhasin."

Tunk left the door open a crack and put his ear to it. "Shit," he whispered, "Evans must've heard something, he's coming this way." Tunk backed away from the door, frantically running options through his head. He watched as the door was cautiously pushed open, and Evans' silhouette appeared in the doorway.

Silence.

"Who's in here, Krill?" Evans said, reaching for the light switch. "You're not supposed to be…"

Before Evans saw anything, Tunk rushed at him, executed a perfect rugby tackle, and bowled him over. The Head Boy, caught by surprise, yelped with agony, fell, and in so doing cracked his elbow on the hallway floor. Somehow, Evans managed to crawl out through the open door and into the passage, where he lay moaning and holding his arm.

Tunk jumped over Evans' prostrate body, fled in the darkness, and kept on going. *Sleeth is on his own,* Tunk thought as he sped down the passage, burst out the back door, and into the night.

In response to the commotion, lights came on. Two nurses came to check on the noise. They had heard cries, saw Evans, and ran to him. The Head Boy painfully sat up as the nurses reached him.

Evans opened his eyes and saw Sleeth flee from a room along the corridor. He called out weakly, "Sleeth, what are you doing here?" Even in a dazed state, Evans was clear-headed enough to wonder if Sleeth had assaulted him.

Despite this activity, Jim Bhasin remained fast asleep in his room at the opposite end of the corridor.

When Sleeth had heard footsteps in the front office coming his way, rather than try to warn Tunk, he ducked into the janitor's closet. Sleeth listened at the door. He was surprised when he heard Evans' voice, then moments later, Evans yelling and apparently hitting the floor.

Sleeth determined that now was the time to make his getaway and he would have, except when he stepped out of the door, he found himself face to face with a nurse, who was rushing to Evans' side. She stopped short and screamed. Sleeth brushed past her and headed for the back door. Just before he got there, he heard Evans' voice: "Sleeth, what are you doing here?"

Nick Krill ignored the uproar, closed the door to his room, and went back to bed. Soon, all was silent. He didn't think Evans had seen Tunk or himself, but he'd clearly heard Evans identify Sleeth. He was pleased that despite his expulsion he hadn't lost his touch. Tunk had tackled Evans and more than likely Sleeth would be blamed.

If asked, Nick would maintain he slept like a baby, unaware that someone came into his room. He reached under his pillow and clutched his gold bracelet. *Quit while I'm ahead.*

★ ★ ★

Tunk ran all the way from the san to Trafalgar. He had no doubt that he needed time to outmanoevre Sleeth. With only a few days left at Blackleigh, he imagined the House as a sinking galleon with Sleeth, the doomed captain, desperate and alone at the ship's wheel. Nearby on a fiery sea, a small lifeboat bobbed up and down on the waves, packed with fleeing rats hoping to escape the deluge.

He asked himself why he'd spent so long in furthering the oaf's ambitions? He'd even branded his arm for Sleeth, but he now regarded his scar as a badge of shame. Tunk wondered why it had taken him so long for a person of his high intelligence to realise the futility of catering to Sleeth, a power-hungry narcissist who only cared about himself.

The break between them was well overdue. Tunk felt confident that Krill wouldn't give him up. As Tunk saw it, the boy clearly had integrity and wasn't a snitch.

If it came down to it, Tunk would swear that he never set foot in the san, but knew Sleeth intended to go there, and "beat the truth out of Bhasin". He'd say, *Sleeth wanted me to go with him, but I refused*. And Sleeth would get the blame for bulldozing Evans.

Most damning to Sleeth, Tunk mused, would be a revelation, if it came out – about Sleeth's oath sworn with other prefects, and his willingness to use all means to eject Simon and other outsiders from the school. Tunk planned to claim, if asked, that his own role was forced under duress.

Tunk envisaged a golden future for himself in greener pastures. He didn't plan on going to university. He wanted to learn the ways of business and come up the hard way. He'd always been fascinated by stocks, shares and profitable situations. A career as a merchant banker appealed. Maybe he'd one day have his own merchant bank. In his usual relentless way, he'd find situations where he could pull a few strings and make things happen.

Years from now, he could see himself returning to Blackleigh on Speech Day. His success would be honoured and admired by the school and the overflow audience. Perhaps he'd be appointed a governor of the school. Then maybe they'd call a new House by his name, even though up till now they'd only named Houses after British victories in battle… There were no limits for one so deserving.

★ ★ ★

William Croat had his own brainwave over breakfast on the same Thursday morning. He always felt at his best while consuming food. His father often advised his overweight offspring to first look after the inner man.

Croat noted with satisfaction that Sleeth was absent from his usual place in the dining room. That was just as well because Croat figured that he'd taken adequate steps to save his own skin, pay Sleeth back for his threats to demote him from being a prefect, and for entrapping him in a dangerous conspiracy. In fact, just in case of trouble, Croat arranged to go by the train at twelve o'clock, a day early, and head for home.

Croat decided that, having been a prefect at Blackleigh, he was primed to move up in the world. Someone as capable and deserving as himself should go to university, obtain a law degree, establish a practice, and join a few selected companies as their legal director and trusted adviser.

Working behind the scenes would be his speciality. No longer "odd man out" among the prefects, the "frog" was ready to leap to his rightful place... on top of the heap after being bred to rule. He would show them all...

Croat reached for another piece of toast and slapped on a heavy smothering of butter and jam. He'd take a fresh bag of doughnuts with him for the train. The inner man was ready for outer glory.

38

REVELATIONS

On Thursday morning, Sleeth was on his way to breakfast, and about to enter the dining room in the Administration Building, when he was handed a note by Rimmer from Waterloo. Sleeth was irritated by the interruption, then became concerned when he opened the note and learned he'd been summoned to the Headmaster's office at 8:15AM.

Quite apart from his not having eaten, he felt the doctor inconsiderate not to have given him notice of the topic of their meeting, nor allow him time to prepare. Then he thought better of the matter when he realised that the Headmaster probably wanted to tell him about Bhasin, in person, and discuss a suitable punishment for the Indian boy.

No one was in the Head's office lobby, and Sleeth presumed that it was too early for Mrs Macnally to arrive. He saw the door to the inner sanctum was already open and that a light was on in the study.

He tentatively knocked. "It's Hugh Sleeth, sir," he said assertively. In response he heard Dr Macleod say, "Come in."

The doctor was seated alone at his desk. He looked up as Sleeth entered and beckoned for him to sit in the empty chair opposite. Sleeth sat, mindful of keeping his back ramrod straight, and looking confident. After all, he reasoned, he was about to leave Blackleigh as a high achiever at a prestigious public school.

He looked across at the photograph of Winston Churchill on the Headmaster's wall, and his mind flashed to thoughts of a general, in history, whom he greatly admired. *What was it Julius Caesar said?* Then he remembered: *"I came, I saw, I conquered."*

The Head was staring at him, but said nothing, Sleeth decided to take the initiative. "I assume you want to see me, sir, about the Bhasin decision. I believe leniency is justified despite his crime. The outstanding issue for us is to determine a suitable punishment."

"Punishment?" the Headmaster repeated vaguely. "No, I have something else in mind."

The doctor's answer annoyed Sleeth, for nothing was more important to him than to conclude the Bhasin matter; that decision in turn would hammer a nail into Simon's coffin.

The Headmaster said, "This is about your report on discipline in Trafalgar and the lack of any follow-up regarding Peter Wynn's expulsion… for starters."

Inwardly, Sleeth felt relief. These requests could be handled with ease, then he'd get the hell out of the old man's office and have his breakfast. "Yes, sir, I instructed prefect Tunk to prepare the extra report. I've seen and approved it. I'm surprised that he didn't send it to you. You can be sure that I'll speak with him today."

"Let me make myself clear," the doctor said, frowning, "my interest in discipline goes well beyond Wynn. I've had alarming reports of extreme bullying in Trafalgar, a breakdown of justice, and a conspiracy among those seniors having power, with the intent to oust innocent juniors from Blackleigh."

The Headmaster went on, "It's hard for me to think of a more serious combination of offences, especially by those in a position of trust. I'd like to have your comments, Sleeth."

Sleeth had to think fast. He had solemnised the commitment of all the conspirators, and his group were sworn to secrecy, Sleeth wondered where the Head was getting his information but first had to quell the attack.

"With my many responsibilities as Head Prefect, and my leadership in the Corps, minor infringements could escape my notice. But as I said in my report, ours is a well-run House, where no such abuses could possibly take place. May I ask you, sir, how you came by such information?"

"It is the duty of a Headmaster to know what transpires in his school. Let *me* ask *you* something. If you were a Headmaster, and you learned that such abuses were occurring, what would be your remedy?"

"I've never heard of such things. I'd be unable to give you an opinion if I felt that all the charges were just based on rumours."

"Let me show you this."

The Headmaster removed from his desk drawer an object wrapped in newspaper and handed it to Sleeth, "I'd like you to open this package."

Sleeth unfolded the newspaper wrapping to reveal a short steel rod to which was affixed a white medal. In shock, he found himself looking at the very gadget he'd created for the branding ceremony, which until now he'd kept safely tucked away in his in his study desk drawer. *How did the doctor come to possess it?* Despite his panic, Sleeth kept a clear head.

"I don't know what this is. I've never seen the object before."

"Then let me refresh your memory," the Headmaster said. "On the metal rod is affixed a DSO combat medal from World War II. I happen to know, because I was fortunate to be awarded the same medal."

Sleeth gasped but said nothing.

"As you can see," said the Headmaster, "this rod, with the soldered combat medal, has been adapted to leave an outline of the medal, when burnt against skin. In this case, the object was used to solemnise a wicked oath sworn by you and four other conspirators."

"I am referring to Tunk, Miller, Snell, and Croat, all of them prefects in Trafalgar, and to *you* as their ringleader."

Sleeth's head was spinning, but he remained silent and rigid.

"Sleeth, I am fully aware of your history of bullying and abuse, and the crimes you instigated as the cabal's ringleader. I've also heard you were in the san late last night when Evans was attacked. Do you have anything to say?"

"I deny these charges," Sleeth said with aplomb deserving of an officer of the corps. "And you can't prove these accusations."

"On the contrary, I have all the proof I need. Take off your jacket and roll up your left sleeve. I've already seen the arms of the other boys – now I'd like to see yours."

"This is an outrage. I won't do it."

"I had the feeling that you might not co-operate," Dr Macleod said. He pushed a button on his phone and a buzzing sounded in the outer office. In the next instant Mark Evans with Phillips and Whiteley, two seniors from Plessey, and both officers in the corps, grabbed Sleeth by his shoulders, where he sat, and pinned him to his chair. Whiteley, from behind, held the edges of Sleeth's jacket, unbuttoned his shirt sleeves, and yanked them towards his elbow, exposing the branded scar.

"Well, what have we here?" Dr MacLeod couldn't resist a momentary smirk.

"I also happen to have copies of the signed letters of agreement between you and Jonathan Simon, with his agreement to leave the school. Naturally, with what I'm about to say, his agreement is no longer binding. They were signed under duress on the basis that Bhasin be punished for a crime for which he was innocent.

"Had you taken the time to question Bhasin after the stolen watch was found in his locker, you might have doubted his guilt. But then it suited you to believe Bhasin was guilty, so you could entrap Simon."

The Headmaster held up the paper, put both hands on his desk, and stared into Sleeth's eyes, long and hard. Finally, he said, "Hugh Sleeth, you are hereby expelled from Blackleigh with a black mark against your record. You will receive a dishonourable discharge from the school corps. If you apply to any university or military college, I will inform the appropriate authorities of your nefarious background. When I'm done, you'll be lucky to find employment in a Welsh coal mine."

In fury, Sleeth shook off the boys holding his arms, turned on his heel, and marched out of the door, his back ramrod straight.

As he stomped out of the Headmaster's lobby, Sleeth reflected that his disgrace derived from his sworn oath to have Jonathan Simon expelled. Instead, he was the one kicked out on his ass. A single word was foremost in his mind: *Revenge.*

★ ★ ★

Jonathan returned to the Houseroom after lunch on Thursday to find an envelope pinned to his locker door. He hurriedly opened it. A meeting was scheduled for him with Dr Macleod in his office at three that afternoon. He'd never been summoned by the Headmaster before and felt apprehensive.

A gentle hand tapped Jonathan on the shoulder and he turned to see Jim Bhasin.

"Let's talk outside." Jim beamed. "I need to update you. They're letting me go home this afternoon for the holidays. The taxi to the station will be here in about ten minutes. Matron helped to pack my trunk."

Jonathan didn't know whether to fling his arms around Jim or shout for joy, but instead they clasped each other's hands.

"What's going on here?" a familiar voice said behind them. "Is this a meeting of the losers' union?"

Jonathan turned to see Gabriel. He never knew whether Whitey would behave like an angel or a demon. More often lately, the demon side outweighed his good days. Either way, Jonathan knew Gabriel could be relied on to dampen his mood.

"I see they let you out?" Gabriel said to Jim. "What a mistake! Are the rest of us safe with you running free?"

"Yeah," Jim retorted facetiously, "Sorry to disappoint you, but I've been cleared of any wrongdoing."

"I doubt that," quipped Gabriel. "By the way, heard the latest?"

"What's that?" Jonathan asked.

The snowy-haired Gabriel flashed a devilish sneer. "There are still plans for you."

Jonathan chuckled. "I'm still waiting for that dorm initiation, if that's what you mean."

"Then you won't be disappointed," Gabriel said cryptically, and walked away.

Jonathan and Jim went out the side door of the Houseroom into the sunshine.

"What does Gabriel mean?" Jim asked.

"Forget him, he's all talk."

They moved away from the House and found a bench.

"Today," Jim said, "after I was told I could leave the san, Evans gave me an update in his study. He told me they've a pretty good idea who stole Mr Morton's watch."

"Who is he?" Jonathan asked, astonished by the news.

"Nick Krill, the first witch."

"He's not even in Trafalgar, and you hardly know him. Why did he have it in for you?" Jonathan asked.

"I don't know, but Evans believes it was Krill."

"I wonder why he did it," Jonathan said.

"I've no idea. Evans told me Krill has closed up like a clam and won't talk.

"And there's more," Jim went on. "When Evans went to the san last night to check on me, someone decked him. Evans' left arm is in a cast."

"Wow," was all Jonathan could muster.

"Here's the biggest news of all: I'm coming back next term, and your agreement to leave Blackleigh is dead as a doornail. I promised Evans not to repeat this to anyone but you."

Jonathan gasped. "How did all that come about?"

"Evans didn't go into details, but I'm sure you'll find out in your meeting with the Headmaster – three o'clock, isn't it?" Jim looked at his watch. "It's time for me to go. I'll call you at home and you can fill me in."

Jonathan walked with Jim to the lobby door. Jim said, "Jonathan, I owe you a big thank you. I always knew you'd get us through."

★ ★ ★

At three o'clock, Mrs MacNally showed Jonathan into the Head's office. Jonathan saw Dr Macleod with Evans, whose arm was in a sling. They were sitting together at the round table where there were two extra chairs.

Jonathan had never been so close to the great man before.

Dr Macleod stood to greet him. The Headmaster was taller than he expected. Jonathan was taken aback when the Head smiled and shook his hand. "Welcome." He gestured for Jonathan to sit next to him. "I've heard good things about you," he said with a genial smile. "Mrs MacNally will bring in some tea."

"Thank you, sir," Jonathan said. Evans smiled at him.

The Headmaster said, "I'm pleased to inform you that I've just got off the phone with Peter Wynn's dad, Trevor, and with Peter himself. Both are looking forward to Peter's return next term."

"That makes me more than happy, sir." Jonathan gave him a large smile.

"The pace of change is often slow," the Headmaster broke in, "but we're making progress.

"Another development I can share with you is our plan to increase the size and scope of the school with the addition of a new House for Girls," he said with a twinkle in his eye. "For this, we're grateful to Peter Wynn's father – his generous donation is of great help. Trevor appreciated our efforts to remedy the injustice to his son.

"I told Mark I was working on something, but I didn't want to say too much until I was sure we could raise the funds. This new House for Girls is long overdue. I'm delighted to tell you that work on the new building, which will take a year, commences at the start of the summer holiday. The final negotiations for Trevor Wynn's gift were handled by an old Blackovian.

"I have more good news. We found out that Sleeth was the mastermind behind the conspiracy against you, Jim, and Peter. I suspect you'll be happy to know that he's been expelled and received a dishonourable discharge from the corps."

Jonathan felt pure joy and vindication upon hearing this news. He enquired, "How did you learn about…"

They were briefly interrupted when Mrs MacNally came in with a pot of tea, milk, sugar, and biscuits on a tray with cups, saucers, and spoons. Jonathan wondered why she'd brought in four cups for the three of them.

"Is there anything you'd like to ask?" the Headmaster asked after Jonathan drank some tea.

"Yes, sir… How did you learn about the abuse and the conspiracy that the three of us faced?"

"Good question," the Headmaster replied. "Mark Evans has, of course, been invaluable. There was also someone else who provided vital input and help. From him we learned that Sleeth made other Trafalgar prefects swear an oath to use any means possible to oust you and the others from the school. It's hard to believe, but he pressured them to brand their forearms with a WWII medal as a sign of their commitment."

"Can I know who the someone is, sir?"

"Yes. In fact, you can even hear from him yourself," the Headmaster answered. He picked up his phone. "Mrs MacNally, please ask our visitor to come in."

The door to the study opened.

Jonathan gasped in amazement. James Flicker strode in. He said with a quick smile, "Hello, Jonathan, looks like your life still isn't boring."

Flicker wore an elegant grey suit with an old Blackovian school tie. He appeared even more confident than when he was a prefect. But he was the same handsome, tall, tanned figure with swept-back brown hair, rimless glasses, and the intriguing fencing scar on his left cheek. He joined them and sat at the table.

"You'd have been a great Head Prefect of Trafalgar, James," said the Headmaster, "but I can't complain. You've done a fine service for the school. Jonathan asked me how we learned about Sleeth's wicked oath. I thought you should tell him."

"Right." Flicker nodded. "As you know, Jonathan, I had plans to make changes in our House. But due to my family situation, I had to leave school. I did, however, keep in touch with the Headmaster, and shared my concerns about our traditions, and the serious abuse of juniors. I knew this would continue in my absence."

Jonathan leaned forward, careful not to spill his tea, and focused on what Flicker was saying.

Flicker went on, "I've known one of Trafalgar's prefects since we were at our London prep school together before Blackleigh. We're good friends, and over the past year we spoke on the phone at weekends.

"Early in the school year, he called to tell me that Croat came to him as usual, to tell him that Sleeth was up to no good. He'd formed a pact with the prefects appointed and directed them to target certain boys in Trafalgar for expulsion by any means necessary. Croat was probably more worried for himself, rather than anything else.

"I suggested that my friend have Croat write up a report from time to time about Sleeth's plans and activities and give it to my friend. He in turn, unbeknownst to Croat, sent the reports to me.

"The source was none other than my friend, Ben Winkler, the only prefect who didn't swear an oath along with the others.

"Croat's reports were sketchy, so I couldn't do much of anything." Flicker looked up at the signed photograph of Churchill on the Head's wall. "Since then, it's like *he* said, 'This is not the end... But it is perhaps the end of the beginning.'"

Jonathan listened intently. His friends hadn't suffered in vain.

"I also had help from an unexpected source," Flicker said. "By chance, you met my cousin, Olivia. She made me promise to do everything I could when she found out that you were in trouble. She also urged me to work for the addition of a House for Girls.

"Olivia asked me to help you. She didn't know the details because you wanted to protect her. That was chivalrous of you, Jonathan. I told her not to worry because I cared about you too."

"That's when I called Bill Croat. We were study mates together and in touch during the term. I found him worried sick that Sleeth's ruthless plans could result in his own expulsion, and finally he told me about the branding and the cabal."

Jonathan could feel his heart pulsing.

"I told him that I was coming up to Enderby shortly. I knew that Sleeth wouldn't destroy the evidence as the medal was too valuable to him, and I explained to Bill what he needed to do. If possible, he should obtain the branding iron, that Bill said Sleeth kept in his office, and take it over to the Headmaster's office, obviously without Sleeth's knowledge.

"For his cooperation, I do recommend that Bill be spared any punishment. And let him leave school without any blemish on his record. We are indebted to Bill for having done this.

"There are no locks on the downstairs doors where Sleeth's study is located. While Sleeth was at the rifle range, Bill exchanged the metal rod with a simple wooden ruler wrapped in the same newspaper, in the hope that Sleeth wouldn't know his branding iron was missing.

"Of course, I told Bill what an idiot he was to get tangled up in any business that has Sleeth as its leader. But he told me he had no choice, if he wanted to remain a prefect. He also said that he'd done as little as possible in order to appease Sleeth. So that's where we are. We have more to do to make things right, but we're on our way."

"Incredible… Thank you, for all you've done," Jonathan said to Flicker.

"Well, it makes life interesting." Flicker smiled.

"I'd also like to thank you too, Evans," Jonathan said. "When I was at my wit's end, not knowing what to do, you came through for Jim and I."

"I was glad to help," Evans replied.

"As Trafalgar's future," the Headmaster said, "Ben Winkler is leaving for university. Two existing prefects are staying, Snell and Miller, but with stern reprimands on their records. Plus, they'll be doing the disciplinary work in the school grounds that Sleeth intended for Jim."

"I never thought much of Snell," Flicker reminisced. "He has a closer relationship with insects than with human beings."

"Quite so," agreed the Head. "I would also have booted Rodge Miller if not for the letter he sent me, advocating clemency for Bhasin."

"Yes," Jonathan said. "Miller told me he'd written that letter and he apologised for harassing me."

"It's helpful to know that about Miller," the Headmaster said. "As for Snell and Tunk, Snell will be demoted and will no longer be a prefect."

"We're also looking at Tunk's involvement, since he will not be returning next term. He insists that Sleeth coerced him into following orders."

Dr Macleod went on, "At the first school assembly, I asked a question. 'Is education just a means to achieve a prominent place in society and earn a good living, or does it have a far greater significance in our lives?' I'm satisfied you three know the answer.

"Thank you, James, for getting involved and for your help with fund-raising."

The Headmaster abruptly stood, and Flicker and Evans did the same. Jonathan remained seated, not knowing what was happening.

"Before you go, Jonathan," Dr Macleod said, "we'd like to thank *you*, most of all, for bearing the brunt of the brutality and never giving up. For fighting the good fight."

He then applauded Jonathan along with Flicker and Evans. Jonathan was so surprised that he put his head down. When he raised it again, he had tears of pride in his eyes, and smiled back.

★ ★ ★

Jonathan and Flicker stood outside the Headmaster's office.

"I head back to London tomorrow," Flicker said.

"I miss you, James," Jonathan admitted.

"Don't worry." Flicker put his hand in his pocket. He gave Jonathan an engraved printed card with his address and phone number. "You can always call me."

"Oh, thanks… for this… and so much more."

"I have a feeling this won't be the last time we meet," Flicker said as they shook hands. "I'll be seeing you. Take good care of Olivia."

Jonathan walked through the Assembly doors and went outside. He stood at the top of the steps, overwhelmed and grateful for the outcome. Yet he recalled Peter Wynn's admonition that at Blackleigh you couldn't ever let your guard down. Jonathan looked up. Above, a dark cloud moved to block the sun. *Is that an omen?*

39

SHOWDOWN

The dorms were less than half-full; many boys had left early for the summer holiday. The rest would depart the following morning on the train from Enderby to Paddington. Heavy trunks, wrapped sporting gear, suitcases, and hand luggage filled the Houseroom. More luggage and parcels blocked the way up the stairs, leaving a narrow alley as the only access to the dorms and studies.

Jonathan left off packing when the matron called him from the door. "Simon, you've a phone message. You can call back in my room," she said. "I'm off for the holidays. When you leave, please close the door and leave the key above the frame." She handed her key to Jonathan.

He offered to help Mrs Ambrose manoeuver her suitcase down the stairs, but she said she'd manage. Matron gave him Olivia's name and phone number.

Has she called to cancel? Jonathan worried. Mrs Ambrose, hands full, had left with the door open. Jonathan picked up her phone and dialled.

"Hello," Olivia answered.

"It's me… You called?"

"Sorry, slight change of plan," she said.

His heart sank.

"There's a farewell party at lunchtime hosted by the sisters. Could we still get together – but at four, for tea?"

"Sure," he answered with relief. "I've so much to tell you…"

"Save it for when we meet. In the meantime, please keep out of trouble," she joked.

Jonathan's back was to the door, when he replaced the phone. His euphoria in knowing he'd soon be with Olivia was shaken upon hearing Sleeth's voice.

"Y-you're go-going nowhere." Sleeth's words were slurred; he'd obviously been drinking.

Jonathan turned to see not only by Sleeth, but also Tunk, Snell, and Gabriel. Sleeth, unshaven, was swaying slightly. He wore a khaki-coloured vest and denims. The others were dressed in T-shirts, shorts, and running shoes. Snell held a putting iron, which he ominously swung backwards and forwards.

"What are you all doing here?" Jonathan said. He gasped. "I thought you'd be on a train to nowhere."

"I've some unfinished business," Sleeth replied, and closed the door.

Gabriel broke in, "I warned you, Simon." He turned to Snell. "Where's Croat?"

"Frog left for home early," Snell replied. "In fact, he left just in time. I've finally acquired a scorpion, but I missed the chance to put it in his bed. That would have been an interesting experiment on what part of his gross body the scorpion would scurry to first."

Sleeth drew himself up to his full height and glared at Jonathan. "I thought I had you," he said, "yet you're still here. But now you'll rue the day you ever heard my name. But first things first. You!"

He unexpectedly turned on Tunk and accused him of taking the branding iron and turning it in to the Headmaster.

Tunk, in shock, replied, "Why would I do that?"

Sleeth sneered, "To save your ass."

Tunk threw up his arms in protest. "It wasn't me. Probably was Croat or Miller – they didn't show up for the retribution, see?"

Sleeth shook his head. "Croat is a coward and Miller's not too smart."

Tunk pointed. "What about Snell?"

Snell raised his golf club like he wanted to hit Tunk with it but refrained.

Sleeth said icily, "No, Tunk, you're the schemer – it was you," and with that Sleeth pulled back his fist and sent a hammer blow crashing into Tunk's face.

Tunk went down sprawling across the room and covered his face with his hands. "Now my other tooth's broken," he moaned.

"Stop snivelling and sit in the corner. A betrayal is what I get from you, after all I've done for you. I'll finish up with you later."

Jonathan cringed at the thought of what might come.

"It's payback time, Simon," Sleeth said as he reached into his pocket. "Let me show you something I found in the armoury." Sleeth proceeded to slip brass knuckles on his right hand. "By the time I've finished with you, Simon, all you'll have left is a face that only a mother could love."

In all the commotion, Gabriel had snuck up behind him, pinned his arms behind his back, and held Jonathan so he couldn't move. He struggled to no avail as Sleeth cocked his right fist.

The door flew open and slammed against the wall. Sleeth turned to see who it was. Miller stood in the doorway.

"I heard wot you lot planned. I'll make you a deal, Sleeth. Leave Simon alone and I'll only break one of yer arms."

Sleeth took a swing at Jonathan, but because he was drunk, it was telegraphed. Jonathan jerked his head back – and collided with Gabriel's nose.

Gabriel yelped in pain, stumbled backward, dragging Jonathan with him to the floor. Now Jonathan was out of Sleeth's reach.

Miller stepped towards Sleeth, in case he had any ideas of kicking Jonathan. But Sleeth had forgotten Jonathan for the time being.

"How did you know about this?" Sleeth asked Miller.

"How could I not know? Gabriel mistakenly thought I'd be joinin' you lot. He told me you were gonna meet in the dorm. But when I heard all the shoutin' next door, I come here."

"You know, Miller, I've prayed this moment would come." Sleeth grinned. "I've always hated your guts. A ring boxer like yourself stands no chance against a street fighter like me."

Sleeth charged Miller, his brass knuckles whistling with the breeze.

Miller easily dodged the blow, spun around behind Sleeth, and delivered a punishing jab to Sleeth's right kidney.

Sleeth, in great pain, turned around to stare at Miller in shock.

"Do you really fink I win the school boxin' matches by fightin' fair?" Miller said. "That's why no one wants to fight me."

Miller dipped down, performed a leg sweep that knocked Sleeth's legs out from under him.

Sleeth hit the floor with a sickening thud.

Miller straightened up and looked down at Sleeth. "This is where the match is over, and they usually raise me arm and announce that I won. But in your case, Sleeth, I'll make an exception, and keep me promise…" Miller stamped his foot down on Sleeth's arm.

Sleeth, grasping his arm, howled in agony, and curled into the fetal position.

Miller shuffled his feet, preparing to go in for the kill.

Jonathan was now on his feet. "Miller… Please… That's enough."

"But his arm ain't broken yet," Miller protested.

"Listen Miller, if Sleeth goes to a hospital, things could turn out bad for you. There'll be an inquiry. Quit while you're ahead," Jonathan advised.

"See… that's why Sleeth's out fer the count, and you're still here. You got brains!"

Jonathan suddenly yelled, "Look out, Miller!"

Snell had crept up behind Miller, and now he swung his putter, with all his might, across Miller's back. Miller turned in surprise, shook himself, grabbed Snell by his scrawny neck, and hurled him across the room.

"Did that revoltin' little insect try to bite me?" Miller asked Jonathan.

"If he did, it wasn't a good idea… I think I'll go now," Jonathan said. "Frankly, I don't want to be around when Sleeth wakes up."

"Yeah, I think we're done 'ere," Miller said, surveying the carnage of boys on the floor. He placed his arm around Jonathan's shoulders. "I'll see yer next term. And Jonathan, from now on, you call me Rodge."

Gabriel reluctantly opened the door. "I can't believe it," he muttered in dismay. "Miller lets Simon call him Rodge!"

Jonathan took the key, and he and Rodge Miller headed out of the room together.

He experienced déjà vu. Last year it was Flicker, and this year it was Miller who he'd turned from a foe into a friend.

40

RIPPLES

Jonathan arrived a few minutes after four at Janet's Café. Olivia was waiting for him outside. She wore a light blue sweater, a yellow scarf, and a blue coat. Her blonde hair was ruffling in the wind. Olivia hugged him and gave him a deep kiss.

"Sorry I'm late," he said. "Sleeth insisted on saying 'goodbye'."

Olivia's eyes went wide. "I was afraid that might happen."

"It's fine," he said, gesturing from head to toe. "As you can see, I survived… in one piece."

Olivia breathed a sigh of relief. "I've a brilliant idea. Let's celebrate by having a posh tea at the Golden Harp Hotel. It's where I used to meet James. Afterwards, we could take a stroll in the hotel garden."

"I'd like that."

Fifteen minutes later, they walked into the stately

atmosphere of the small country hotel. A portly, elderly man at the reception desk raised an eyebrow to convey he was checking them out.

Jonathan looked around. On the faded off-yellow walls were oil portraits of long-gone local notables, displayed in heavy gilded frames, with subdued lights overhead. Most of them had lived in the times of Blackleigh's early years. Their names, titles, and the portrait artist were inscribed in black italic letters on small tarnished gold bands, at the base of each frame.

The proud figures, likely once masters of nearby country estates, were long forgotten. *What had they left behind?* Jonathan wondered. *A name and a portrait.* He thought about the names of old boys, inscribed in gold on the Trafalgar Houseroom lockers. They too were gone. What mattered was to live life to the fullest and make each day count.

"There's a tearoom off the lobby. Let's go there." Olivia took his hand and led the way.

In the spacious, ornate room, Olivia steered Jonathan to a table in the corner set for two, with a vase of blue forget-me-nots on a white linen tablecloth. He took off his coat and they sat and studied the menus.

Olivia placed hers aside, having made up her mind. With all the excitement they both realised they weren't hungry. A waitress arrived promptly, and they ordered something simple: tea, and for a treat, scones with jam and cream.

"This is the table where James and I recently met. He called me yesterday evening at school," she said, "and told me about your meeting with the Headmaster."

Jonathan put his hand on top of hers. "Thank you for the surprise, getting James involved."

Olivia let loose with her best modest smile. "Now seriously, Jonathan, how did you survive your encounter with Sleeth… the so-called 'goodbye'?"

"Well… you'll never guess who came to my rescue."

Olivia thought for a moment, then tossed her hands in the air. "Not a clue."

Jonathan chuckled. "Miller."

Olivia looked back at him and rolled her eyes. "You're not serious?" she gasped. "The same Miller who came after us in the theatre?"

"Yes, that Miller, but it appears he's changed. According to him, he had a 'revelashun'."

"A what?" She giggled.

"He meant a 'revelation'. Rodge Miller and me are now friends. He even wants me to call him by his first name."

"Wow, you must be doing something right."

He laughed.

"You forget what's most important," she said.

"What's that?" Jonathan asked.

"*You* showed them how *one* person, despite the odds, can make a real difference."

"But I had help," he admitted. "You were there for me, even when you weren't beside me." He paused, trying to find words. "I've never met anyone like you."

"You haven't lived that long." Olivia fluttered her eyelids.

They finished their tea and Jonathan paid the bill.

In a gentle breeze, they walked in the tended gardens. No one else was there. Jonathan saw an occasional rose bush in bloom and flower beds bordered with blue thyme. He breathed in and the lawn gave off the distinctive aroma of freshly cut grass.

They found a bench under a willow tree, sat and gazed into a lily pond. He thought, *It was worth everything for this!* He realised that he'd quite forgotten he was only fifteen years old.

He spontaneously turned and kissed her lips. Olivia put her soft arms around his neck and placed her cheek against his. He caressed her hair and became lost in the moment. Turned on by feelings he'd never known, Jonathan wished this could last forever.

After their embrace, he asked, "I wonder if we could get together over the summer?"

Olivia's eyes went downcast for a moment. *How am I going to tell him this?* Then she forged on, "I've missed my father terribly. I've been talking with him, and he agreed that I'd spend the summer with him in New York."

"Alright, let's see each other in the autumn, after your return."

"Jonathan…" Olivia hesitated. "There's more. Through my father's connections, he got me an audition at Juilliard. If I'm accepted…" She was unable to finish.

Olivia's heart was breaking, along with his, but at the same time, the opportunity to study music at Juilliard would be her biggest dream come true. And if not Juilliard, who knew what unpredictable changes life would bring?

She put two soft fingers under his chin, lifted his head back up.

"Would you like a glimpse of the future?" she said coyly.

Jonathan had lapsed into silence. In a fleeting moment, he'd gone from feeling on top of the world to plummeting down in despair.

"Yes… yes," he finally said, and smiled hopefully. "Please show me!"

Olivia took out two coins from her purse. "There's one for you and one for me." She blew a soft kiss on them and tossed the shillings into the air. He followed the glinting objects. The silver coins broke through the mirrored surface of the pool. Two small ripples, each enveloping the other, grew into one and reached the edge of the pool where they sat.

"There it is… the future!" she exclaimed. "In the large circle." She placed her hand in his. "We've both a ways to go. Everything happens in its own time. For now, let's just hold on to what we have."

Jonathan looked deeply into Olivia's eyes. He didn't know what to say. But whatever came to pass, he already knew he'd never forget her for the rest of his life.

ACKNOWLEDGEMENTS

My thanks:

To those who told me my first stories and to those who encouraged me to write, Daphne Lewis, Hazel Singer, Elsie McNally, Joe Bain at Stowe School, Prof. Walter Anderson at UCLA.

To my Editor: Cliff Carle

To my readers: Jonathan Lewis and Simon Lewis

To those at the Book Guild Ltd: Philippa Iliffe, Lauren Bailey, Rosie Lowe and Jack Wedgebury.

ABOUT THE AUTHOR

Michael Leon Lewis was born in London, England, and educated at the Hall School in London, then at Stowe School, where he won the annual school poetry prize.

In 1968, he immigrated to Los Angeles and graduated from UCLA, Phi Beta Kappa, with a BA in English and subsequently from Loyola Law School, passing the California State Bar.

In 1979, he founded a real estate investment company with his brother and won numerous beautification awards for projects undertaken on the Los Angeles Westside.

Michael served as vice-president on the board of trustees at UCLA Royce 270 for the Performing Arts, and as president for two years on the board of trustees for the Los Angeles High School for the Arts.

Michael Leon Lewis is devoted full-time to writing, is a long-time member of a literary group, and plays the classical guitar.